Anise couldn't help ~~around Gre~~ ~~and give him a heartfelt hug.~~

"Thank you." Noting how perfectly she fit in his arms, Gregory held himself in check long enough to ask, "For what?"

"For tonight." She stepped out of his embrace so that she could look into his eyes. "I haven't felt this carefree in a while and I really appreciate your taking me out." She looked at his bedroom eyes, his juicy lips, and the slight dimple begging to be touched. "There's something I'd really like to do with you."

There was a fleeting thought of what Mrs. Williams might think about her niece returning home in the early morning hours, or even the next day, but looking at the desire in Anise's eyes, Gregory knew that he'd have to take his chances and let the chips fall where they may. Pulling her back into his arms, he nuzzled her neck and murmured, "What would you like to do with me?"

Also by Zuri Day

Lies Lovers Tell

Body by Night

Lessons from a Younger Lover

What Love Tastes Like

Lovin' Blue

Love in Play

Love on the Run

Heat Wave (with Donna Hill and Niobia Bryant)

Published by Dafina Books

A Good Dose
OF
Pleasure

A Morgan Man Novel

ZURI DAY

Dafina
BOOKS

Kensington Publishing Corp.

http://www.kensingtonbooks.com

DAFINA BOOKS are published by

Kensington Publishing Corp.
119 West 40th Street
New York, NY 10018

All Kensington Titles, Imprints, and Distributed Lines are
available at special quantity discounts for bulk purchases
for sales promotions, premiums, fund-raising, and educational or institutional use. Special book excerpts or cus-
tomized printings can also be created to fit specific needs.
For details, write or phone the office of the Kensington
special sales manager: Kensington Publishing Corp.,
119 West 40th Street, New York, NY 10018, attn: Special
Sales Department, Phone: 1-800-221-2647.

Dafina and the Dafina logo Reg. U.S. Pat. & TM Off.

ISBN-13: 978-0-7582-7512-7
ISBN-10: 0-7582-7512-9
First Kensington Mass Market Edition: October 2013

eISBN-13: 978-0-7582-7526-4
eISBN-10: 0-7582-7526-9
First Kensington Electronic Edition: October 2013

10 9 8 7 6 5 4 3 2 1

Printed in the United States of America

*This book is dedicated to all of my Zuri
(beautiful) readers/supporters/fans.
Writing for you is my pleasure. One Love!*

ACKNOWLEDGMENTS

I would like to thank Dr. Geoffrey Connors, Assistant Professor of Pulmonary and Critical Care at Yale School of Medicine's Department of Internal Medicine, for his insight and advice on emergency room procedures. Also a HUGE hug to editors Ellen Winkler, Robin Cook, and my angel, Selena James. Editors rock!

1

She couldn't do it. After waiting two months, three weeks, four days, six hours, and a few nervous minutes, Anise Anna Cartier couldn't find the courage to open the envelope and discover her fate. Heck, it had been an easier act to change her name from Shirley Anne Carter to the one she now bore, and that's something that had belonged to her for twenty-five years. This dream right here, the fate of which she now held in her hands, had only been hers for a matter of months.

"Boomer, what do you think it says?"

Her best friend, a Bernese mountain dog that weighed almost as much as its owner, wagged his tail and trotted over.

"Here," she continued, holding the envelope down near the dog's nose. "Do you want to read it and tell me?"

Boomer sniffed the paper, then walked back over to his pillow and plopped down on it. For him, the paper obviously didn't convey that it was something to eat.

She reached over for a pair of scissors that was on her messy worktable, amid acrylic and oil paints, brush sets, various types and scraps of paper, block pads, cold and hot press sheets, matting, frames, tissues, a soda can, and a half-eaten bag of potato chips. Her hand shook as she used the sharp edge to slit the envelope, the one showing the company name, The Creative Space, in the return address.

The Creative Space. Leaving her hometown of Omaha, Nebraska, and becoming a student at the Kansas City Art Institute, she'd quickly learned that in the art world it was the place of legends. She'd known nothing about this Los Angeles treasure until she was eighteen years old. That's when her favorite art teacher and now mentor, Jessica Price, told her all about the place where she'd fallen in love with art and with the man who was now her husband and father to their four kids. The place that was like an exclusive club—an artist couldn't just show up there, he or she had to be recommended and/or invited. That's how Anise had gotten the inspiration to live her dream of moving to Los Angeles and learning from the best. The invitation to move to LA had come from her aunt, Aretha Williams. The recommendation had come from Jessica.

Her phone rang and, as had often been the case

with the woman Anise swore was psychic, it was Jessica.

"I got it," Anise said by way of greeting.

"You did? Congratulations!"

"No, I'm not sure whether or not I got the internship, but I got the envelope." Silence. "I know, I should open it, huh?"

"Uh, that's normally how people find out they've been accepted into the mentorship program at The Creative Space!"

Anise's scream caused Boomer to lift his chin off his paws and sit up on his haunches. He watched dispassionately as she tore open the correspondence, ripped out the single sheet of paper, and let the envelope fall to the ground.

Anise scanned the contents quickly. "'It is our pleasure to inform you,'" she read, her voice rising with excitement, "'that you have been accepted for an internship at The Creative Space for our summer season, beginning June first.' Oh my goodness, Jessica, that's only six weeks away!"

"Then I suggest you get off this phone and get busy packing! And if you need any help at all, Shirley, I'm just a phone call away."

"I appreciate that. And by the way, Shirley doesn't exist anymore."

"Come again?"

"I changed my name."

"What? Why?"

"It doesn't fit me. Never has, really. My legal name is now Anise."

"Okay." The way Jessica drew out the word suggested there was more she wanted to say, but didn't.

"I don't expect you to understand."

"It's not that. I'm just surprised is all. But, hey. Whatever floats your boat sails mine."

Anise laughed. "Thanks, Jessica."

"Do the people at The Creative Space know about this change?"

"They will as soon as I respond."

"What about what's-his-name? How does he feel about your new moniker?"

"I couldn't care less how Joey feels. What I do is no longer his business."

"So your on-again, off-again love life with him is off, again?"

"My on-again, off-again situation is over. Finished. Kaput. I swore that the last time I was with him was the last time, period. And I mean it."

"You've said those words before."

"Yes, but this time they come with almost two-thousand miles of distance getting ready to be between us. This will undoubtedly aid my resolve. I've known Joey most of my life. He will always be my first love. But without a doubt I know that he's not the one I'm supposed to spend the rest of my life with. It's time to move on."

"Good for you. With no ties binding you to Omaha you can move to LA and truly spread your wings. And who knows? Your soul mate could be a mere plane ride away."

"I have sent a message to Derek Luke to tell him I'm coming."

Both women laughed at this inside joke. Upon seeing the movie *Notorious*, a movie based on the life of the late rapper Biggie Smalls starring Derek Luke, Anise had sent a copy to Jessica and explained that her future husband had a leading role.

"Listen, sweetie, the kids will be barging through the door any minute now. I need to run and get dinner ready. But remember, if you need me, don't hesitate to call."

"With everything I've got to do, keep your cell handy."

"You got it. Bye, Shirley."

"Anise."

"Right. Anise. Anise. Anise." Jessica made a tune of the name as she worked to memorize it.

"Now you're being silly. But I appreciate you. Thanks so much, Jessica. For everything."

Anise ended the call and looked around as if the answer to prepping oneself for relocation was somewhere in the room. Just thinking about all she'd have to do in such a short time caused Anise to almost hyperventilate. There was the matter of settling her mother's estate, which included putting her mother's house—where she had lived for the past six months—on the market. Then there was the daunting task of handling what remained of her late mother's legal and medical bills, distributing and/or disposing of her mother's material possessions, looking for some type of employment in Los Angeles and, shortly after she arrived on the West Coast, finding a place to stay. Sure, her aunt had told her she could live with her as long as she wanted, but Anise knew in time she'd want her own place.

With a final look around, Anise spotted her iPad. She walked over, fired it up, and, after settling on the couch, opened a clean note page. She set up several headings and began listing all of the things needing to be done, in order of importance and time frame. The more she organized, the more she relaxed. Yes, it would be a challenge to complete all these tasks in only six weeks, but she knew the key to finishing anything was simply getting started.

2

On the other side of the country, 1,542 miles from Omaha to be exact, Dr. Gregory Morgan looked at his caller ID and thought *WTH?* Last week it had been Venita blowing up his phone after getting the number on the pretense of using him as a reference. Venita was a beautiful brunette and a capable nursing student who hoped to one day work alongside him. That would truly be fine with Gregory. Alongside him was one thing. Beneath him, which he'd discovered was her real MO, was quite another.

The month before that it had been Pamela, a woman he'd known since college. They'd run into each other on the streets of Beverly Hills. He'd been genuinely glad to see her and had readily accepted her request to have drinks and catch up. He agreed on sipping and reminiscing, but her thought was to get him caught up in the affairs of her life, and after hearing her hour-long diatribe about an abusive husband, a cheating ex, and a son just put on Ritalin, he knew that dating her was the last thing he wanted to do. He even turned down her request to give her son a professional diagnosis. "I'm an emergency doctor, not a psychiatrist," he'd told her, before offering the name of a colleague in the mental health field. She declined the information. He'd had only three words for her when she invited him to continue their reunion in the comfort of her home. No. Thank. You.

And now it was his friend-with-benefits calling. Again. He and Lori Whitfield had known each other since childhood, after meeting as neighbors in the town of Long Beach. They'd dated in high school, kept in touch through college, and would scratch each other's itch in between relationships. He liked Lori because they were both on the same page: driven professionals who believed love and marriage took a backseat to goals and aspirations. She was determined to succeed in Hollywood, so when he heard she was dating an up-and-coming director, he'd thought it was a career-enhancing hookup and wished her well. But then she'd called a week ago, with doubts on whether or not her latest liaison was really a good idea. Already her producer partner was showing signs of insecurity and possessiveness. The last thing needed, she'd explained to the doctor, was an industry player blackballing her career. Gregory had agreed, and had gone over to make her feel better. After a hot and hearty "tune-up," he'd brought his behind home like he always did, totally prepared to hear about the next guy not long from now. Instead, she'd invited him to breakfast the next morning. Strange, he'd thought, considering that the bedroom was the only place they usually assuaged their appetites. But he went anyway. They were friends, after all, and a man had to eat. Ten minutes into the meal and he knew why his intuition had thrown up a warning sign. For the first time since he'd known her, Lori started talking about marriage and motherhood, about not getting any younger and about not wanting to grow old and die all alone. He'd listened and tried to offer consoling advice. She was a dear friend, one whom he couldn't imagine trying to throw hints of interest in his direction. If anybody knew where he stood on family, it was Lori. He'd come from a good one and one day envisioned being a husband and dad. But that would come later, after he'd fulfilled his goal of becoming known as a pioneering physician and ensuring his late father's legacy.

Women chasing Gregory was not a new thing. Since childhood he, his older brother, Michael, and his younger brother, Troy, had always had their share of attention from the females. The Morgan Magic, Michael used to call it. Michael had always taken full advantage of the attention, but Gregory had been too focused on school and work to have more than one woman at a time. Lately, even one woman had proved too much, which was why he felt the arrangement with Lori was so advantageous. Looking at the caller ID again, he thought maybe not. Maybe his FWB good thing was about to come to an end.

He reached for the phone and prepared to push the speaker button, realizing the irony of his life starting to look a little like the one his brother used to live, the life he'd teased Michael about before he got married. Michael used to juggle more women than could fit through the revolving doors during lunch hour at Macy's. Gregory didn't understand how Michael had done it. Because here he'd only been juggling a few women for a few weeks via telephone calls, and having a night of good sex every now and again, and he was emotionally exhausted.

"Hey, Lori, what's up?" He made his tone sound busy even though at the moment he was only half watching ESPN.

"Shortly, I'm hoping it's a certain part of your anatomy," she purred. "I've got a light afternoon and thought I'd stop by."

"You're a tempting morsel, but unfortunately I have to pass."

"I thought you were off on Tuesdays."

"I don't have to go to the hospital, but I'm still working, doing some research from home."

"You know what they say about all work and no play?"

"And you know what they say about keeping one's eye on the prize."

"Please, you cannot be serious. You know that you're already the hospital staff's darling."

"I'm talking about another prize—the research grant. They'll be making a decision soon and I'm being proactive. If I get named as the recipient, hitting the ground running will be an understatement. I want to be able to start making a difference from day one."

"Spoken like a true Morgan man."

Gregory smiled. "You know it."

"Speaking of, how are your brothers?"

"Busy conquering the world; you know how we do it."

"Um-hmm. Do I ever know how you do it."

"Listen to you, being a bad girl."

"That's the best kind." A pause and then, "Oh, I need to take this call."

"Is that your man?"

"I don't have one of those."

"Does he know that?"

"Ha! Bye, lover."

"Bye."

Gregory hung up the phone, turned off the television, and stretched out on the couch. He thought about the research grant, and how getting it would be the impetus to all of his dreams coming true. Helping people in a way he felt he couldn't help his father had been a driving motivation since his father's death years ago. Now, he was closer than he'd ever been to this dream becoming a reality. No one would distract him from this goal. No one would detour him from this date with destiny.

Nobody.

3

Almost six weeks to the day from when she received her acceptance letter from The Creative Space, Anise landed at Los Angeles International Airport. Her aunt, Aretha, met her curbside, just outside baggage claim. "Hello, Shirley," she said, giving her niece a heartfelt hug.

Anise hugged her back, and after they'd placed her luggage in the trunk and settled into the car, she said, "Aunt Ree, please call me Anise." At her aunt's questioning look, she continued. "Mommy named me after my grandmother, and while I loved her dearly, I always hated that name. Shirley never fit me. I've done a lot of soul searching since my mother's death. Her passing taught me how short life is and caused me to think a lot about how I want to live the rest of it . . . on my terms. It's time to mark a brand new chapter, to live my life a whole different way. That began with changing my name. It has legally been changed to Anise, Anise Cartier."

"Cartier?" Aretha asked with raised brow. "Like the watch?"

"You could say that," Anise replied with a laugh. "But when the idea came to me to change my first name, it's not what I had in mind. Carter sounded too plain to go with Anise so I just spiced it up a bit."

"No pun intended, huh?"

"Ha! That's right, auntie. No pun intended."

"Hmm." Aretha looked at Anise with an unreadable expression. After turning from Sepulveda Boulevard and merging into the parking lot otherwise known as the 405 Freeway, she shrugged and gave her niece's leg an affectionate pat. "I think Shirley is a pretty name. Changing it sounds extreme to me. But I'm happy that you're taking control of your destiny, baby, so make no mistake, I'll support you every step of the way." There was a sparkle in Aretha's eye as she continued. "Welcome to Los Angeles, Anise Cartier." She pronounced the last name with a haughty accent and elaborate sweep of her arm, causing them both to break into laughter. Anise's heartbeat increased as she took in the sights whizzing past her. *I'm in frickin' Los Angeles, California, baby!* Just as she thought this, a warm breeze swept across her face and settled around her shoulders. This had happened several times in the past few weeks. *Mommy.* Anise batted away tears at the knowledge that her mother was indeed with her, and seemed to approve of this journey to a new life.

The next morning, Gregory Morgan turned onto his street, having just finished a rare twenty-four hours straight at the hospital, almost half of them in surgery. His usual grind was twelve, twelve-hour shifts a month, but last night a seven-car pileup during rush hour traffic had occurred on the 10 Freeway, leaving one person dead and a dozen critically injured. UCLA's emergency room had been filled to capacity and beyond, with him and a team of four other doctors working round the clock to save lives. Fortunately, they had. Aside from the young man who'd died when his vehicle had spun out of control and been broadsided, no one else had died as a result of this unfortunate accident. Yawning deeply, he rubbed his eyes, already envisioning at least eight uninterrupted hours of deep, dreamless sleep on his king-sized memory foam mattress.

He was four houses away from his own home when he saw her: a darkly tanned treat, all legs and booty with shoulder-length hair pulled back in a simple ponytail. Beside her was a dog that could have doubled as a Shetland pony. Gregory couldn't ascertain whether she was walking her dog, or the dog was walking her. *Hello, neighbor!* He slowed to watch how her butt cheeks seemed to wink at him with each long stride, how the muscles in her calves became defined when foot met pavement, and how her arms and legs flowed in effortless synchronicity. As his pearl white Mercedes cruised alongside her, she tugged her huge dog to the side of the road and glanced over at his car. Their eyes locked. Gregory's breath caught in his chest. *Wow.* She was as beautiful from the front as she was from the back: big eyes, pert nose, big juicy lips that had him licking his own. Without realizing, he'd slowed his car almost to a stop, temporarily mesmerized by the bewitching natural beauty now half smiling, half frowning as she once again neared his car.

He was straight-up busted and too tired—and interested—to care that she'd peeped his stalkerish behavior. Also missing from action was his recent decision to lay off the ladies and put all of his attention to his medical research. Right now, Gregory was interested in researching something else. Pressing on the brake, he pushed the button to ease down the window on the passenger side and blessed her with a grand piano smile. "Good morning."

"Hey," she said, with about as much enthusiasm as a nun in a porn store. The beast growled. Gregory frowned. *Great. You can ride it in a rodeo and then have it guard your house.* Both owner and dog kept it moving.

Undeterred, Gregory released the brake and pressed down on the gas pedal. He glimpsed a hint of a smile before she turned her head. "Oh, it's like that? You're going to just throw a 'hey' over your shoulder and keep running?"

"Yes," the stranger replied, her eyes slightly narrowed and daring as she answered. "It's *just* like that." She broke into a sprint and cut through a neighboring yard, her four-legged protector right on her heels.

Gregory turned the corner. Beauty and the beast were nowhere in sight. He peered further down the street before turning into the alley that led to the detached garage at the back of his Hancock Park home. *That was fast. Where could she have gone?* After parking the car, he walked through the rarely enjoyed backyard that had been meticulously landscaped and into the two-story traditional home he'd purchased for a steal when the housing market collapsed several years ago. The back door opened into a hallway with the laundry room on one side and a mud closet on the other. A short walk and a turn landed one into the updated gourmet kitchen, which anchored the open-concept living space next to a mahogany staircase. Gregory didn't notice any of this as he retrieved a glass of orange juice from the refrigerator before mounting the stairs and heading for the master suite. He didn't think of his marble-encased shower with the dual rain forest showerheads as he undressed and stepped into the soothing water stream. As he washed away the tension of the stress-filled shift he'd just finished, Gregory was only vaguely aware of his surroundings. He was too busy thinking about sun-kissed skin and a dazzling smile from the stranger who'd told him it was "just like that."

4

Anise exited the shower and wrapped herself in one of Aunt Aretha's big fluffy bath towels. That she was actually in LA, not to visit but to live, still felt like a dream. Last night, she and her aunt had engaged in just a bit of small talk before back-to-back yawns revealed exactly how tired and drained the past few months—especially the toll of dealing with her mother's death—had left Anise. Aunt Aretha had mentioned a breakfast date with her gentleman friend followed by a hair appointment this morning, but she'd also promised to take Anise to a famous LA eatery for lunch. Having slept a solid eight hours, enjoyed a brisk walk with Boomer followed by a long, hot shower, Anise felt wide awake and ready to begin . . . well . . . the rest of her life.

"Okay, what's for breakfast?" Anise mumbled to herself as she looked inside her aunt's refrigerator. Seeing a carton of eggs, cheese, and English muffins, she decided to make a quick breakfast sandwich to go along with her tea. Once done, she went into the dining room where earlier she'd placed her cell phone and iPad. This morning's goals were simple: check e-mails, add her résumé to several job search sites, and create a new Facebook page to go with her new name. Thankfully, her mother had left a small amount of money in savings and Anise figured that this, combined with the money from her mother's life insurance (less the outstanding medical bills and other financial obligations) and finally, proceeds from the sale of the house, should allow her to live comfortably for at least a year or more, even without a job. Maybe even two if she budgeted correctly and stayed away from the malls.

She logged on to her Gmail account. The name on the first e-mail that caught her eye did not surprise her, Joey L. Brown, next to his account address: brownsugarballer@gmail.com. Yes, he was the former high school heartthrob who'd led their school football team to the state championships. That he'd gone after her, the artsy one, instead of the head cheerleader had definitely gained him points. And yes, he could be as sweet as sugar. Which is why that day he'd come over unannounced, she'd ignored every loudly clanging warning bell in her head and let that fool in her house. One thing had led to another and the night ended with his hands on her waist and her naked butt in the air. That the man laid pipe like a certified plumber was undeniable. It was the weakness that had led to his being her off-again-on-again-off-again boyfriend since they were juniors in high school. A freak leg injury the summer after graduation had put his plans of college and pro ball on permanent hold, but it didn't stop their physical exploits. Even when it became clear that not only would there be no NFL check to pay the mortgage but also that his athletic build and sexy smile wouldn't cover a car note. Even when rumors began to swirl that maybe there'd been something going on with him and the cheerleader after all. No matter. The madness had continued off and on and long distance, during the four years she'd attended the art institute, getting dual degrees in photography and art.

After graduating, she'd met the type of man that she thought she could marry: smart, educated, gainfully employed. And then had come the fourth date. The night when she saw his dick. The sight of it had literally taken her breath, and not in a good way. Aside from a baby's, a number two pencil, or a drinking straw, she'd never seen anything so round and thin. But chiding herself on being whipped by Joey's generous tool, she'd smiled, drank two glasses of wine, undressed, got into bed, and gave having sex with a straw a good old college try. It was the one time in life where she'd faked orgasm. It was also the last time that she saw this particular "pencil." Shortly after their breakup had come the news that her mother was sick. She moved back home to take care of her and hooked back up with Joey. Big mistake. But at the time, in her line of reasoning, a big mistake beat a thin one any day. But still, wrong was wrong, which is why that last "see you later, bye" screw with Joey should not have happened. Not even in California for forty-eight hours and this wannabe ballplayer— whom she'd not let back into her house again after that night—had continued blowing up her cell phone and was talking about spreading some brown sugar on the West Coast. It was a free country so he could travel where he wanted. But if he arrived in the City of Angels, he wouldn't see her. For her the last time was really the last time. Sexy smile, nice body, big dick and all . . . she was done.

The ringing cell phone startled Anise out of her musings. Grateful for the distraction, she barely looked at the caller ID before answering. "Hello?"

"Hi, Shirley?"

Anise winced. It had only been a week and her new moniker was barely official but still it fit her like a second skin. Shirley never had. Recognizing the voice of the man who was handling her mother's modest estate, she responded, "Hi, Bob. I changed my name to Anise, remember?"

"Oh yes, of course," he said with an uncomfortable chuckle. "I'm sorry, Anise. Changing one's name is not a common occurrence here in Omaha. In fact, you're the first person I've ever heard do such a thing." Being that Bob was in his sixties and, outside of college, had rarely left the state where according to one slogan the possibilities were endless, Anise was not surprised.

"How are you doing?" Bob asked.

"Okay, I guess."

"I lost my mom ten years ago and it still hurts. My prayers are with you."

"Thank you."

Bob cleared his throat. "I'm afraid I have a bit of bad news."

"I just buried my mother, Bob. Can't see how I can get news that's any worse."

"Well, that's for sure." An awkward pause and then, "There's a slight problem selling the house."

This caused Anise to sit straighter in the dining room chair. "What kind of problem?"

"It appears there is an outstanding loan where the house was put up for collateral. The bank wants to collect and has filed an injunction to do so from any monies made from the sale of the house before they're dispersed to you as the beneficiary."

Anise sighed. Mentally, she'd already added this money into her budget. So this was the last thing she wanted to hear. "Mom didn't mention a loan to me. What did they say it was for?"

"Some type of medical treatments."

"But she had insurance!"

"Early on it appears she tried some type of alternative treatments that her insurance didn't cover."

"So what does this mean? Will there be anything left over after the bank—*and you*—get their part?"

"I sure hope so, but it depends on how much we can get for the house. Fortunately the market is creeping back up and she'd just had the bathrooms and kitchen renovated a few years back. I'll work with the Realtor to get the very best for you, Anise, but in the meantime I need to overnight some paperwork for you to look over and sign." He explained what he'd be sending and confirmed her mailing address before hanging up the phone.

With the joyful aspects of her "new life" effectively dimmed, and memories of her mother renewing her grief, Anise decided it was time for a break. It was a beautiful, hot day so she decided to do something she'd never think about doing in Omaha: put on one of her new bathing suits and get some sun. Last year, when they were on clearance, it had taken her a moment to decide to buy the skimpy bright orange two-piece that left little to the imagination. Even now, she figured that the only place it might see action was in her aunt's backyard. But the halter-style top showcased her naturally full breasts and the boy shorts gave a little peekaboo to her juicy round cheeks. If she ever went to Jamaica, she'd reasoned, she'd put a smile on the face of an island man. She changed quickly, took her reheated cup of tea to the backyard, and plopped down on one of the patio chairs. Boomer promptly clomped over, both tail and tongue wagging. As if sensing her sadness, he made a sympathetic sound, placed a paw on her thigh, and balanced himself on his hind paws to lick her leg. The act of empathy brought tears to Anise's eyes, ones she didn't try and wipe away. "I'll be all right," she whispered to Boomer, who rested his head in her lap. "I'm just feeling overwhelmed, you know?"

Boomer barked.

"Yeah, you do know." She petted the gargantuan Bernese mountain dog's soft fur, feeling the pain slowly retreat and the tears subside.

Boomer raised his head from her lap and continued barking.

"Whatever you're saying I agree, my friend." In one long swallow she drank the remainder of her tea and gave Boomer a final pat. "Now shush up while I embrace the California lifestyle by soaking up some sun."

Turning over onto her stomach, Anise settled into a comfortable position on the cushioned lawn chair and while taking deep, even breaths began to relax.

5

He had to be dreaming. Because in all the time he'd lived here, Gregory had never heard a barking dog. Not that he could remember. Not where his sleep was interrupted.

Then there it was again: another bark, more sustained and much too close by. Gregory turned over, a frown marring his handsome face. He wasn't dreaming. Unfortunately he'd been torn from a deep sleep. He was now wide awake and more than a little perturbed.

Woof!

"You've got to be kidding me!" Gregory huffed as he threw back his covers, bounded out of bed and marched to the window on his master suite's north side. *If I see the mongrel that's causing this racket, I'm going to be hard-pressed to follow the Hippocratic Oath and do no harm! I'm going to . . .*

At the sight that greeted him upon reaching the window all words, indeed all thought, fled from his mind. There they were again, those delicious round butt cheeks and shapely legs that he'd admired not too long ago. The ones that had dared to run away from him. The ones that right now, against his will, made his dick begin to harden. *Damn, you're fine.*

She turned over, stretching her right leg to its length while bending the left one at the knee. When she threw her left arm over her face to shield her eyes from the sun, her generous breasts jiggled. Gregory found his nose almost pressed to the windowpane as his narrowed eyes took in the hint of a dark brown areola peeking out from beneath the bright orange material. She settled against the lounge chair, her right hand lazily running across her stomach and settling at the top of her swimsuit bottoms. Gregory imagined what lay beneath those shorts: soft curls, bikini wax, tiger stripe? His mouth watered as images of his tongue against either of the three possibilities rose unbidden in his mind.

You're pitiful man, you know that? Yes. He knew.

No longer in a ponytail her hair lay carelessly around her face, with tendrils teasing her neck the way his tongue longed to do. The man whom the late Sam Morgan had instilled to be respectful felt a bit guilty, perverse even, ogling this stranger without her knowledge or permission. But Gregory couldn't stop, couldn't move; her effortless beauty made him powerless to turn away. Couldn't stop his thoughts either—scenes of them together—her body hot, naked and willing, lying in his arms.

She's in Miss Williams's yard. Is that her daughter, a relative, or the child of a friend? Without another moment to think about it Gregory walked to his closet, pulled on tan drawstring pants and a black tee, and his leather sandals. There was only one way to find out the identity of this stranger. She'd gotten away once. This Morgan man didn't intend on that happening again.

Boomer, who'd been content watching grass grow, began barking again.

"What is it, boy?" Anise asked, sitting up and stretching.

Boomer trotted over to the tall fence made of brushed cedar planks which, combined with various vines and bushes, enclosed Aretha's backyard. *Woof!*

Anise got up from the lounge chair and padded barefoot across the soft grass. "Do you smell a dog on the other side of this fence? Or a cat, maybe?"

Woof! Woof!

Anise carefully opened the seven-foot tall gate, her eyes cast downward to an area she thought the assumed four-legged friend would occupy. Instead of paws she saw a pair of big feet, buffed nails, nice sandals. She jumped back in surprise, even as her eyes quickly traveled up tan-colored casual pants, black tee over what looked to be a toned set of abs and up into the brownest, most gorgeous eyes she'd

ever seen. She ignored the rush of heat that hit her
punanny, steeled herself against his killer smile and
lickable dimple, and suddenly remembered that
she was scantily clad. Crossing her arms to cover
her chest she casually addressed him. "Oh. It's you."

Boomer now barked ferociously, turning in circles and trying to get past Anise and protect his
charge. Acutely aware of how skimpy was her bikini
top, Anise battled between exposing the tops of her
girls or risking a possible dog attack and lawsuit.
Common sense won out. Reaching for her guard
dog's collar she secured him to her side and spoke
with authority. "Boomer! Stop!"

"Sorry," Gregory began as he looked at Boomer's
ferociousness and took a step back. But when his
gaze went from the furry dog to its foxy owner, he
halted his retreat. His decision to come directly to
the backyard and not the front door had been the
right one. She looked even better up close than she
had in the window: skin that appeared dewy and
soft made his hands long to rub themselves across
it. "I didn't mean to startle you. But a dog, this dog
I presume," he nodded at the canine, "woke me up.
I followed the sound and . . ." The man's gaze returned to Anise's face. He smiled and held out his
hand. "Gregory Morgan. I live next door," he finished with a cock of his head in the direction of
his home.

"Shir—um, Anise Cartier," Anise replied as they
shook hands, the reversion back to her old name a

clear indication of how much this man unnerved her. She knew that she probably should be offended at the way he ogled her and in hindsight wished she'd donned a cover up but one, she hadn't planned on anyone seeing her and two, considering the way she was taking in his fine frame, not to mention the thoughts she was having on what could possibly be done with said fine frame, she couldn't even be mad. "You're the one—"

"Who you dissed this morning? Yes, that would be me."

Now it was her turn to apologize. "Sorry. It wasn't personal."

"That may be," Gregory drawled, and placing his hands over his heart, continued. "But I was deeply offended. Nothing short of letting me take you out for dinner"—Boomer pushed his big head between Gregory and Anise—"minus your guard dog, will make me feel better."

"Then I guess you'll keep feeling bad, because we won't be going out. I'm not real good company right now."

She watched as Gregory studied her more closely, his eyes narrowing as she assumed he noticed her reddened eyes. "Are you not feeling well? I can help you."

Anise snorted, thankful that his comment finally stilled her fast-beating heart. "Yeah, I just bet you think you can. You've got it going on in the looks department, but does that tired line actually work on girls out here?"

Confusion showed on Gregory's face before reality dawned. "Oh no, you misinterpreted my meaning. I'm a—"

"Look," Anise interrupted, with a talk-to-the-hand motion adding emphasis. "I'm sure you're amazing. Just not right now, okay?" Without waiting for an answer, she closed the gate, walked across the yard and back inside her aunt's house.

Yet for the rest of the morning, as she changed from swimsuit to shorts and then looked for jobs, called her college teacher's contact, and messed around searching for people to friend on Facebook, she thought about the raw masculinity of her aunt's neighbor . . . and his kind, concerned eyes.

6

"How was your morning?" Aretha asked, as soon as she and Anise had settled into her car.

"Pretty good. How was your breakfast date?"

"Girl . . . after more than twenty-plus years of being single, I think I've snagged a good one."

"I'm happy for you, Aunt Ree."

"What about you, Shirley—sorry, sweetie, I mean Anise." She paused. "It might take a minute for me to adjust to calling you that."

"I understand. I've slipped a couple times myself. You know what? Just think about what I am to you."

"What's that?"

"A niece!"

"Ha! Now *that* I can remember." Aretha switched the radio from her preferred talk show station to one playing smooth jazz and turned down the volume. "So, Anise, how many broken hearts did you leave behind in Omaha?"

"None that I know of," Anise readily answered.

"Well, we need to do something about that. You're a young, talented, beautiful girl. There's no reason why you shouldn't have a fine young thing warming your bed at night."

Anise looked at her aunt in surprise. Her mother, Carolyn, God rest her soul, would never have made a comment like that. In fact, Anise had rarely been able to discuss her somewhat voracious sexual appetite with her conservative mom. Anise had loved sex from the moment she'd given her virginity to Joey during her junior year of high school. But it had taken only one offhand comment shortly after she'd returned to Omaha and hooked up yet again with her high school ex to know that what she deemed "free-spirited" her mom called "promiscuous." Looked like she'd come over fifteen hundred miles to find an older woman who was on the same page as herself.

"I don't think I'm ready for a relationship," Anise said after a lengthy pause. She gave Aretha a brief rundown of her escapades with Joey. "I want to concentrate on my art, so I'm not looking for anything serious. But it might be nice to have a friend to hang out with, show me around the city."

"If you're lucky, he'll know his way around a bedroom, too!" Aretha said with a chuckle. "And I know just the man."

Aretha noted Anise's skeptical look yet continued nonplussed. "He moved next door to me about two years ago. His name is Gregory. He's as fine as a GQ model dipped in a Hollywood heartthrob; could give brothahs like Shemar Moore and Boris Kodjoe a serious run for their hard-earned money. Plus, he's successful, a medical doctor. If I were about twenty years younger I'd go after that man myself! I think he's . . ."

Anise knew her aunt was still talking but she hadn't heard a word past "doctor." Her mind was filled with the last few words she'd exchanged with the stranger: "Are you not feeling well? I can help you." Now she knew her assumption had been grossly incorrect. She thought he'd been hitting on her when he'd simply been—

"Anise! Have you heard a word I've said?"

"Sorry, Aunt Ree . . . I was thinking about your neighbor." This time it was Aretha's turn to look flummoxed. "We've already met." Anise gave a brief rundown of the morning's happenings.

"Well, now. Sounds like divine order to me. When are y'all going out?"

"After the way I blew him off . . . probably never."

"Girl, please. He's a man, isn't he?"

Anise turned from looking out the window to gaze at her aunt. "Yes, but so what?"

"And you were wearing a bikini while talking to him?"

"Yes."

"Honey," Aretha said, giving Anise's body a pointed perusal. "I don't think you're quite aware of what you're working with. That you acted unaffected around him—something that I doubt he's used to—probably piqued his interest instead of turned him off."

His wasn't the only interest now stimulated. "Do you know anything else about him, besides his being a doctor?"

A smile scampered across Aretha's face. Anise had tried to ask the question innocently enough, but Aretha knew the inquiry was anything but. Any woman would be a fool to live that close to perfection and not want to try and get a little piece of it.

"Now mind you this isn't firsthand. He and I haven't said more than a handful of words since he moved here. But a while back there was an article on him and his brothers in a local magazine, with a pictorial spread and everything. And judging from the way they look, honey child, there are probably few women who tell them no. Have you heard of Shayna Washington?"

"The track star?" Aretha nodded. "Sure, I've heard of her; even own a pair of her Triple S sneakers."

"Gregory's brother, Michael, is married to her."

"Really?"

"Yes, indeed. All of the Morgan boys are very successful; at least that's what the article said. Michael owns the sports agency that represents Shayna, Gregory works in ER. Then there's another brother who works security for celebrities."

"A bodyguard?"

"I guess so."

"He sounds more my type," Anise honestly admitted. "I tend to gravitate toward bad boys."

"Oh, Lord . . . you sound like your auntie now, and that's not necessarily a good thing. I admit those Tupac types can get your blood stirring. Just depends on whether you're looking for a good screw or a good man."

"Aunt Ree!"

"What? At the end of the day that's what we're talking about, right? Just keeping it real, niece. Isn't that what y'all young people do?"

"We're obviously not the only ones!"

Aretha chuckled. "I call it like I see it, girl. Life's too short to pussyfoot around. Emphasis on p—"

"I got it!"

"I don't mean to embarrass you," Aretha said, with a laugh. "But you don't have to hide nothing from me. Your aunt hasn't only been around the block; I've been around the city and the state, and had a helluva good time doing it, too. Still . . ." Her voice tapered off as she found a parking space near the restaurant touting the best chicken and waffles in the country.

"What?" Anise, noting her aunt's sudden seriousness, lowered her voice as well.

Aretha executed a perfect three-point parallel park, turned off the engine, and faced Anise. "It's okay to have fun and all, but sometimes I wish I'd paid more attention to what would be good for me over the long haul, instead of just what would bring me pleasure in the moment. If I had, I might not be fifty-five and childless, and have been divorced all these years, just now meeting another man who might put a ring on it. Have fun, but if you want the husband and the kids and the white picket fence . . . don't wait too long."

They went inside the eatery and the conversation meandered from men to Anise's mom. She shared with Aretha as much as she could about the half sister that her aunt regretted not knowing better and Aretha told Anise about the father the two women had in common. It wasn't lost on her that in both generations life had repeated itself: just as with their mothers, neither sister had ended up with a man in her life. Up until this very moment Anise wouldn't have said this mattered. But the more she thought about her aunt's handsome neighbor with the sexy smile, nice body and kind eyes, the more she thought about taking her aunt's advice. *Have fun. Don't wait too long.* By the time they arrived back in Hancock Park, Anise had pushed past pain, fear, and feigned indifference . . . and formed a plan.

7

As soon as she'd refreshed the water in Boomer's bowl, Anise headed for the guest bedroom and her art supplies. Adrenaline flowed through her, not only because art was her passion but also because of the project she had in mind. During the drive home from the restaurant she'd thought of various images for the card she'd design to put in Gregory's mailbox. Serious? Funny? She'd gone back and forth and in the end had decided on drawing something that reflected her personality. As tempted as she was to try and impress someone who seemed quite impressive, she decided to just be herself. She also tried to convince herself that despite her aunt's perspective she wasn't planning to get into anything sexual with the doctor. She held on to this lie for about two seconds and then admitted the truth: the man was gorgeous, his body was banging, and she figured if his hands and feet were any indication he could easily clear the six-week-old cobwebs out of her cootchie and thrust any memories of Joey right out of her mind.

After lining her charcoal pencils up on the make-shift desk that was in actuality a vanity and placing her card stock on the board she'd found in Aretha's storeroom to act as a workable surface, she set up her iPod and got to work. Humming to a variety of hip-hop and R & B tunes, and looking continuously from the mirror to the card stock, she quickly sketched out the picture that she'd envisioned. Then, after switching to a calligraphy pen, she placed a simple message inside the card. While waiting several moments for the ink to dry, her mind kept refusing to be swayed from thoughts of Gregory and instead created sexual fantasies starring Anise and her neighbor. One of them involved both of them nude: her painting him and then him pumping her. Her body warmed at the thought. Normally she wouldn't consider sleeping with someone she barely knew, but hey, hadn't her aunt encouraged her to see if he knew his way around the bedroom? Who cared if he thought her loose and fast? She'd be moving in a matter of months if not weeks and then, as big as this city was, likely not ever see him again.

After testing the ink to see if it was dry, Anise placed the card inside an envelope, slid into her favorite jeweled flip-flops, and marched over to Gregory's mailbox. She thought about it, but the woman entertaining daring thoughts about sexing a near stranger wasn't quite bold enough to knock on his door. The card would have to be enough. She slid the envelope through the mailbox slit, went back into her aunt's house, and tried to busy herself with organizing her life. After checking on her shipping and finding out that her artwork and other pertinent boxes had not yet arrived at the storage space she'd rented, she turned on the TV and tried to get caught up in a marathon of TV One's *Unsung*. But she couldn't. All she could think about was what kind of tune old boy would be singing when he read her card.

Gregory stretched as he awoke to a waning sun and a quiet house. Glancing at the clock, he was happy to see that after what turned out to be a welcomed interruption from his shut-eye this morning, he'd slept all afternoon. It was a little before six pm and, because of the long shift he'd just pulled, he had three glorious days off. His usual schedule of twelve on, twelve off, with off days midweek, left him little time for a social life. He planned to not waste these next few days and immediately thought about the attractive woman who was staying at his neighbor's house. The one who'd made him wish that he'd been more, well, neighborly. *Anise.* He'd met Aretha Williams shortly after moving into his home but aside from rare, brief conversations near their garages, had had little contact with her. After their brief encounter, Gregory realized he still didn't know much about the beautiful woman obviously staying next door besides her name. *Could that be Miss Williams's daughter?* And then an even bigger question: *Did it matter?* Granted, girlfriend was exquisite. But she seemed to come with a lot of attitude. Gregory had never had to work to get a woman and he didn't plan on starting now. Especially with what was coming up on his plate. If his dream came true, a relationship was the last thing he'd have time for. Working in ER and juggling this new venture would be enough drama; he didn't want to also have to deal with it in his personal life.

Having made the decision to curb his interest in something new and stick with the familiar, Gregory reached for his cell phone. It rang in his hand. "Hello?"

"Hey, baby."

"Hey, Mama." Gregory put the call on speaker and rolled his nude body—also exquisite—out of bed.

"Did you get my message?"

"You called my cell?"

"No, I left it on your home phone."

"Oh. No, I haven't checked my home phone in the past couple days." While strolling into the massive walk-in closet, he told his mother about his recent grueling schedule.

"I worry about you, Gregory. Y'all boys all work so hard."

"We got it honest."

"That you did," Jackie Morgan replied, and Gregory could hear the smile in his mother's voice. He pulled on a pair of linen drawstring pants as she continued talking. "You all's daddy was one hard-working man. That's just one of many things I loved about him." Conversation stilled, as both thought of Samuel Morgan, the father who'd been larger than life, the one whose shoes each son would spend their lives trying to fill. "Speaking of Sam, have you heard any word yet?"

Gregory immediately knew what she was talking about, the multimillion-dollar research grant for which he was now a finalist. The grant he wanted more than air to breathe. The grant that would allow him to fulfill a dream and honor his father. "I haven't heard anything since they narrowed the field from ten to three."

"I don't know what's taking them so long. Don't matter who else submitted their application. There's no doctor out there better than you!"

"Spoken like a true mother," Gregory said, with a smile. "But I appreciate your saying that. I'm so close I can taste it, Mama. Being able to study and possibly save lives with the kind of injuries that took out Daddy."

"That would be a blessing, son. Listen, baby, I

have to run. Robert's on his way to pick me up and I'm not dressed."

"Hot date, huh?"

"The temperature of my dates is none of your business." Gregory laughed. "But listen, I called to see if you had checked your mail, but since you haven't even checked your messages I doubt you've done that either."

"No, I stopped by my mail center on the way home. Didn't see anything from you though."

"Oh, I'm sorry, Greg. I gave Michelle your home address. It's so rare that I send you anything by mail that I forget about the PO box."

"Who's Michelle?" Gregory asked with a frown.

"Nobody you have to worry about stalking you," Jackie readily replied, correctly reading her son's mind. "Michelle is Robert's sister, and she's helping me plan his Fourth of July retirement party."

"Oh! Okay, nice. Robert is finally going to hang up the gun, huh? Does Troy know this yet?" Robert moonlighted at Troy's security firm. That's how he'd met their mom.

"Yes. Robert told him on Monday."

"Well, tell Robert I'm happy for him. And I'll definitely help him celebrate. I'll go check the mailbox now."

"Okay. Thanks, Greg."

Gregory opened his door and took a deep breath of sunshine. He took the key that was kept on a holder just inside the front door and unlocked the wrought-iron mailbox the previous owner had installed. To his surprise, the large container was stuffed. Then he remembered why. His housekeeper undoubtedly emptied the box periodically but she was back in Mexico visiting a sick relative. He hadn't even thought to mention his mail to the substitute that the agency had sent. Amazing how much junk mail the postman could deliver in two short weeks.

Back inside, he went to the dining room table and began separating the many advertisements and spam mail labeled to "occupant" and "current resident" from the two envelopes addressed to him. Both were cards. He quickly recognized his mother's return address label on the first one, but the second one intrigued him. It only bore his name: no address, no return address, no stamp. *Hmm.* He opened the envelope, pulled out the card, and came face to face with a caricature of the woman next door. *Great artwork.* There was no doubt that the woman drawn on the card was meant to resemble the woman he'd just met—Anise. Not only did the oversized face with the wide eyes and big lips look just like her, but the woman in the drawing wore a sexy, orange swimsuit, identical to the one he'd checked out from his bedroom window and longed to remove once he saw her up close. The one that was making him rise again with just the mere memory. The card was meant to be comical and the fact that she was biting her big toe did the trick. He adjusted himself and laughed out loud. Opening the card, he read:

Dear Gregory:

Hi, I'm the woman next door who earlier today put my foot in my mouth when you asked how I was feeling. My aunt told me that in fact you are a doctor. So, as a way to apologize, drinks are on me.

Anise

He murmured her name aloud, noting the phone number below said name before again looking at the well-drawn picture. Caricatures were meant to exaggerate the features of the person illustrated, but the big booty that she'd been drawn was all too real. He thought about who could have drawn this picture of her and felt an unexpected pang of jealousy. And, again, blatant desire. Gregory forgot all about the attitude and potential drama that not long before had had him ready to steer clear of the caramel cutie who gave him shade. He also forgot about calling Lori, his friend with benefits. Instead he reached for the phone and, when she answered, said, "Anise? Hello, it's Gregory. I just read your card."

8

Without his physical presence distracting her, Anise took note of something. Gregory's voice sounded as amazing as his body looked. Earlier, she'd acted nonchalant when she saw him, but there wasn't one of his seventy inches that she hadn't noticed. She liked that he wasn't the over the top muscular type guy, like Joey, the kind who looked like they lifted weights for breakfast. If she were to guess, she'd say he was packing major artillery in the crotch area and since hard, round butts were her weakness, she planned to check out what he was working with at the very next opportunity. A purely artistic observation, of course.

"Hello?"

"Oh, yes, I'm here." Anise silently chided herself for letting her instant daydream get in the way of real time conversation. "I was distracted."

"Look, if this is a bad time—"

"No, it's fine. I was on the Internet but I'm done now."

Silence, as each waited for the other to speak. And then they both did . . . at once.

"So where are you—"

"Hey, sorry about—"

Another second of silence before Gregory continued, "Please, go ahead."

"I apologize for dissing you earlier. I never would have guessed that you were a doctor."

"No worries; it was an honest mistake." Gregory reared back in his chair, liking the conversation, and the sound of her voice. It was silky, and a tad raspy. Sexy. Just like her. "I like your name. It's a spice, right?"

"Yes."

"So can I assume that you're sugar and spice and everything nice?"

Anise smiled, even as she rolled her eyes. "You can assume whatever you want, with that lame comment."

"Lame?"

"That's what I said."

"I thought it was creative."

"Ha! Whatever."

"Speaking of . . . your mother must be one of those creative types."

The unexpected mention of her mother snapped Anise's fleeting good mood. She remained silent, unable to think of a witty comeback.

"I'm sorry; did I say something wrong?"

"No, it's just that . . . my mother died recently. It's been difficult."

Her sadness and vulnerability came through the phone. A surge of protectiveness filled Gregory's chest. For some inexplicable reason he found himself wanting to take this woman in his arms and hug her hurt away. Yes, she was gorgeous and yes, he'd enjoy making slow, passionate love to her, he didn't doubt that. But there was something more he felt for her. Crazy, since they'd just met.

"I'm sorry for your loss. I know how it feels to lose a parent. Look, I didn't mean to bother you earlier. I really didn't. Probably the last thing you need right now is someone trying to get a date."

It has to beat suffocating under the sadness of missing Mommy. "Actually, it's probably exactly what I need to take my mind off things. By your calling I'm assuming you're accepting my drink offer?"

"If we can get through sharing a glass without wanting to break it over each other's head, perhaps we can do dinner, too."

"Ha!" This was the most lighthearted Anise had felt in months. And why couldn't she wipe this smile off her face? "That might work. Are you free tonight, or would tomorrow be better?"

Gregory checked his watch. Seven o'clock. "I haven't eaten yet and can be ready in thirty minutes. What about you?"

"Is this a casual date?"

"Sure, why not?" For the past year Gregory felt he'd split his apparel time between suits and scrubs. Dining in jeans sounded like a nice change of pace. "I'll ring your door at seven-thirty."

"I'll be ready."

9

Thirty minutes later, Gregory rang his neighbor's doorbell for the very first time. He had a mack daddy greeting prepared for Anise, and was a little surprised when Aretha answered the door. "Oh, uh, hello, Mrs. Williams. How are you doing?"

"Fine, doctor. Come on in! Anise said to tell you she'd be down in five minutes. I told my niece it was a shame that we've been neighbors all this time and I've never thought to invite you over."

Ah . . . so Anise is her niece. "It's totally understandable, Mrs. Williams. Besides, my schedule is so hectic that being home is rare."

"I can imagine the life of a doctor keeps you busy . . . among other things."

Gregory wasn't only Samuel's son, but Jackie's, too. And he'd heard that I'm-trying-to-get-in-your-business-without-seeming-to-try-and-get-in-your-business tone too many times. "I like your home," he said, in a none-too-subtle change of subject. "Amazing how our homes look similar on the outside but the inside layouts are totally different."

"Yes, the previous owners totally renovated your home about five years ago. They did a beautiful job."

"So you've seen it?"

"Yes, I did a walk-through when it was on the market. Forgive my rudeness. Can I get you something to drink? I just made some citrus tea."

"Oh, no, ma'am. I'm fine."

"Ooh, Lord, I know I'm older, but whenever I hear 'ma'am' I start looking around for my mama!"

Anise walked in amid their laughter. "Hello, doctor." The twinkle in her eye said she was playing; only later would she find out that it was with fire.

He paused before speaking, partly to drink in her loveliness, partly to cool this undeniable ardor that came up whenever he was around this natural vixen. Later, he'd tell himself that it was because she was different from the type of woman he usually dated, but right now all he wanted was to be alone with her. "Good evening, Anise. Are you ready?"

"Yes."

They said good-bye to Aretha and then headed out to Gregory's Mercedes. "You look nice."

"Thanks."

Gregory hung behind just slightly, just enough to check out how Anise's booty was filling out her skinny-legged jeans. Denim had never looked so good. He liked her style, too; kind of bohemian is how he'd describe it, totally unlike his usual designer-clad, name-dropping, diamond-dripping dates. Yes, the change of pace felt good. When he stepped up to open her door, he caught a whiff of her scent. His manhood jumped and he resisted the urge to kiss her the way he wanted to, just under the wispy strands lying at the nape of her neck. Rounding the car, he took a moment to breathe deep and adjust himself in his pants. *Calm down, man. Dang!* If he or, more precisely, his manly member was going to insist on acting like a randy teen in heat . . . it was going to be a long night.

Unbeknownst to Gregory, Anise also appreciated the few seconds of space while he walked around to get into the driver's seat. It had taken all of her willpower to act nonchalant in front of a man who looked better than any specimen she'd seen on paper or in person. She was sure he had women coming and going, and plenty to tell him how great he was, but he didn't come off as cocky or conceited. *He doesn't have to, girl. No need to act like that when you're the real deal.* She offered him a smile as he slid onto the soft leather seat.

"Buckle up." She did. "Do you like reggae music?"

Anise's surprise was obvious. "Yes. Do you?"

His smile brightened the car's interior. "Don't look so surprised, sweetheart," he said, putting the car in drive and heading down the street. "I like all kinds of music. I know a nice little spot not too far from here. It has a nice, relaxed atmosphere, a stellar house band, and some of the best jerk chicken outside of Jamaica."

"Sounds good."

"You won't be disappointed." Gregory glanced over and observed Anise taking in the sights. "So . . . where are you from?"

"Omaha."

"Nebraska?"

"Now who's sounding shocked?" Anise said with a laugh.

"I would have guessed you were from a larger city—Chicago maybe, or Atlanta."

"Why?" Anise asked, genuinely interested to hear his answer.

Gregory shrugged. "You have this casual, innocent air; I guess that's the small-town side. But there's also a sophistication about you."

"Omaha is small compared to LA, but it's the biggest city in Nebraska."

"What's the population?"

"About half a million." Gregory tried not to laugh but failed. "Oh, so I'm your comic relief, now? Are you laughing at my hometown?" She tried to sound chagrined but couldn't stop the big smile spreading across her face. Nor was it lost on her that she hadn't felt this happy since the day her mother left and the world stood still. The generic topic of conversation calmed both of their nerves and they settled into an easy camaraderie, like they'd known each other longer than a day.

"What about you? Were you born here?"

Gregory nodded. "Born and raised in Long Beach, about forty minutes from here."

"Snoop Dogg's hometown!"

"Hmm, into reggae and hip-hop . . . a woman after my own heart."

"Yes. Like you, I'm into all types of music, almost anything artistic really. I never would have guessed a doctor would get down on that type of music."

"Dre does!"

Anise chuckled, finding it refreshing that such an attractive man could spout such dorky jokes. "True."

"Everyone who grew up in Long Beach, especially in the 90s, were proud of our homegrown artists: Snoop, Nate Dogg, Warren G, RBX, Daz Dillinger. Butch Cassidy and Lil' ½ Dead."

"Wow! I've never even heard of some of those rappers."

Gregory's look was flirty, sexy as he licked his lips and drawled, "That's how we got down in the 2-1-3, baby."

Anise watched his tongue like it was giving directions. She was sure Gregory had no idea how good he looked to her right now, how every time their eyes met her heart went pitter-patter and how every time he opened his mouth she heard another reason to like him. *An educated, handsome medical doctor who loved hip-hop and jerk chicken?* Anise got the distinct feeling that things in sunny southern California were about to get interesting.

They reached their destination. Gregory watched Anise reach for the door handle. He placed a light hand on her arm. "Let me get that." He bounded from the car and opened her door. She exited and found herself within inches of the lips she'd admired while watching her date converse. Neither moved and once again, that undeniable attraction swirled around them.

Gregory's eyes drooped, his long lashes obscuring his dark brown orbs. "Are you hungry?" he asked, his voice low and suggestive.

"Very," was Anise's daring reply.

As they turned and walked into the restaurant both knew that neither of them had been talking about food.

10

"Oh my God, this is so good!" Anise had just cleaned the meat from a chicken leg and licked her fingers without shame. They had enjoyed drinks at the bar while waiting for their table and learned more about each other in the process. Gregory had told her more about growing up in Long Beach and Anise had admitted that before this trip, she'd never gone farther west than Denver, Colorado.

Gregory's heart swelled as he watched Anise's unabashed glee at eating good food. She was a breath of fresh air from the women he usually dated: those who either ate like birds, could barely enjoy a generous bite for fear of ruining their lipstick, or would never, *ever*, lick their fingers in public. The way her tongue caressed her forefinger filled him with heat, imagining how it would feel to have her lick something else.

Anise wasn't faring much better. She'd never wanted to be a piece of chicken more than at this moment. The way Gregory wrapped those succulent lips around that thick poultry leg made her jealous of the bird. She wanted to suggest that there were other legs he could use his lips on, and then she'd return the favor . . . on one of his legs.

Determined to shift his focus, Gregory reached for his fork and speared a nicely grilled carrot. "Who drew that picture of you on the card you gave me?"

"I did."

A raised eyebrow showed his surprise. What she didn't see was how relieved he was that some male artist hadn't feasted on her beauty. "I'm impressed. You're very talented."

"I'm glad you liked it."

"I did. Very much. Is drawing a hobby you developed while watching the tumbleweeds roll down the middle of the dusty road in your hometown?" His dazzling smile made the dig easier to handle. His assumption that her passion was a hobby? Not so much.

"For me, art is not a hobby," Anise explained, a note of chagrin in her voice. "It's my career."

Gregory didn't have to use his medical expertise to know he'd hit a nerve. "Sorry, I didn't mean to offend you."

"Apology accepted." She relished her last bite, a tender, perfectly seasoned plantain, before pushing away her plate. "What about you? What made you decide to become a doctor?"

"My dad."

"Is he a doctor?"

"No, he worked in the shipyards. An on-the-job accident caused his death. I felt so helpless, wished I could have helped save him. From then on, healing people became something I wanted to do."

"How old were you?" Anise asked, her demeanor having immediately changed from playful to sympathetic.

"Sixteen."

"I bet you still miss him."

"Every day."

A moment and then, "What kind of medicine do you practice?"

"I'll be happy to share that with you one day. But tonight"—Gregory's eyelids dropped, and thick curly lashes hid his true intentions—"I don't want to talk about work. Right now," he continued, rising from his chair as the band eased into a Bob Marley classic, "I want to escort your sexy self out on that dance floor and see some of those Midwestern moves."

"You sure you can handle that?" Anise asked, also standing and moving toward the small dance floor.

"I will or die trying!" Gregory reached for her hand and then pulled her into his arms, where he'd wanted her to be all day. As the band played a Bob Marley tune that asked if it was love that he was feeling, Gregory was content to simply be feeling Anise's body so close to his own.

He felt even better than she'd imagined. His shoulders, broad and muscular, his freshly shaven chin brushing up against her temple, his scent enveloping her much like his arms. She didn't mean to but before she knew it her body was moving against his, her soft breasts saluting his rock hard chest. He noticed immediately, evident by the way his arm tightened around her waist and his hand moved down to her gluteus mound. *Did he just cop a squeeze? Like my booty was a piece of fruit?*

Yes, he did. And she didn't mind his skilled exploration. Not one little bit. In fact, she thought one good turn deserved another, and ran her hand across his backside. *Umm. Round and firm, just the way I like it.* Gregory just pulled his head away from hers, made eye contact, and smiled.

"Does my ass meet with your approval?" he asked, surprised yet pleased at her audacity.

"Does mine meet yours?"

"Absolutely."

"Ditto."

They laughed, then both went back to behaving themselves.

After dancing through most of the band's first set, Gregory placed his hands on Anise's shoulders, gave them a sexy squeeze, and steered her back to their table. "All right, you win. You've outdanced me."

Anise smiled as she wiped a sheen of sweat from her brow, taking the moment to touch him again as well by wiping a bead of sweat from his classically handsome face. "That was fun!"

"I'm glad you enjoyed it, Anise. Maybe we can do it again before you go back home."

"I'm not going back to Omaha. I live here now."

"Oh." In light of this information, a myriad of thoughts vied for attention in Gregory's analytical mind. It was one thing to enjoy a fling with a neighbor's visiting relative . . . but Anise had moved here? *Will she continue to live with her aunt?* That arrangement could be like ice water on a hot affair, especially if what he was feeling for Anise was just a short-term physical attraction. "Do you think you'll be able to find your muse in such a big city?"

Instead of answering, Anise just looked at Gregory and smiled. There was no need to tell him that she was looking at it.

The ride back to Hancock Park was quiet. They shared small talk but were mostly content to listen to the diverse sounds from Gregory's iPod. When they reached his garage and she stepped out of the car, Anise couldn't help but place her arms around Gregory's neck and give him a heartfelt hug.

"Thank you."

Noting how perfectly she fit in his arms, Gregory held himself in check long enough to ask, "For what?"

"For tonight." She stepped out of his embrace so that she could look into his eyes. "I haven't felt this carefree in a while and I really appreciate your taking me out." She looked at his bedroom eyes, his juicy lips, and the slight dimple begging to be touched. "There's something I'd really like to do with you."

Now we're talking! Do I have condoms? There was a fleeting thought of what Mrs. Williams might think about her niece returning home in the early morning hours, or even the next day, but looking at the desire in Anise's eyes, Gregory knew that he'd have to take his chances and let the chips fall where they may. Pulling her back into his arms, he nuzzled her neck and murmured, "What would you like to do with me?"

"Sketch you." Immediately, her fantasy of drawing him nude flashed in her head. She dismissed it just as quickly.

"Yeah, baby, I want to do that, too. . . ." *Wait. Rewind. Did she just say "sketch"? The good time we've just had and baby girl wants to sketch instead of screw?*

"Great!" Anise embraced him once more, her full breasts pressed against his chest. She kissed his cheek before stepping out of the embrace. "Thanks for agreeing to be a subject. Will tomorrow morning work? The light around ten is perfect."

Gregory was still stuck on the things he'd like to do right about now, none of which involved pen nor pad. But his intuition told him not to push. "Sure, Anise," he said, running a strong forefinger down her cheek. "That sounds fine."

They gazed into each other's eyes and the energy

shifted. The dim light that filled the garage cast a magical glow. Gregory's eyes dropped to her lips, slightly pursed, and to the increased heart rate evidenced in a way that only a doctor would notice.

Anise watched how Gregory's eyes had shifted. Hers lowered as well. As if choreographed, they leaned in toward each other and soon, their lips were touching. Doing what each had wanted to do all night. It seemed the most natural move in the world. Anise's eyes fluttered closed as she felt Gregory's cushy lips against hers and his strong arm slide around her waist. She tilted her head, only vaguely aware that her arms had once again found their way around his neck, all too conscious of how his tongue was darting against her closed lips, requesting entry. She complied. The kiss deepened, causing a soft moan to escape from her mouth in spite of herself. Nipples strained against lace. Gregory felt them. His manhood hardened inside his boxers. Anise felt it. The knowledge of his desire made her stomach clinch, and her inner walls contract. The intensity, and the truth, surprised her. She wanted that—all of him—inside her. *Now!* This undeniable idea slammed against the voice of reason also going off in her head. The fact that she was in a garage, mere feet from her aunt's house, with a man whom she'd just met, ready to take him on the concrete floor.

Gregory's thoughts were dangerously similar. One hand had moved to cup the butt he so admired, and that he'd squeezed earlier, and push her lower body closer to his desire. The other hand's fingers entwined themselves in Anise's hair allowing him to push his tongue deeper into her mouth, swirling, lapping, darting in and out, and making both of them hot for more. He kissed a trail from her lips to her neck and back, ready to push aside fabric and take a pebbled nub into his mouth.

Sanity intervened.

Gregory broke the kiss, resting his forehead on Anise's. "That was a bit presumptive of me," he murmured, trying to still his rapidly beating heart. "But I won't apologize."

"No need. It's what I wanted," Anise said, swallowing her disappointment as she took a step back. "Thank you for a wonderful evening."

"Let me walk you to your door."

They reached the back door to Aretha's home and said good-bye to each other, and to a night that neither wanted to end.

11

After a night where she tossed more than a salad on the cooking channel, Anise finally gave up on trying to sleep and got out of bed. She threw on a pair of gray sweats, a white tee, and sneakers and headed downstairs for Boomer's morning walk. It was just after seven-thirty but she wasn't surprised to smell coffee and hear her aunt in the kitchen. One of the first things she'd learned about Aretha is that she was an early riser.

"Good morning!"

"Good morning, Anise." Aretha eyed her niece speculatively. "You're up bright and early."

"Yes, well, Boomer needs to go out."

"I can take him if you want to sleep in." Anise was too flustered to realize what her aunt was implying. "Didn't get a lot of rest last night? Late night with the neighbor?"

This finally got Anise's attention. "The night was

not what you're thinking, Aunt Ree. I was home before midnight."

"Well . . ."

"Well, what?"

"Are you going to make me pry it out of you by syllable and vowel? How was your night with the doctor?"

Magical, amazing, left me feening for more! "It was nice. We went to a restaurant that features reggae music. Good food, good drink, good music. I enjoyed myself."

"And after that?" Her raised brow and devilish expression left no doubt as to what she was asking.

"After that he brought me home, walked me to your back door like a perfect gentleman . . . and said good night."

"Uh-huh."

"Really, auntie! That's what happened."

"If you say so. But that love mark on your neck says otherwise."

Aretha's laughter followed Anise as she hurried the short distance to the half bath near the kitchen. Sure enough, the brownish red mark on the side of her neck was one she darn sure couldn't have put there herself. She fingered it lightly, warming more from the memories of how the mark got there than from any embarrassment its presence caused.

"Okay, Aunt Aretha," she said upon returning to the kitchen. "We shared a passionate kiss . . . but that's it."

"Well, that's unfortunate."

"Ha!"

"Girl, I'm just messing with you. How you conduct your love life is none of my business. But if it were, I'd be doing a lot more than just kissing . . . but that's just me."

Boomer barked. Perfect timing. He was ready to go outside. Anise was ready to make the great escape. This type of openness was new to her, and as one who didn't grow up with siblings or a lot of girlfriends with whom to share lifelong secrets, she'd have to make a conscious effort to get used to it. But she liked Aretha's genuineness, and her determination to keep it real. They were traits that later would serve Anise well.

"No need to rush things, auntie. We just met. But we plan on getting together again." She told Aretha about Gregory posing for her later that morning.

"Something told me I wouldn't have to worry about you," Aretha said with a smile. "I'm not trying to get ahead of things . . . but I've got a feeling."

Anise smiled and signaled for Boomer. He came at a quick trot, and as they headed out, Aretha added, "And when you come back, keep that horse you call a dog outside!"

An hour later, Anise was back at home, showered, and ready to eat a light breakfast before heading over to Gregory's house. She'd been delighted to return from her walk with Boomer to a text from Gregory, confirming their "date." After responding, she'd jumped into the shower and taken the next hour to check her e-mails, handle a little business, and eat a light breakfast before embarking on her first artist project in LA. Picking up her easel, paper, and drawing tools, she headed out the back door and over to Gregory's house. Just the thought of being behind closed doors with that man made her panties moist. If he made love as good as he kissed . . .

When the doorbell rang, Gregory shut down his Internet program and closed the device. He'd gone back and forth about what to wear for this, his first session as an artist's model, and when he couldn't decide, he just put on a robe. A part of him hoped the sketching could be postponed for something a little more creative, but if not, he had some outfits laid out upstairs. He'd let the artist decide.

"Good morning, sunshine!" Gregory stepped aside so that she could enter before twirling her around and gathering her in his arms. "I missed you!"

"It's only been a few hours," was Anise's sarcastic reply. But secretly . . . she was thrilled. Within seconds of the hug she became aware of the fluffiness of the material next to the tie-dyed mini that she'd donned for the visit. She stepped back. "Did I catch you fresh out of the shower?"

"Not exactly. Give me an injured patient or

accident victim of blunt force trauma and I'm calm, collected, and totally in control. But you've pulled me totally out of my comfort zone, woman. I had no idea what to wear."

"So . . . can I assume you have nothing on underneath there?" *And have I dreamed of drawing you naked so hard that my wish is becoming reality?*

"No, I don't. But before you assume"—*the truth*—"that I'm naked for any other reason than your work, I have several outfits laid out upstairs in my master suite. I just thought it would be easier for you to tell me what you wanted rather than me keep changing clothes."

If I told you what I wanted, trust me, no sketching would get done. "No worries, Greg. We'll decide on the wardrobe in a minute. Is it all right to call you Greg? Or do you prefer Gregory?"

"I'll answer to either."

"Okay, good." Anise gave a quick look around the open-concept living space on the first floor. They stood in the foyer, but she could see the living space beyond them, combined with the dining area and what she imagined was the kitchen that completed the L-shaped space. The sun was pouring into his floor-to-ceiling east-facing windows, as she'd imagined. And speaking of imagination . . . hers was running wild. Gregory's near-naked state had sent her for a serious artistic loop. In her imagination, she'd pictured him either in a tailored black suit, a casual shirt and slacks, or maybe hospi-

tal scrubs. She'd drawn her share of nudes during
her freshman year at Kansas City Art Institute and
while it had indeed been her fantasy, she'd not
given one serious thought to drawing the doctor
naked. Until now.

"Let's go back by the windows; let me see you in
natural light."

The air was palpable as she followed Gregory
into the main living space of the home's first
floor. He was barefoot—and naked, she reminded
herself—beneath the type of fluffy white robe
you'd find at a five-star hotel. *Naked, the way you've
envisioned.* The moment was surreal, as if Anise was
the observer of her own life story, both taking part
in the play and being totally separate from it at the
same time. Everything about Gregory Morgan had
her discombobulated. As they walked she took in
the well-appointed, color-coordinated space: soothing hues of blues and grays, with stark white walls
and light bamboo wood flooring. She also noted
that any art on the walls was negligible, the place
almost bare, yearning for her contribution. But
more than anything she noted the marvelous abun-
dance of sunlight pouring in from the east wall,
casting a naturally spirited light across his living
room. Her eyes settled on a set of oversized leather
chairs that flanked the massive stone fireplace. The
chairs were a dark gray with ebony feet. She immediately envisioned Gregory's naked body draped
over the large chair, his gaze focused away from

her, confident, charismatic, and without a care in the world, with the fireplace blazing and maybe one other element in the mix. *Boomer!* In her mind, the picture of man and best friend came together in an instant. Considering the animosity of their first meeting, however, Anise decided to get the main subject drawn and then, if needed, sketch in the dog to complete what would be a cozy, homey scene.

"I like your place," she said at last.

"Thank you. I don't get to enjoy it much but when I do, it's a purchase I don't regret."

Anise nodded, fully in artist mode. She set up her easel and placed down a blank, white sheet of paper. Then, looking around, she noticed a set of upscale portable TV tables, strategically placed under the window. She walked to where they were, pulled one back to the center of the room, and placed on it her leather bag of supplies: brushes, pencils, oils . . . the works. It had been more than two years since she'd sketched a live subject—one of her favorite things to do during her freshman year at Kansas City's AI. A myriad of emotions swirled around her as she adopted a detached persona to check out the environment. The color palette that he'd chosen for his decor was a perfect backdrop for his deeply tanned body, right down to the mostly tawny brown abstract rug that anchored this part of the room. She walked over and centered the big leather chair next to the fireplace. It wasn't lit, but she could draw in the details. Noticing the shards of light pouring in, she pulled the chair forward and placed a chenille-covered ottoman near the base so that Gregory could stretch out. She looked over and noticed his intent expression as he watched her obviously in her element.

"Okay," she said once an awkward moment of silence had passed. "I think I'm ready to place you in the scene." He walked over, stood next to the chair and turned for her next command. It came quickly and both were turned on by its implications.

"Let's start by having you sit in the chair with one leg on the ottoman. But first . . . lose the robe."

12

The request was unexpected, said casually, yet authoritatively—a total turn-on. In Gregory's world, he was the authority, the one in charge. Nurses and operating staff followed his dictates to the letter; women he dated followed his lead. This was a new experience. He quite liked it.

"Should I put some music on first?" he asked without turning around. He was talking while willing his soldier to stand down. "Or something to drink?"

"What's the matter? Second thoughts?"

"Not at all." *Good. I can finally turn around.* "It's called good manners."

"Because you're not the first nude I've drawn," she continued, in an irksomely casual tone. She talked while positioning her pencils, smudgers, and other items near the easel. "We did dozens as freshmen in college, making me very comfortable while drawing the male body."

"I'm glad to know we'll both be comfortable."

Pondering the salacious implications of his comment, she turned to place the paper on the easel. He untied the robe and let it hit the floor.

"Okay, so just"—*Oh. My. Word.*—"sit in the chair and get comfortable." Now it was Anise's turn to regain her composure. Sure, she'd expected toned, but not perfection. From waist up he was almost hairless, and she loved a clean chest. He was toned but did not look addicted to working out. Everything was perfectly proportioned. *Ev-er-y-thing! On second thought, I could use a tall, cold glass of something right about now!* She kept these thoughts behind what she hoped was a detached veneer, while she did a couple of totally unnecessary things like pull out some items she had no intention of using and arranging charcoal pencils that she didn't even see. All she could see in her mind's eye was—

"Is this okay?" Gregory had sat in the chair and struck an easy pose: left leg bent, right leg straight, manly masterpiece hanging lazily over right leg, arm draped across the back of the chair.

"Umm . . ." Thankfully back in full artist mode, Anise ignored her remoistened panties and eyed the pose critically, observing light angles, shadows, and body lines. "Place a leg on the ottoman, much as you would if deep in thought. Good. Can you place a knee up and rest your elbow on it, placing your hand against your . . . yes . . . that's it." She gave a curt, unfazed nod, as if not affected at all.

Liar. She was *totally* affected. Her nether stickiness was proof. "Very good. Let's get started."

Anise picked up a pencil and was almost immediately in a zone. This was the first time she'd drawn like this since her mother's transition. Although the card had been hastily put together, it had reminded her how much she'd missed working. For her, creating was like breathing. Since her mother died, she'd been living with almost no air. Continually glancing between her subject and the paper, her pencil and charcoal masterpiece began to take shape. So did a decision: sooner or later she was going to damn the consequences and sleep with the doctor.

She wasn't the only one thinking about sex. Anise's professional, seemingly totally unmoved veneer had a brother twisted. *Is she really so focused on drawing me or is she just not interested?* Gregory was confident but not cocky. He didn't have a different woman every week like younger brother, Troy, or older brother, Michael, before marriage. He knew his way not only around the bedroom but around a woman's body, and lying here naked while a woman he barely knew captured his image was supersexy and unlike anything he'd ever done before. And he'd done plenty. Though his profession was one of conservatism, in the bedroom Gregory liked to unleash his inner freak. The thoughts going through his mind were definitely freaky.

"How long is this going to take?" he asked. He

didn't really care, just wanted to get his mind off freaky things so he could keep his soldier soft.

"Not long if I just do a simple sketch. Getting restless already?"

"Just wondered; don't think I'd make a good model though."

"I have a feeling you can do whatever you put your mind to."

He looked at her. "Really?"

"Don't change the pose! Keep facing forward, the way you were."

"Oh, okay." Gregory turned his face back to its original position. "Why do you say that?"

"I would think that anyone who becomes a doctor has the discipline to do anything." When he didn't answer Anise paused, looking up from her drawing. "Am I wrong?"

"No, you're right."

"You also have the right body proportions to model," she said, making long, bold strokes across the paper. "The female artists would have loved for you to be a model in our class. Most of what we sketched was the average, everyday man."

"I think you just paid me a compliment."

"Don't let it go to your head. I'm sure I'm not the first woman to say that you're a handsome man."

He lifted his hand and shrugged.

"Stop moving!"

"Dang, woman. I thought we were just having a little fun here. This feels like work!"

"I am working. Now be quiet so I can concentrate." Gregory broke the rules and cut her a look that conveyed he wasn't used to taking orders. "Please."

For the next fifteen minutes the only sounds in the room were from drawing instruments meeting paper. Then Anise placed down her pencils, stepped away from the easel, and announced, "I'm done."

"Does that mean I can move a muscle?"

"Was it really that bad?"

"No, I'm just teasing. I was getting a little chilly though."

"Then by all means, put on your robe."

He stood and reached for the robe lying next to the chair. Keeping his back to her, he hurriedly put it on. No matter. In the few seconds it took to grab the fleecy number, Anise drank him in like a two-hundred dollar bottle of Krug. His butt was the stuff that dreams were made of, all hard and round with dimples above the humps. *He looks good going and coming. Yes, indeed.*

He turned to catch her staring at him. "What?"

She quickly diverted her eyes. "Nothing."

Yeah, I've got your nothing, baby, and I want to give it to you. "Can I see it?"

Can I touch it? "Sure."

He walked over and joined Anise in front of the easel. "Wow." He stared at the perfect rendering of him: face, arms, legs, penis. The attention to detail was amazing; it was if the man in the picture could get up and walk out of it. "Impressive."

"You like?"

He turned and looked at her. "I do."

She shifted; and so did the atmosphere. "I'm glad," she murmured, looking at his eyes, and then his lips. "Because I enjoyed drawing you."

"Good, because forgive my forwardness but now there is something that I think I'd enjoy."

"What's that?"

"This."

Their lips collided and, much like the night before, the kiss sent shock waves through both bodies. Big G below instantly got harder than M.C.'s hammer and Anise felt an intense throbbing sensation between her legs—a signal that every part of her was ready for this moment. Their breathing increased, her hands slipped inside his robe to do what she'd wanted to do all morning: feel his bare skin.

Gregory abruptly broke the kiss, yet kept his arms tightly around her. "Remember what you said earlier," he whispered into her ear. "About me being able to do anything I wanted?"

"Yes," was Anise's breathless reply.

"Right now I want to take you upstairs and make long, slow love to you." He stepped back to look into her eyes. "May I do that?"

Of course not! There is no way I'd sleep with you.

We just met! Of all the unmitigated gall, the inflated ego and contemptuous conceit—wait. Did I just say yes . . . out loud? And why are my feet moving in his direction? Traitors. Her mind was willing to pass on this tantalizing morsel, but the flesh was all in.

She took Gregory's hand as he led them up his ornately-designed staircase. She'd vacillated before, but at this moment not one part of her doubted that in this house, with this man, was exactly where she wanted to be.

13

They reached the master suite. Gregory left her side and walked to the sitting area, just around the corner in the L-shaped room. Soon, slow notes from a sexy saxophone floated around the corner. He came back to the middle of the room where Anise stood motionless. Taking her hand and gazing into her eyes, he smiled at the innocence he saw there. "Are you nervous?"

"Should I be?"

He ran a lazy finger up her arm, peering at her through lowered eyelids. "No."

"Good. Because I don't want to do anything that you don't want to do."

"I want to do everything."

He wrapped his arms around her and whispered into her ear. "I'm glad to hear that you want me as much as I want you."

I probably shouldn't. This is way too fast. But this

time her arms betrayed her, wrapping themselves around Gregory's waist.

For a moment they just stood there, rocking back and forth to the jazzy music. Slowly, he ran his hand up and down her back. She shivered, and ran her hand across his perfect ass. Encouraged, he placed a kiss near her temple, and another one on her cheek. Soft. Reverent. She kissed his cheek. He kissed his way to her lips and when he reached them they were waiting, slightly parted, welcoming his tongue even before it arrived. He swiped her parted lips before thrusting his tongue deep inside her warm mouth, swallowing the gasp that escaped from her lips. He felt her nipples pebble against his chest. She felt his desire protruding through the robe, its heat scorching the thin material of her tie-dyed mini. The material was an intruder, a barrier to what she wanted to feel—flesh against flesh.

He felt it, too.

Even if he'd tried to deny it, the log pressing against her stomach and the hand creeping beneath the silky fabric of her dress would have given him away. He eased his hand up her leg to her booty, fingers scorching her skin. Her passion skyrocketed, so much so that her scalp—and other body parts—tingled. His hand continued to move until with surgical precision a skillful finger slowly made its way down the crease of her butt . . . *ah* . . . with just enough pressure applied to make her wriggle against him in search for more. Even as his hips gyrated to a lover's rhythm and his tongue kept time. Even as she matched him note for sexual note, as if they'd been making this kind of harmony for years.

"I want to see you." His voice was low yet demanding. He stepped back and reached for the hem of her dress in one fluid motion and with another, pulled the material over her head. His eyes narrowed as he took in her pert breasts and hard nipples straining against the pale yellow lace, the creamy expanse of her flat stomach, and what appeared to be a bald mound beneath a matching thong. *Nice.* The color of her undies seemed to kiss her skin the way the sun might. *Good idea.* He placed his lips on her shoulder, slowly moving his head back and forth as his fingers sought and found one of her nipples, rubbing it through the lace. She placed a hand on the back of his head as he continued his oral exploration: grazing her chin as he passed to the other shoulder, down her collarbone and oh . . . so . . . slowly licking the cleavage her push-up created. Soft. Tender. Standing became too much of a chore and she buckled against him.

It was the only clue he needed to take this dance from vertical to horizontal. He led her to the bed and guided her to a sitting position. With their eyes locked he untied the robe and let it fall.

Booyow!

So excited was it in its freedom that had she been

leaning forward Big G would have hit her in the face. It waved its greeting, the head full and round and perfectly mushroomed, a hint of love juice gleaming in the late morning sun.

Her mouth watered.

He placed a guiding hand on the back of her head. As if she needed any encouragement. She didn't.

Her tongue darted against it—tentatively, teasingly—before she opened her mouth to take him inside. Air escaped between his gritted teeth. Hips moved forward and back and forward again. She grabbed his girth and slid to the floor, tongue swirling, hand squeezing and rubbing the length of his shaft. It had been forever since she'd loved with total abandon, since she'd taken a walk on the wild side and let herself go. Not since . . . *her mother died.*

Her rhythm faltered; her hand fell to her side.

Gregory too stopped moving. "Anise . . . are you all right?"

Her aunt's wise words rang in her ears. *Have fun. Don't wait too long.*

Her hand reached up and once again found the massive weapon she'd so enjoyed painting. Fingers wrapped around it as her tongue got to know the length of him, as it ran against the pulsating vein on the underside of his dick. She placed her hands on his firm buttocks. His hips resumed their slow rotation. Tears threatened from the pleasure and pain of it all.

He felt the need to please her. Thoroughly.
Completely.

Pulling himself away from her, he reached
behind her to undo her bra, then eased her on the
bed. "You're beautiful." She remained silent but
her eyes clearly communicated her longing. It was
his turn to kneel and, starting with her toes, he lav-
ished love with his tongue: on her ankles and shin,
the sensitive spot behind her knee, her trembling
thighs. Gently pushing her legs apart, he kissed the
inside of her thighs and smiled when they trem-
bled. *Oh, you like that.* He kissed them again. Pushed
her legs farther apart. Air hit her nub and that,
along with anticipation, left it quivering and totally
exposed.

He kissed it.

She thought she'd explode right then.

Making love to her with his tongue, he christened
every crevice of her feminine flower, sliding first one
finger inside her, and then another. Lapping,
nipping, tasting her over and again—her love
juices coated the inside of his mouth, leaving a glis-
tened sheen on his lips. She tasted like ambrosia.
He couldn't get enough. But he tried, plunging
deeper and deeper until her nails dug into his
shoulders and she cried out her release.

But it was only the beginning.

He rose off his knees, slid his body alongside hers
and seared her with a kiss. The scent of her essence
wafted around them, heightening the experience,

propelling him on. He couldn't wait another moment. Her body was calling and he had the answer. He rolled over, opened his nightstand and pulled out a condom. Ripping the foil with his teeth, he kept desire-filled eyes on her as he rolled the magnum rubber over his magnum manhood. Her eyes fluttered, hips lifted. This pleased him. She was ready. He began slowly, steadily, knowing it would take a moment for her to adjust to the Morgan miracle—that long, thick piece of pleasure that drove wild every woman it had ever known. Her muscles involuntarily clenched at the intrusion. He felt her take a deep breath and relax. Another couple inches slid inside. He kissed her: slowly, deeply. Another few inches in. And thus the dance continued until feeling her warm and wet around him, he pulled out to the tip and plunged in to the hilt, fully sheathed inside her. The weirdest feeling overcame him. Being inside her felt like coming home.

She welcomed him with open arms, her legs wrapping around his. They settled into a rhythm that went from fast and frenzied to slow and sure. He thrust and plunged, over and again, seemingly unable to go deep enough, long enough. There was a primitiveness that he felt, one he couldn't explain. He wanted to own her, brand her, make her his. Later, he'd ponder these foreign feelings but right now his body tried to execute his heart's desire. He shifted them until he was behind her, and continued his glorious assault. Reaching around for her breasts, he played with her nipples as he pounded her flesh. She shimmied back against him, reaching her hand beneath them to tickle his sac. Not to be outdone he ran a long hard finger down the crease of her buttocks, running his thumb around the rim of her brown star before he eased it inside her.

"Oh!" Surprise quickly turned to pleasure. "Yes! That feels so good!"

"You like that?"

"Uh-huh."

"So you're a freak?" He slowed the pace as he talked to her, his thrusts sure and powerful, making sure that she felt every delicious inch, even as he continued to play with her ass. "Huh?" His voice was low and hoarse with desire.

"Yessssss."

"That makes two of us."

Once again they changed positions. His tongue and fingers became intimate with every part of her body; a medical exam could not have been more thorough. When they shifted again it was so that she could ride him cowboy style. He palmed her luscious booty while gazing into her eyes, her butt slapping against his thigh an erotic lullaby that he knew he'd never tire of hearing.

For minutes (or was it hours?) they showed each other sensual appreciation. Then, as if a volcano were erupting, their movements quickened to a feverish pace, moans and groans filling the air.

"Ah, I'm coming!" Anise exclaimed.

Gregory grunted with each hard thrust and soon joined her in going over the edge. Their bodies were slick with perspiration as they lay there entwined, catching their breath and marveling at the experience. For several moments, they simply lay there, feeling each other's heartbeat. He placed a soft kiss against Anise's temple as they shifted and spooned against each other. "That was wonderful. Thank you."

The pause was long enough for a train to drive through it. "You're welcome?"

Her perplexed answer caused Gregory to burst out laughing. "Ah, you're a breath of fresh air, baby girl. You make me laugh." Anise placed her hand over his but remained silent. "What are you thinking, babe?"

A pause and then she turned to look at him. "I don't think I've ever been thanked afterward." Gregory kissed her on the neck. "And I'm thinking about how crazy it is that I'm lying here having just made love to a man I didn't know two days ago." She turned to face him, vulnerability in her eyes. "It's not something I normally do."

"You don't seem the type," he replied, running a finger across her cheek. "Regrets?"

Anise shook her head. "Not a single one."

"For the record, I don't engage in much casual

sex either, not only for health or emotional reasons but to keep my reputation intact."

"Guys think about such things?"

"This guy does."

She settled back against his chest. "Because you're a doctor?"

"Because I am a man of principle and conviction, who sees the big picture and who has big plans. And yes, being a doctor is part of that."

"So tell me about these big plans."

"Maybe one day I will."

Gregory's phone rang. He reached across Anise to retrieve it from the nightstand. "Ah, man, I forgot," he said, after looking at the caller ID. "Yes, I'm late." He listened for a bit and then asked, "Is Michael there?" Anise got out of bed. He watched as she slipped into her tie-dyed mini. "Slow your roll, brother. It's not like I've never had to wait for you. Besides, you're sure in a hurry to get your butt kicked. See you in thirty minutes."

14

Gregory smiled and shook his head as he entered the athletic club's parking lot and spotted his brother's flashy ride. Pulling up next to it, he made quick work of parking, retrieving his duffel bag, and heading into the gym. Five minutes later, he was heading to one of several basketball half-courts where his brother stood making three-pointers from the top of the key.

"That's right, get your practice in," he said, starting trash talk upon arrival.

"'Bout time you got here," was Troy's reply. He walked over and gave his brother a fist pound. "What's her name?"

"What's whose name?" Gregory took the ball from Troy, dribbled a couple times, and then executed a flawless layup.

"Oh, it's like that, huh?"

Gregory threw the ball to Troy and began stretching. "Like what?"

"We just set up this game yesterday. Who made you forget your plans in less than twenty-four hours?"

A smile. Silence.

Troy dribbled the ball a couple times, took a shot, rebounded the ball, and continued bouncing near where Gregory now stood. "So this must be somebody new, because if it was Lori, you would have said that straight out. Or Lisa would have mentioned it when I saw her last night."

At the mention of the brothers' childhood neighbors, twins who'd been friends with benefits for years, Gregory stopped midstretch. "Oh, man. Don't tell me you're screwing Michael's leftovers. That's nasty."

"No, man. Unlike our brother, I do have certain standards when it comes to the women I sex." He tossed the ball to Gregory. "So was it Lori?"

Gregory shook his head, bouncing the basketball. "I haven't been with homegirl in a while; well, once since I escorted her to the Image Awards. She's seeing some hotshot Hollywood producer, remember?"

"I can't believe you'd give up that honey. She's hot!"

"Yes, she is." He tossed the ball to Troy.

"Even more . . . I can't believe she'd give you up."

"How do you figure?"

"You know that girl loves your dirty drawers. You tell her to jump; she asks how high." He shot the ball back to Gregory.

"What happened to Michael anyway?" Gregory took a shot, missed, and went to retrieve the ball. "I thought he and Shayna were home this week."

"They are," Troy replied. "Got called to a last minute meeting concerning Shayna's clothing line."

"Wow, marriage to that sistah domesticated a man I thought could not be tamed." He threw the ball back to Troy.

"Looks like somebody else is being tamed, too. What's her name?"

Gregory stole the ball back from Troy in mid-bounce. "Why are you trying to get all up in my business, son? Don't have enough of your own?"

"Please. You wish you could play as hard as I do."

"No, I don't."

"Whatever, man. Key up."

The two began playing. Gregory dribbled twice, faked to the left, and then sank a turnaround jump shot.

"Lucky shot."

"Ha!" Gregory loped back to the top of the key. "Well, just so you know . . ." He took one step in, aimed, and sank a three-pointer. "I'm going to be lucky all day long."

"Whatever. Play, fool."

The two brothers jostled, poked, prodded, and sweated for the next thirty minutes. Gregory won the first game of twenty-one. Troy won the second. Soon game number three was on and poppin' with the score tied at eighteen.

Troy had the ball. "You know what's getting ready to happen, don't you?" he teased, lazily bouncing the ball at the top of the key.

"You're getting ready to miss," Gregory replied, crouched in a defensive stance that showed he was ready to pounce as soon as Troy took a step.

And he did. But his six feet were no match for his younger brother's six-foot-four. Troy's fadeaway jumper bounced around the rim before going in. "Yes!"

Gregory gave his brother dap as they both headed for their towels and water bottles near the wall. The gleam in Troy's eye reminded Gregory of when they were young. "You've got me to thank for that big ego of yours."

"How's that?"

They reached the water. Gregory took a healthy swig. "I've been letting you beat me for a long time."

Troy's grin was one of total disbelief. "Is that right?"

"Of course!"

"Okay." Troy stroked his goatee in an exaggerated fashion. "Well, I appreciate that." He looked at his watch. "All right, man, I'm out."

"Me, too." They gathered their things and headed toward the parking lot.

"You talk to Mama?"

"Yes. She called about the invite she'd sent me; I'd missed it because she sent it to the home box that I never check."

"I think she and Robert are getting pretty serious."

"Those are my thoughts exactly. In fact, I thought she was calling with a wedding announcement."

"How would you feel about that?" Troy asked.

"I'd be happy for her. Nobody will ever replace Daddy but Robert's a good man."

"That's what I told her," Troy said, as both men placed their bags in the trunks and closed them. "And that was after I reminded her that a man wasn't going to buy the cow if he was getting the milk for free."

"Whoa, man!" Gregory cracked up. "You actually said those words to Jackie Morgan? Out loud?"

"Yeah, and I have a feeling that at the next Sunday brunch there's going to be hell to pay!" He leaned over and gave his brother a shoulder bump. "We're working a private party after the Lakers game tonight. I can get you in."

"Thanks, bro, but I've got plans."

Troy eyed him curiously but then shrugged and walked around to the driver's side of his car. "Talk to you later, man."

"Anise," Gregory said, after Troy had opened his door.

"What?"

"Her name is Anise." With that, Gregory got in his car and drove off.

15

Anise sat back, closed her eyes, and examined her emotions. There were a myriad of them, but one dominated: happiness. As foreign as it seemed, she allowed herself to acknowledge that she actually felt hopeful for the first time in months. Even before her mother died, there had been a pall around the house. They tried to be cheerful, but when one knew there were days or months instead of years and decades to someone's life, there was only so much smiley face to go around. She'd even taken the advice of an art therapist that her mentor, Jessica, knew, and had painted and hung beautiful art in her mother's home: sunsets, flowers, children laughing and playing with dogs. Her mother had loved the paintings, would stand in front of them and smile. But she still died.

Sighing, Anise looked around the comfortably

appointed living room. Thoughts of her mother were replaced by thoughts of her ex-boyfriend, and the sex they'd once shared. She'd considered theirs a perfect love life. But it had never been magical, like what had happened with her and Gregory. Sex with Joey had never made her feel as though she were floating on a cloud, without a care in the world. As if on cue, guilt began to settle around her like a shawl. Joy faded. *Carefree? Seriously? How can I be happy in another man's arms with my mother barely gone? Is it right, Mommy? Is it okay for me to go after my dreams, when so many of yours were left unfinished?* Tears welled, and she did nothing to stop their flow. "I miss you," she whispered into the space, and immediately felt Boomer's wet nose nudge her ankle. She looked down at him and petted his fur. "I miss my mommy, you big old mutt."

Boomer whimpered and prepared to jump up on the couch.

"Oh, no you don't, you mangy stranger," Aretha said, coming around the corner. "You'd better get your paws . . . oh, baby." Her tone changed with one look at Anise's watery eyes. "I'm sorry. I didn't know he was trying to comfort you." She placed her shopping bags on the coffee table, sat next to Anise, and rocked her in her arms. "It's all right, baby. Cry as much as you need to for as long as you want. It's all right."

They stayed this way for a while before Aretha

spoke again. "How did it go with the doctor this morning? Did you get to paint his picture?"

A smile skidded in between anguished tears, and a bit of Anise's melancholy lifted. Would the emotional roller coaster ever stop? She nodded, sitting up and reaching for a tissue from the box on the table. "I did a drawing with pencils and charcoal. And it felt good to sketch again." *And to make love.* "I'd really missed it." *And the feel of a man's arms around me, of a hard body over me.* "I felt happy. And then I thought of Mama and felt that I didn't really have the right."

Boomer rested a paw on her leg and began licking her hand.

Aretha looked at the niece she loved like a daughter even though they'd spent so many years apart. "You have every right," she replied, compassion mixed with concern. "Carolyn would not want you to put your life on hold because hers has ended. To the contrary. She'd want you to grab that steering wheel called your future and ride that baby until the wheels fall off! My mother and I are also close, and I can't imagine the type of pain you're going through."

Anise's cell phone rang. When she made no move for it, Aretha asked, "Are you going to get that?"

"It's probably Gregory. We were supposed to go out tonight."

"What do you mean 'were'?"

Anise shrugged. "I don't know if I feel up to it."

"Why don't you take a nice hot shower, get dressed, and meet that fine specimen of a man. Your feelings will catch up to you soon enough."

"Maybe I will," Anise said with a sigh. "At least if I'm talking to him I can't think too much."

"I know that's right! Not with that fine form of flesh sitting in front of you." Her voice lowered, softened. "Your mother would want you happy," Aretha repeated. "And I want that, too. Plus, I want you to help me get a question answered that I've been wondering about."

"What's that?"

"Whether or not my neighbor has a big dick."

"Auntie!"

"Thought that would bring out that pretty smile."

Anise leaned over and hugged the woman she'd not spent a lot of time with but felt she'd always known. Kindred spirits, she and her aunt. That's how she felt.

"To have feelings of happiness doesn't mean that you're not grieving your mother, that you don't miss her every moment of every day. I have friends whose parents have been gone for decades and they are still missed."

"That's what Greg said. His dad died when he was sixteen and he still misses him every day."

Aretha nodded. "Carolyn will always live on through

you. Those memories will always be there"—she pointed at Anise's chest—"in your heart."

"Thanks, Aunt Ree."

"You're welcome." Aretha gave her a hug. "Bruce and I are going to the casino on Saturday. I'd love for you to join us. That is, if you and the doctor don't have plans."

"No, he'll be working Saturday."

Aretha's brow rose. "Already knowing his schedule, I see. Go on, girl!"

"It's not like that, Aunt Ree. It just came up in conversation."

"Uh-huh. What else came up?"

"On that note . . ." Anise jumped off the couch, rushed past her, and up the stairs.

"Hehehe . . . all right, Anise. I'll stop teasing you, girl. I'm just glad you two got along good." Aretha followed behind her. Anise would have been shocked to learn what Aretha's intuition (and the glow on Anise's face) strongly suggested—that Anise already knew the answer to her question regarding Gregory's penis size. Aretha had the distinct feeling that her niece and the good doctor had not only gotten along, but gotten it on. *Don't worry about your baby, Carolyn. I think she's adjusting to LA just fine.*

16

When Gregory called her from his car a few hours after they'd parted and suggested they spend more time together tonight, Anise hadn't hesitated. Which is why she now found herself once again having dinner with him.

"This is nice." Anise sat in the chair Gregory pulled out for her and took in the room while he walked to the opposite side of the table and took his seat.

"Last night, we went casual. Tonight, I want to show you off."

"Show me off? Doesn't this feel like we're moving a little fast?" Yes, she'd slept with the man after barely knowing him twenty-four hours . . . but still.

"We're just having dinner," Gregory replied with a shrug. "We both have to eat; why not together?"

His point was valid, yet Anise still found herself seesawing between wondering what in the heck was happening with this near-stranger and being very happy that it was going on. And then there was the guilt for feeling joy. She tried to relax. "That aquarium in the floor is beautiful. I almost didn't want to step on it for fear of the glass cracking."

"You're probably not the first one who's had that thought. But I've been assured that the acrylic used to create that showpiece could withstand an earthquake."

"Oh! Don't remind me. That's the one thing that terrified me about moving here."

"They're not so bad. Most of the time we don't even feel them. There might be one happening right now."

"Greg!"

He chuckled. "Okay, I won't frighten you. But seriously, I've lived here all my life and can still count on my fingers the times I've felt anything more than a tremor."

"What does it feel like?"

"Have you ever been in a building when a large truck rumbled past and felt the room shake just a bit?"

"I don't think so."

"It's hard to explain it. But if one ever happens, I hope I'm there to keep you calm."

Anise placed an elbow on the table and her chin

in her hand. "I still can't believe I'm here in LA. This is crazy."

"What made you decide to move here?" Gregory asked, placing his napkin in his lap.

"My aunt invited me." Anise positioned her napkin as well. "Soon afterward, I got accepted into a coveted art program. Everything just came together and here I am."

"Congratulations."

"Thank you."

"I must admit my total ignorance when it comes to the art world. Is it a lucrative career?"

"It can be. But like many creative arts careers—actor, dancer, singer musician—an artist draws for love, not money."

Gregory grinned and responded, "If only love could pay the bills."

"If only getting paid wasn't all people thought about!"

The waiter came to take their order. Perfect timing. Anise used the interruption to calm down. It wasn't Gregory's fault that much of her life she'd fought her mother's admonitions to "get a real job." Carolyn had loved her, but had never understood that when it came to Anise and her career as an artist . . . there was no plan B. She wondered if anyone could.

"I admit that I'm a bit touchy where my art is concerned. Painting and photography aren't the most respected professions in the Midwest and I've spent most of my life defending my career choice."

"Which you shouldn't have to do, with me or anyone else. I admire you for following your dreams."

"Thank you."

"So your next drawing can be of me with foot in mouth."

"Okay, but based on what you just said, I guess I should charge you."

"Ha! Fair enough."

As the waiter set down glasses of lemon water, the smiles at the table signaled a silent truce.

"I don't expect you to understand how I'm feeling. Nobody probably questions your decision to become a doctor. I know you weren't being judgmental. It's my stuff, my preconceived notion about how someone like you would be."

"Someone like me?"

"You know: respected, successful . . ." *Fine, sexy, packing . . .*

"Oh. Thought I'd be stuck up, feeling that an artsy person such as yourself was beneath me." He cocked his head and with a devilish wriggle of his brows, added, "Wait a minute. For a wonderfully delicious period of time this morning . . . you were."

Anise swatted his arm, grateful for lighthearted banter. "Stop it."

"I didn't want to then—I don't want to now." He watched her take a sip of water, remembered how those lips felt on his skin. And wanted to feel it again. "How'd you get your name?"

"It's kind of a long story."

"I'm not in a hurry."

"Actually, the reason is simple: I didn't like the name I was born with. So I changed it."

"See, opening up to me isn't so hard." He leaned against the back of his chair. "Anise is different, interesting. How did you choose it?"

"I was looking at a list of spices and liked their sound. But Cinnamon sounded like a stripper, Saffron sounded like a woman with an Adam's apple." She paused when Gregory chuckled. "And salt and pepper had already been taken."

"Anise . . ." The name floated out of his mouth, Anise would swear, on a sultry breeze. He reached out for her hand, leaned over, and kissed it. "I like the way you taste." Those soft, wet lips against her skin, and memories of the magic they'd earlier worked on other parts of her, had her squirming. The food arrived just in time.

"Mmm, this smells delicious." Anise immediately picked up her knife and fork and sampled the braised short rib she'd ordered.

Gregory smiled at her obvious enjoyment of the dish, before taking a bite of the herb-roasted halibut he'd selected.

"I think," she said midchew, wiping her mouth

and finishing the bite, "that this is the best rib I've ever eaten."

"I thought the Midwest was known for barbeque."

"Kansas City or St. Louis, maybe. Omaha is more steak country. But I don't eat those as much."

"Do you have siblings?"

Anise shook her head. "It was just me and my mom."

"You two must have been very close."

She nodded and, not wanting to fall back into sadness, changed the subject. "What about your family? My aunt told me that you have brothers."

"So you've been grilling your aunt for information have you?"

"Didn't have to; she was more than eager to tell me about her," Anise used air quotes, "fine young neighbor."

"Remind me to thank her." His comment was repaid by her smile. "What did she tell you?"

"That one of your brothers is married to Shayna Washington, and the other one is a body guard."

"She did her homework."

"Says she read about you guys in a magazine."

"The information is definitely out there. It's not hard to find." He finished his bite and looked at Anise thoughtfully. "I think my family will like you. I want you to meet them."

"I don't know, Gregory. I think it's a little early for me to be meeting family."

"Are you saying you don't want to meet my family?"

"No, I'm just saying . . ." The sentence died as she noticed how Gregory's attention had been drawn to someone behind them. She resisted the urge to turn around, and didn't have to wait long to see what had shifted his mood.

17

Had she imagined it? By the time the handsome blue-eyed blond walked up to the table with his date, not a trace of what she thought she'd seen on Gregory's face remained. In place of the split second of annoyance and anger was a genial smile.

"Hello, Gregory," the blond man said. "Fancy meeting you here."

"Drew." Gregory reached out and shook Drew's outstretched hand. "I guess great minds think alike."

Drew placed his arm around the woman beside him. "Khloe, this is Gregory Morgan, the darling of UCLA Medical Center's staff."

Khloe shook Gregory's hand. "Hello."

Drew turned to Anise. "Drew Fordham."

She shook his hand. "Anise Cartier."

"Anise Cartier?"

"Yes."

Drew smiled, an unmasked flirtatiousness in his voice. "It is a pleasure to meet you, Anise Cartier." He turned to his date. "Like me, Gregory has set high goals for himself in the medical field. In five, ten years he'll probably be the head of ER. Huh, Greg?"

Gregory's smile stayed firmly in place. "Perhaps."

The two men eyed each other. Tension joined them as a guest at the table.

"Honey," Khloe said a bit nervously, "I think our table is ready."

"You two have a nice evening." Drew gave one last smile to Anise before walking away.

While watching Drew leave, Anise asked Gregory, "What was that about?"

"We're both being considered for a very lucrative research grant. Whoever gets it will leave their post at the hospital to conduct research in the medical field of our choice."

"Becoming head of ER sounds like a big deal. You'd leave that to do research?"

"That was his way of saying that he'd get the grant."

"Oh."

"He likes to play games."

"The vibes I picked up between you two didn't feel like a game to me."

"For either of us, being the recipient of the

grant would be life changing, and do wonders for our career."

"How so exactly?"

Gregory waited while the waiter refreshed their glasses of wine. "Much like art is your passion, medicine is mine. When my dad died, I felt so helpless; all I wanted in life was to be able to have helped him. He died of a specific type of brain injury caused by blunt force trauma; a piece of equipment snapped off a crane and hit him in the head. If I get the grant, I will research ways to heal this type of trauma, which right now is almost always fatal. If my team and I are successful, and lives can be saved as a result of this research, it will be like a dream come true. And a tribute to my father."

Anise was momentarily silent, taking in all Gregory had said and realizing what an incredible man this was. *How did I step off the plane and walk into his arms? How did I get so lucky?* Immediately the answer came to her. *An angel named Carolyn was looking out from above.*

"That's a beautiful thing to want to do for your father, and for the world. I can relate to having a dream like that. Part of the reason I'm so driven to achieving my dream is for my mother. When she was my age she wanted to be a dancer. But a career in the arts was a foreign concept in Omaha, Nebraska, and especially in my grandmother's household. She was discouraged from pursuing her dream, of going to New York and trying out for the

Alvin Ailey troupe, and instead encouraged to get a real job. Unfortunately, by the time I shared my dreams with her she'd become much like her mother and instead of encouraging me to be an artist she suggested I become a teacher, like her."

"But you didn't."

"I couldn't," Anise said with a shake of her head. "I loved my mother but I couldn't see me living in Omaha, teaching children for thirty years, retiring, and dying. I didn't want to leave this earth filled with what-ifs, not even having tried to do what I wanted. You know?"

Gregory smiled. "You know that I do." He picked up his glass, raised it in a toast. "Here's to living our dreams."

Anise smiled. *He gets it! He understands.* "Cheers."

The evening continued with conversation flowing as smooth as the wine. But the fact that Drew was breathing the same air as him was never too far from Gregory's mind. *What is he doing here? Did he somehow get wind of my plans and purposely show up?* Admittedly, this probability was a long shot, and prior to becoming a finalist for the grant, Gregory wouldn't have given the coincidence a second thought. But it was no secret that Drew was a ruthless overachiever out for fame and fortune. Whatever his back story, Gregory felt this guy was obviously one with something to prove. All during this grant process Gregory and the third finalist, Ken Burrows, had remained cordial. But Drew made it clear to anyone who would listen that *he* was the one who should be awarded the money. *His* research was the most important. No one wanted the grant worse than *he* did. Gregory begged to differ on that one. But he had no doubt that Drew would do just about anything to win.

Not that Gregory wasn't used to certain doctor jockeying. The world of medicine was a competitive field. But some of Drew's latest shenanigans were borderline criminal, not competitive, ones that if successful against him could potentially cost him not only the grant but the right to legally practice medicine.

"Gregory, did you hear me?"

"I'm sorry; I was momentarily distracted."

"Well," Anise cooed, "I'm known to have that type of effect on men."

Gregory chuckled, and the dark thoughts about Drew dissipated. For the moment. But he was Jackie Morgan's son and he was definitely going to follow the advice she'd drilled in all of her children: sometimes paying attention is the only price you have to pay.

Gregory didn't trust sly-smiling Drew for a minute, and he'd most definitely be paying attention. Believe that.

18

The next day, Anise woke up bright and early. Her date last night with Gregory had energized her. Hearing how close he was to his dream made her determine to live her own. In short order she walked Boomer, made a protein smoothie, plopped down on the bed in the guest room, and fired up her iPad. There were a few new e-mails but one immediately caught her eye. Clicking on it, she read:

Hello, Anise: This e-mail is to confirm our meeting tomorrow. As we previously communicated, please bring your portfolio, and anything else you feel showcases your talent and artistic style, and helps us know you better. Jessica raved about you and from the samples we have seen, we are excited to have you join us. If you have any questions, please don't hesitate to call us. See you soon! Dawn.

Anise reread the e-mail from The Creative Space's director, then stood and paced the room. She was stoked! Big time. Is this how it felt when dreams came true? She didn't know. She'd never experienced getting what one truly wanted. At one time she'd wanted things to work with Joey, for him to get an NFL contract and for them to take things to a more exclusive level. Didn't get that. She'd definitely wanted her mother to live. *Definitely* didn't get that. But there were moments when she'd felt that she was on the right track: when she graduated in the top ten percent of her class, when she had some of her work featured at Kansas City's famed Nelson-Atkins Art Gallery, and when Jessica Johnson agreed to be her mentor. Yes, this moment rather felt like those. Only better.

She began to calm down, and after grabbing a glass of juice from the refrigerator returned to her iPad. She continued scrolling through her mostly spam e-mails until she reached a friend request from her newly created Facebook page: Art by Anise. The name she thought both catchy and concise had just popped into her head one day and right after creating the page she'd purchased the URL with the same name: ArtbyAnise.com. *Must be catchy enough since I'm already getting requests!* She went over to the popular site and clicked on the friend request from Art-n-Sol. The name didn't ring a bell at all, so she browsed the profile. It seemed that whoever it was had just set up his profile, too, since there were only a few photos and even fewer comments on the time line. The profile picture was a famous Michelangelo painting. She clicked on the "about" link and read the scant information: male, single, living in LA. Under employment, he'd written "sales". They had one friend in common— The Creative Space Arts Center. She accepted his friend request, eager to grow her circle of friends in LA, especially ones with an interest in art.

Ready to add to her whopping total of five new Facebook friends, one of which was Jessica and another of which was Dawn, Anise sent requests to all of her college friends before typing the name Gregory Morgan into the search engine. Although several pages came up under this name, none of the faces were her fine doctor friend. *Interesting*. She then typed in the brother's name, Michael Morgan. A public page for Morgan Sports Management came up immediately.

"Wow," she murmured, "almost fifty thousand likes." She spent several minutes scrolling the page before clicking on Shayna Washington's picture and going to her page. Shayna had even more likes than her husband. Anise checked out her page, reading the posts and looking at the pictures. Most of them centered around Shayna's career as a track star. On a whim, Anise put Shayna's name into the Web site's search engine and found a personal page. She clicked on that and went to the photos on that page. As she'd assumed, the photos on this page were personal. One of the first ones shown was from some type of get-together where Anise quickly recognized Shayna and Michael. On one side of them was Gregory with a woman gorgeous enough to walk a runway. On the other side was a man Anise believed had to be the other brother, the security guy. She took a closer look. All of the brothers were handsome but for her, Gregory looked the best. At this thought, a warm fuzzy feeling came over her. "Stop it, girl, y'all are just friends." That's what she mumbled to herself. But deep down, she knew that what she was beginning to feel for him was much, much more.

Someone else was examining feelings on that morning. Gregory sat in the breakroom. He was supposed to be reading the medical journal before him but for the past several minutes his mind had been on Anise. The more he considered it the more he realized that quite a few of his thoughts had involved her lately. Even as he smiled, he wasn't totally sure how he felt about that.

"Hey there, Greg." A distinguished-looking doctor in full scrubs garb stepped into the room.

"Dr. Meyers!" Gregory closed the magazine that he'd been busy not reading. "How did the surgery go?" One of his mentors, Aaron Meyers also often served as a surrogate dad.

Dr. Meyers pulled off his cap and sat in a chair

facing Gregory's desk. "He'll live to see another day."

"Then that's a job well done." He reached over and shook Dr. Meyers's hand.

"Gregory? Are you all right?"

Gregory slowly shook his head. "Not really."

"Want to talk about it?"

Gregory looked out the window, and then at Dr. Meyers. Without a word, Dr. Meyers cocked his head in a gesture for them to leave the room. They didn't say another word until they reached the older physician's office.

"Okay, Gregory. What's on your mind?"

"I don't know if I should say anything. You'll probably think I'm just being paranoid."

"Well, you know what they say. Just because you're paranoid doesn't mean they're *not* out to get you." Dr. Meyers then feigned looking around. "And I don't know who *they* are, so keep your voice down."

The men laughed.

"In the past couple months," Gregory spoke into the silence, "I've had things happen that haven't occurred in all my years of practicing medicine, including my internship."

"Such as?"

"I had a motorcycle victim come in, did the emergency surgery. Wrote up a report and left it for his assigned doctor, except when Dr. Foster asked for the report from the file clerk, it was missing. It's happened twice more since then."

Dr. Meyers's brow furrowed, but he said nothing.

"Last week, I prescribed pain medication for a patient. When the paperwork got to the nurse, the dosage listed was five hundred twenty-five milligrams. She thought it strange and double checked it with the physician on duty, who immediately corrected the amount. Fortunately for me, before ending my shift I'd shown the report to one of the interns on duty, Venita, and she vouched for what had been on the original request. If not for the keen observation of the nurse on duty, I could be facing some serious charges." The ensuing silence was palpable. "Do you think I'm crazy, that these are just a couple of unfortunate events and that I'm imagining attempts at sabotage that really aren't there?"

"I don't think you're crazy," Dr. Meyers responded. "Money and ego make men do strange things. Medicine is a competitive field. And considering you're a finalist for a multimillion-dollar grant, you're wise to be extra cautious."

Gregory took a deep breath and exhaled slowly. They looked out of Dr. Meyers's window, which faced an inner courtyard. For a moment, both got caught up in nature, their thoughts flying along with the scampering birds, their emotions running hot and raw, like the sun. Finally Dr. Meyers resumed their conversation. "I had lunch with one of the foundation board members this week. He's good friends with the Rosenthals."

The Rosenthals were behind the philanthropic organization spearheading the grant. Gregory was all ears. "They've made a decision?"

"Not yet. But I do have news." Dr. Meyers leaned forward. "There's a big building in Santa Monica that will be gutted and totally renovated to house the recipient's research center. The building belonged to Abram Rosenthal's grandfather and has been tied up due to a fifty-year lease. The lease expires in August and the tenants will be given notice to vacate by either August or September, if they haven't been told already. They want to fast-track the renovation so that the center will be on track for a first of the year unveiling. They're planning for the facility to be top of the line, state of the art, and they're going to make the opening and dedication a huge social event to raise even more money. Heck, if you're the recipient, I may have to come and work for you!"

"I included a competitive budget for staff, doctor. I'd hire you in a heartbeat." Gregory smiled at the mere thought of hiring staff for his dream center. He'd waited a long time, often wondering how what he wanted could possibly happen. Soon, he would find out. "You said a total renovation, huh? I sure hope they plan on getting input from whoever ends up being director."

"I'm sure they will. You've juggled a hectic

schedule since your college days. But I have a feeling that if you win this research grant, time is going to become even more elusive. Are you ready for that? No time for yourself? No personal life?"

"That's pretty much how I live right now!"

"Can I give you some advice?"

"Sure."

"You're one helluva doctor: focused, motivated, dedicated. But try and find the balance, Greg. Helping to save lives makes me happy every day, but Susan, my kids and grandkids? That's where I find my true joy."

Dr. Meyers got a page and left the office. Gregory headed to the men's room. He thought he'd been preoccupied before, but the good doctor had just placed even more on his mind, like where he'd been finding joy lately. The answer was easy— Anise.

19

Anise navigated the hallowed halls of The Creative Space, looking for the lime green door with the brightly painted sun that Dawn had said was her office. On the way, she saw several studios, a couple of them filled with artists at work. In one, a dreadlocked brother with his back to the door sculpted from clay; in another, a woman with bright red streaks throughout her honey blond hair, wearing a paint-streaked T-shirt and skinny jeans, pondered on a canvas that Anise couldn't see. Her heart skipped a beat and the smile happened before she was even aware of it. Yes! This was going to be wonderful. She could meet so many people here, create so many pieces for the art gallery that would one day be the culmination of her dreams. This big, drafty building where so many artists had spilled their aspirations and painted their hopes and sculpted vast arrays of yesterdays already felt like home.

"Dawn?" she said, standing at the blinding lime, yellow, and orange door.

"You must be Anise," the vivacious redhead said with a smile, rising from a chair barely visible behind stacks of art books, portfolios, and other knickknacks on a crowded desk in a crowded room. She bypassed Anise's hand and gathered her in a homey embrace. "Ah, none of that formal nonsense." She turned, gathered a stack of magazines sitting on one of two chairs in the room, set it on the floor, and gestured for Anise to sit. "Excuse the mess. Sometimes it's worse."

"No problem. You probably know where everything is."

"That's why I don't mess with it. If it got straightened up, I wouldn't be able to find a thing!" She noticed Anise holding her portfolio and reached out her hand to take it. "So . . . welcome to LA and The Creative Space!"

"Thank you. This place is awesome. It's like I can feel the presence of all the other spirits who've ever created within its walls."

"It is like that." Dawn nodded. "Which is why it will be such a bummer if some powers that be have their way."

"What do you mean?"

"Lydia Rosenthal-Bolton, the woman who founded The Creative Space, secured a fifty-year lease on this building. It expires this year."

"What does that mean?"

"We may not be able to renew the lease."

"There's a chance for another company or organization to take over the space?" From what she'd seen during the walk to Dawn's office, Anise couldn't imagine that happening.

"We received a notice regarding their intent not to renew the lease. We're trying to fight it but . . . never mind that," Dawn said with a shrug, as she continued to flip through Anise's work. "Let's talk about this amazing artwork! You're good."

"Thank you."

"So . . . as you may know, the waiting list here for studio space is up to eighteen months, but after seeing the samples Jessica sent along with her letter, we were happy to fast-track your internship. And, I may have another great piece of news for you. You're looking for employment, correct?"

This question definitely got Anise's attention. "Yes."

"And you were previously working as an administrative assistant in Omaha?" Anise nodded. "Well, my assistant is experiencing a difficult pregnancy and has been ordered on bed rest. We were going to go through a temp agency to find a replacement for three to four months, but if you think you can carve out four hours a day, five days a week from your creating time to help me here in the office, we'd like to offer the job to you. Are you interested?"

Can life get any better? Anise thought with a smile. "I am totally interested."

Two and a half hours later, Anise left Santa Monica on a natural high. She would forever be in debt to her favorite art teacher and mentor, Jessica, and to the friends of this teacher still on the The Creative Space board. Because of the death of her mother, Anise had been given a "special circumstance" exemption and the normal waiting period for a studio of up to two years had been waived. And instead of finding a job, one had found her! Again, her mother was smiling down upon her, helping her reach her dream. That she and Dawn had become fast friends was a nice plus; and the other artists she met there seemed warm and friendly.

After leaving The Space, she'd driven north to Venice Beach to look at a couple of apartments she'd seen online. Her first choice would have been to both live and work in Santa Monica but right now those tony beachfront apartments were a little too rich for her blood. *Maybe if Bob gets things settled with that bank and he sells the house* . . . Again at the thought of Carolyn, a bittersweet smile scampered across Anise's face. "I'm doing it, Mommy," she whispered, even as she noted the pain at her mother's memory was not as severe this time. "I'm living the dream . . . for both of us."

The rest of the afternoon and evening passed quickly. She logged on to Facebook and was soon engaged in an instant message chat with her newest friend, Art-n-Sol. He'd complimented her on her art, asked about where he might purchase a piece and before she knew it they'd gone on to more personal topics such as where she was from and when she'd moved. Normally she wasn't so forthcoming but Art-n-Sol was funny, flirty and seemed harmless enough. Before she knew it an hour had gone by. She logged off of the social network, checked emails, fed and walked Boomer, and cooked a light dinner for her and Aretha. At ten o'clock she took a shower, dressed in jean shorts and a baby blue tank top, went downstairs and watched a little TV.

At twelve-fifteen her phone rang. "Hello, doctor," she purred.

"Ooh, baby, I like the way you say that. Makes me think about Marvin Gaye and some sexual healing."

"Hmm, I just might be able to help you if that's the cure." They laughed. "Are you at home?"

"Just got in. I'm going to jump into the shower; you're welcome to join me if you'd like."

"I just took one myself, but if you leave the back door open, I'll come on over."

"Done. Just lock it behind you and"—his voice lowered—"bring your fine self on over here and crawl between my sheets."

His words and the none-too-subtle meaning behind them caused a nana-based squiggle that had Anise clenching her thighs. She turned off the television and after a quick glance up the stairs, she looked at Boomer. "Be quiet," she whispered, getting up and beginning a creep toward the back door. "And don't start barking when we go outside." She placed a couple dog biscuits on the patio pillow she'd purchased. Once he settled down on it she gave him a quick pet. "I won't be gone long."

Within minutes, Anise was turning the knob to the door that entered a short hallway beside Gregory's gourmet kitchen. The lights were turned dim. Anise took a few seconds for her eyes to adjust and then walked toward the stairs. Her heartbeat increased as she began to climb them; something about their midnight rendezvous had her feeling naughty and frisky and ready for fun.

20

"Gregory?" She walked inside the master suite and heard the shower going. Continuing to the bathroom door, she announced, "Babe, I'm here."

"Make yourself comfortable," he said over the sound of the water spray. "I'll be right out."

Anise turned and walked back into the master suite. She bypassed his spacious bed and for now his invitation to wait for him in it and instead, took the opportunity to scrutinize his surroundings. Her critical artist eye approved. His was a modern, sophisticated style and the home was so tastefully done that she wondered if he'd hired an interior designer. *Probably so,* she thought, noting how the gray-navy theme from downstairs continued here, with black and white added for dramatic results. She strolled over to a large walk-in closet. Everything was neat and organized. Stepping inside, she noted his platinum jewelry, wallet, and cell phone on the chest of drawers. The cell rang,

causing Anise to almost jump out of her jean
shorts. Peeking over, she read the name: *Lori*. A
female. Her mind immediately went to the picture she'd seen on Shayna's Facebook page. The
stunning woman with her arms around Gregory.
Insecurity poured over her much like the shower
water she heard pouring over her naked friend.
Is she his girl or something? And if so . . . what am I?
Hearing the shower shut off, she stepped out of the
closet and walked over to the sitting area, a cozy
space with a love seat and two chairs flanking an
elevated fireplace.

Gregory soundlessly came up behind her and
wrapped her in his arms. He smelled like goodness
and mercy following you all the days of your life.
"There you are." A nuzzle on the neck was followed
by a soft bite of the earlobe. "I thought I told you
that I wanted you in bed, naked, and waiting."

She turned in his arms, slightly disappointed to
discover that he'd covered up his birthday suit with
low-riding black shorts. "You said all that?"

One kiss; soft, lips barely touching.

"I said between the sheets and figured that I
wanted you naked was a given," Gregory replied.

"You know they say one should never assume."

Another kiss, nuzzling, enjoying the feel in each
other's arms.

"That saying ends with something about asses,"
Gregory murmured. "Kind of how I'd like to end
my night . . . squeezing yours." His hands moved up

and down her back before going lower, cupping her butt.

Her hands appreciated his wide shoulders, and moved down his arms, even as his tongue flicked her lips for permission to enter and she opened them to comply. The swirling began.

And so did his ringtone.

"Darn it." Gregory pulled away. "Sorry, I meant to turn that off." He walked into the closet and after retrieving the phone, silenced the ringer before setting it on his nightstand. He walked back to where Anise was now sitting on the love seat.

"Booty call?" she asked, wondering if he'd tell her that someone named Lori was calling.

"No, that was a woman named Lori, a childhood friend."

Wow, he was honest. Brownie points! "Interesting."

Gregory peered at her, looking for the whole meaning behind that word. "How so?"

"There's not one person from my childhood with whom I'm still in contact. What's so special about this girl?"

"It's not just her but her whole family. She is a twin and in high school her sister, Lisa, used to date Michael. I used to date Lori. Our mothers are friends."

"And you and Lori are still friends."

"Yes."

With benefits? she wanted to ask. But didn't.

Gregory walked toward the bedroom door.

"I'm going to grab something to drink. What would you like?"

"What are you having?"

"Just sparkling water for me; I have another twelve-hour shift tomorrow."

"That sounds fine for me, too. Except mixed with orange juice if you have it."

"Really?"

"Yes, it turns it into sparkling orange."

"Come help me make them."

"Okay."

Ten minutes later they were back upstairs with their sparkling drinks and a bowl of chips. They walked back over to the love seat. "So," Gregory began after they'd settled down. "Tell me your good news."

Anise reached over to give his shoulder a squeeze. "In a minute," she said, getting up and standing behind him. "You are so tight."

He lowered his head. "Umm, that feels good."

She continued for several minutes. "Ah, you're starting to loosen up now."

He placed his hands on hers, stopping the massage. "I'm ready to hear all about your meeting. But I'm exhausted and your skillful fingers are putting me to sleep. Can I listen from a horizontal position, without clothes?"

21

Naked and snuggling against each other, Gregory asked Anise, "Okay, how did the meeting go, baby?"

"It went pretty amazing." She told him about her teacher's connection with the place where she'd be interning. "Because of their friendship I won't only be learning from some of the best painters in the country, but the director's assistant is going on maternity leave, so I'll also have a job!"

"I'm excited for you, Anise," Gregory said, though truth be told, there was more exhaustion than excitement in his voice.

"What makes it so special is that the place I'll be working at, The Creative Space, is very hard to get into. In its heyday people stayed on a waiting list for years. There is a little problem, however, something about their fifty-year lease being . . . Gregory? Are you asleep?"

A soft, gentle snore was her answer.

Anise sighed and slowly moved away from him, hoping to get out of bed without waking him up. As soon as there was air between them, he pulled her back against him. The action may have been automatic but it felt good. She'd come over with the intention of doing some bedroom gymnastics, but it had been a long time since she'd simply snuggled. She nestled her booty into his curved form, feeling his limp member against her cheek. *I'll just lay here for a little while. Until he's in a deep sleep.* Soon, however, she was knocked out, too.

Hours later, the dream seemed all too real. Someone lightly nibbling on her ear, even as her nipple was tweaked into hardness, and speaking of . . . a certain length of hardness pressed against her backside. Anise squirmed as her body came alive with the ministrations, her legs parting so that the finger rubbing the entrance to her heat could gain entry. It felt so real, almost like the arms were actually around her, the tongue was really gliding down her neck, the powerful piece of manhood was actually easing its way into—

Her eyes flew open.

She sat straight up. "What time is it?"

"Time for me to give you what we missed last night," Gregory responded, deftly turning over Anise and placing her beneath him in one fell swoop.

Anise glanced at the clock. *Seven am?* "Shoot! I

gotta go. Aunt Ree is an early riser!" She hopped out of bed and into her shorts, almost in one motion.

Gregory cracked up.

"Yeah, whatever, Gregory," she responded, hopping on one leg to get her other into the opening. "I'm glad I'm your comic relief." Looking around she continued, "Where's my bra?"

"Behind you." Indeed. Gregory watched her swaying breasts following her twisting torso, his eyes dropping down as she bent to retrieve the lacy secret. Her butt was perfect. Period. Blood surged to his already hardening shaft because her creamy skin was more tempting than keeping a bag full of unmarked bills found in your backyard. He rolled out of bed. "Are you going to leave me like this?"

One look behind her and she knew that she couldn't.

It was the dick: that marvelously curved, perfectly mushroom-tipped, exquisitely rigged and ready mass of manliness.

She dropped to her knees, partly in answer, partly because her legs could no longer hold her. Her right hand started itching. She wanted to draw it, like this: hard, thick, bobbing and weaving like a drunkard at Mardi Gras. But since she didn't have paper or pen she did the next best thing. Slinking forward on her knees, she lifted her head . . . and kissed it. Once. *Bob.* Twice. *Weave.* She stuck out her tongue and tickled his fancy. A slight hiss escaped through Gregory's clenched teeth. Anise smiled. *Fancy effectively tickled.* She felt a hand against the back of her head. *Stop teasing*, it seemed to say. "Please," Gregory moaned. So she did.

Thirty minutes later, a still wet, satisfied Anise eased toward her aunt's backyard gate. She'd fairly run through the shower in Gregory's suite, just enough to hit here and wash there before once again jumping into her clothes and heading home. She hadn't been to church in years but prayed that Aretha (and Boomer) were still sleeping.

Please, Boomer, she pleaded, hoping to telepathically connect with her canine friend. *Don't*—

"Woof!"

Geez, can you bark any louder? Anise hurried inside the gate. "Shut up, Boomer!" Now hers were the teeth that clenched. Boomer didn't care about her attitude. He jumped up, his paws landing on her arm, tail wagging as she shooed him away. He gave her a look. *Is that all you've got?* Anise could have sworn he smiled as he jumped up again. She knelt down so that they were face to face. "Listen." Boomer gave her a big tonguing on her cheek. "Ugh. Listen, don't lick!" she hissed, and then, considering all the licking that had taken place in the last thirty minutes, almost rephrased her statement. Grabbing his fluffy cheeks, she continued. "When I open this door I need you to be quiet.

Okay?" Feeling that his look was one of "your secret's safe with me," she eased open the storm door and slipped her key into the lock. Then, with the stealth of a cat burglar casing the White House, she eased open the door ever so slowly, turned once more and placed a finger to her lips before pushing the door all the way open, letting Boomer run in before she quietly closed and locked the door, turned around, and looked directly into the twinkling eyes of her aunt.

Anise gasped and jumped in surprise.

"Good morning!" Aretha said with a chuckle.

"I, uh, I was hoping I'd get back from, uh, walking Boomer before you got up. Hope we didn't wake you. I decided to walk him first and feed him later."

"Really?" Aretha looked at Boomer and back at her. "Well," she said, her mouth twisted in humor. "Considering you've been walking him since midnight last night, I'm sure that dog is hungry!"

"Okay, I'm busted," Anise said, embarrassed even though she knew that her aunt would not judge. "We were talking and then I fell asleep."

"Anise, you do not have to report to me. I'm just glad to know you've met a friend." After a beat she added, "Now, what did y'all talk about?"

"Nothing because he fell asleep. But it was what I'd wanted to share with you anyway, except you were spending time with a man yourself! It's about my interview yesterday."

"Is this good news?" Anise nodded. "Then hold that thought. I've just been waiting for a reason to break open this sparkling Moscato. We can make mimosas. It's time to celebrate!"

22

"What's up, man?" Gregory walked into his brother's bright, airy home in Hollywood Hills and gave him a shoulder bump.

"Keeping it moving," Michael responded, with an affectionate pat on Gregory's back. "You know how we do it."

The two brothers turned toward the sound of the opening sliding glass patio door. "About time you got here," Troy said to Gregory as he set a tray of grilled vegetables on the table. "Five minutes a side, son, and those steaks will be done."

"You want a beer?" Michael threw the question over his shoulder as he walked into the kitchen.

"Sure." Gregory joined Troy, who'd retrieved a bowl of marinating beef and walked back outside. Within seconds Michael joined them, three brewskis in hand. "Where's Shayna?" Greg asked.

Michael handed Gregory a bottle and set Troy's on the patio table. "Out with her girls."

"I was beginning to think y'all were joined at the hip, as much time as you spend together."

Greg held up his bottle. The brothers clinked glass.

"That's how it is when you're married both personally and in business," Michael said.

Troy laughed as he maneuvered the steaks around on the grill. "That's how it is when you're whipped."

"Whatever, dog. You wish you could have it like I do."

"Naw, I'm still in the club that believes variety is the spice of life. Right, Gregory?" Silence. "Oh, wait. I forgot. You're off the hunt for a minute."

"Why's that?" Michael asked.

"You haven't heard?" Troy responded. "Greg's got a new boo thang."

"Word?" Michael took a swig of beer and looked speculatively at his brother. "When did that happen? I wasn't out of town a week."

"All I know is the sister is so bad your brother forgot our basketball game, the one we've been playing damn near every week for the past four years."

"I know you're not trying to start a conversation about missing b-ball time. You've got that record hands down," Gregory retorted.

"At least I call!" Troy turned the steaks.

"Look, at least I made it and I was only thirty minutes late."

"Who is she?" Michael asked.

Gregory told Michael about Anise. "I don't know what it is, but I have to admit, I'm feeling her."

"It's been a minute since you've had some," Troy said, walking over to the table with the steaks. "You're feeling that tang, man." He put down the plate and dodged Gregory's punch as he walked into the house.

"So what's so special about this one?" Michael asked.

Gregory shrugged. "She's just cool, laid back, doesn't have to go all Hollywood on a brothah. I guess it's that Midwest vibe."

"Doesn't sound at all like Lori."

"Please. The total opposite. Flashy chicks are all right for a night on the town or a short-term affair but deep down I've always been attracted to someone more laid-back and low-key, who handles business behind the scene."

Michael's look was questioning as he responded, "Sounds like you're ready to get married!"

"When I find the right woman then, yes, I'm ready. You and Troy are born players but I actually don't like juggling phone numbers. I remember being ten, eleven, staying up on a Friday night with Mom and Dad watching the Tonight Show. They had this easy-going camaraderie, with the ability to read each other's minds and finish the other's sentences. At times they'd look at each other as though they were the only ones in the room. Made me feel almost like a trespasser. And made me want to experience what a love like that felt like."

Michael looked at his brother with newfound appreciation. "Wow. That's beautiful, man."

Troy walked back out on the patio carrying the grilled vegetables and a loaf of bread from his favorite bakery.

Michael immediately reached for the tongs. "These look good," he said, referring to the squash, tomato, broccoli, cauliflower, and red bell pepper medley. "What'd you do to them?"

"Marinated them in a light vinaigrette and then tossed in a little feta."

"Dang, man," Gregory said, cutting up the medium rare steak before him. "You sound like a chef on one of those cooking channels."

Troy sat down. "Bon appétit."

For a while the only sounds heard in Michael's beautifully landscaped backyard were the gurgling of the fountain and the tinkling of silverware against porcelain plates. Finally, Gregory wiped his mouth and took a drink. "What's happening in your world, Troy? Anything exciting?"

"It's Morgan Security, baby. Everything we do is exciting."

"Man, don't make me throw up this good steak," Michael teased, around a mouthful of food.

Troy chuckled. "Seriously, we've got some nice contracts coming in. We've been approached by the LA security officials who work with the Secret

Service to help with some major political detail, including the First Lady. There also might be a pretty cool job coming down the pike on the music front." He paused, both to take a swig of his beer and also for effect. "We might handle the West Coast leg of Gabriella's tour."

This got a reaction from both of his brothers.

"And get paid for it?" Michael asked.

Gregory added, "Dang, if it meant guarding her, I might change my mind about owning a gun!"

"It's a tough job," Troy said with a shrug, "but somebody's got to do it."

"That's a stunningly beautiful woman," Gregory said, of the new one-name pop sensation whose superstar status was quickly eclipsing that of Beyoncé, Rihanna, and others. "You sure you could handle that?"

"With pleasure," Troy said, his confident smile leaving no doubt that he meant what he said. "What about you, Greg? What's up with that multimillion-dollar grant?"

"Down to three finalists, all of us doctors at UCLA med: me, Ken Burrows and Drew Fordham." Gregory's brows knit briefly, before he reached for a bottle of water and took a drink.

Troy's eyes narrowed. This security man didn't miss much, especially when it came to the brothers he'd looked up to and tried to emulate his whole life. "How are you feeling about your chances?"

Gregory shrugged. "I have a 33.3% chance."

"It's got to be higher than that," Michael countered. "Where's your confidence, bro?"

Troy stopped eating. "Why do I get the feeling that something's going on that you're not telling us about?"

"Because you're an investigator and a protector." Gregory playfully punched his brother's arm. "Your life's work involves getting those types of feelings."

"Nice if that was your attempt at a compliment. But you didn't answer my question."

Michael stopped eating too.

They both looked at Gregory. "It's nothing, really." He placed a few more grilled vegetables on his plate. In the ensuing seconds, the only sound heard was that of his silverware touching the plate. After a couple more bites and the continued curious looks from his brothers, Gregory wiped his mouth and sat back. "Over the past couple months there have been some unusual occurrences . . . that's all."

Troy crossed his arms. "Explain these unusual occurrences."

Gregory told them about the erroneous chart dosage, missing files and a couple other instances. "We're always training interns, there have been several new staffers lately. That these things are happening as a decision on the grant recipient nears could be mere coincidence."

"Or it could be sabotage." Troy pulled out his

cell phone. "I think it's time for me to check out your competition."

"I'm not that worried about it. Me and Ken have always been pretty cool and while Drew seems the type who can be shady, I think it's mostly bluff and hot air."

Troy's thumbs flew across his cell phone keyboard. "Even so . . . watch your back."

"Haven't I always? You know we've all dealt with haters since back in the day. I'm well aware of mine and not just the two I'm going up against for the grant. Troy, I know it's probably useless to say this but checking up on either Ken or Drew is really unnecessary."

"Perhaps," Troy finished entering information and pocketed his phone. "But I'm just doing my job, brother. Just doing my job."

The three men spent the next few hours enjoying each other's company, something that these days was all too rare. By the time he returned to Hancock Park, Gregory had forgotten all about his younger brother's somber warning regarding his haters. But in the not too distant future . . . he'd remember.

23

Gregory headed to the hospital locker room a full thirty minutes early for his shift. There was a song in his heart and a pep in his step, and if anyone had asked, he would have had to admit that a certain spice had positively affected his mood. As soon as he stepped inside the locker room door, this mood ended.

Of all the people who'd be in here now. A few of the men Gregory had had in mind when talking to his brothers; Drew was among them. Just like he'd later told Michael and Troy, he couldn't help it if others believed that he got treated like the golden child. For the most part, Gregory didn't let his co-workers jealousy bother him. He knew how hard he'd worked and how much he'd sacrificed to build a stellar reputation in the medical world. As far as he was concerned, the naysayers could go kick rocks. He walked past the row they were in and continued to his locker.

"Greg."

He kept walking, speaking to the ER doctor whose locker was next to his, one who wasn't jealous of Gregory's success because he'd achieved enough of his own. "Hey, Matt."

"Hey, buddy. How's it going?"

"Another day, another life saved, right?"

"That's how it's supposed to work." Matt closed his locker. "Are you participating in the charity golf tournament next week?"

"No. I have another commitment."

"That's too bad. I was looking forward to showing you how the game is played."

"Ha! Is that right?"

Instead of answering, Matt laughed and walked out.

Footsteps, and then Drew was around the corner, with his cocky grin in Gregory's face. "Did you hear the news?"

"What news?"

"About the location for the new research center."

"Yes," Gregory said, knowing that several colleagues had received this news, including the other candidate, Ken Burrows. Because the building would house more medical companies besides the research center, it was interesting news. "Most of us received that news, Drew."

"That old artist building," Drew continued, "called The Creative Space."

Gregory absorbed this news as he removed his

street clothes and reached for his scrubs. He hadn't given much thought to the building's current tenants. "Never heard of it," he said at last. *But why does that name sound familiar?*

"Lots of great restaurants, a block from the ocean; that is going to be a great locale." When Gregory remained silent, Drew continued. "I hear they're leaning my way. Your study of the brain sounds intriguing but with heart disease being the leading cause of death in this country, my research is more timely, makes more sense."

"I'm glad you think so," Gregory said, moving around Drew to place his things in a locker. "I think Ken's special focus on cancer is extremely relevant. But it's not up to us. It's up to the committee. And I for one am content to wait and see what they decide."

"Waiting is probably your best bet." Drew placed a stethoscope around his neck. "Me, I'm picking out office furniture. See you later. Hey," he stopped at the end of the lockers. "The woman you were with the other night. Anise, right?"

Gregory said, at once on alert, "What about her?"

"She's a pretty lady. A natural beauty; not someone I'd peg you to be with."

"I don't see how that's any of your business."

"Hey, don't get defensive," Drew said, backing up. "I thought perhaps she was just a platonic friend that you were taking out to dinner. If that was the case then—"

"It's not the case. So back off."

"You bet, buddy. I meant no harm. See you later."

Gregory shook his head as Drew left the locker room. *Jerk.* Still, something that had been said bothered him. The name of the building where the research center would be housed. *The Creative Space.* An uneasy feeling surrounded this news, a feeling he didn't quite understand. And a question, still on his mind as he left the locker room and walked to the nurses' station. Where had he heard that name before?

24

It had only been two days since they'd made love, but Anise was jonesing like a crack addict in a drug house. So in the middle of apartment hunting, dealing with the moving truck that had arrived the Monday before and working at the center, she was excited to be taking an afternoon to spend with Gregory. Also, given the news about the center that she'd read on Facebook and that Dawn had confirmed, she could use the distraction.

So now, after getting to the center early and putting in a four-hour shift, Anise had left at noon, gone home, fed Boomer, changed clothes, and now leaned back in the soft leather of Gregory's Mercedes as they sped down the highway.

"Where are we going?" she asked.

"To the beach."

"I love it!"

"Have you gone to the beach since you moved

here?" Anise shook her head, missing Gregory's pleased expression. "Yes, I'm sure you will love it."

The day was beautiful: blue sky, lush green trees, and a sunny seventy-five. The midday traffic was light as Gregory hit the 10 Freeway and headed to Malibu. He reached for his iPod and, after scrolling through hundreds of selections, settled on a group of hip-hop/R & B. Soon, Nelly was telling the world about country grammar.

"Oh, man!" Anise exclaimed. "I haven't heard that song in forever!" She sat up, snapping her fingers and grooving to the beat.

"What do you know about this?" Gregory asked. "You had to be what . . . five when it came out?"

"If I were five, we'd be illegal," she quipped.

"How old are you?"

"Twenty-five."

"Oh, okay. I thought you were closer to twenty-one."

"How old are you?"

"Twenty-nine. An old man."

"When do you turn thirty?"

"August eighth."

"A Leo. No wonder."

"What does that mean?"

"Your sign is the lion, and every Leo I know thinks they're the king of the jungle. Or queen, as it goes."

"And we're not?"

"Whatever."

"I feel totally old school in saying this but . . . baby, what's your sign?"

"My sun sign is Sagittarius, but my rising is Pisces with a Libra moon."

Gregory gave her the side-eye. "Yeah, I've got something rising for your moon all right."

"Ha!"

The easy banter continued as songs from their childhood, tween and teen years played. They'd exited the 10 and hit the Pacific Coast Highway when the voice of R. Kelly floated through the speakers. As soon as she heard the first notes, for Anise, the atmosphere changed. She turned her head, the scenery suddenly blurring as tears pooled in her eyes. She tried to surreptitiously wipe them away.

But Gregory noticed. "Memories of your mother?" he softly asked, placing a hand on her arm.

She moved, avoiding his touch. "It was one of her favorite songs. We used to sing it together when I was around nine years old." Anise continued, her voice dropping even lower. "When we finished she'd hug me and ask, 'Do you believe you can fly?' And I'd say yes. . . ."

Gregory looked over at Anise, with concern in his eyes. For a moment, only the message of touching skies and spreading wings filled the car's interior. Then he turned the music down a notch.

"You'll always miss her, Anise. I won't say it gets better but it does get easier." Silence, as she continued to look out the window. "My dad has been gone for years now. But it's a rare day that goes by that I don't think about him. He loved old-school, seventies style. When he was home, that's all you'd hear in the house: the Spinners, Chi-Lites, Main Ingredient, Stylistics."

"My mom loved those groups, too," Anise said, the merest of smiles on her face as she turned to look straight ahead. "Every now and then she and her teacher friends would get together and after I'd gone to bed, they'd pull out the Marvin Gaye and Barry White."

"Well, if she liked them then you can't leave out Teddy Pendergrass!"

"Oh my gosh, yes!" Anise's smile was genuine now; tears gone, eyes sparkling with happier memories. "He was so nasty, always singing about closing doors and turning off lights."

Gregory started imitating Teddy P. "Turn 'em off!" he growled.

Anise looked at him and burst out laughing.

"If you're anything like your mother, she was a strong woman," Gregory said, turning serious once again. "Not many people would pack up and move across country; having only one relative . . . and a dream."

"Figured a new location would help start my new life. There wasn't anything keeping me in Omaha."

"I'm glad about that."

She looked over and smiled. "Me, too."

He turned on the stereo, grabbed his iPod,

scrolled over to his old-school section, and once again, the mood changed. The song was upbeat— Bill Withers and his classic tune, "Lovely Day." Slowly, Anise's head began to bob to the beat. *It is a lovely day,* she decided. Once again, Gregory reached over and held her hand. This time . . . she did not jerk away.

25

"Wow. This is beautiful!" After almost twenty minutes of winding up and around a two-lane road, they'd turned into a long, narrow driveway that opened up to a home boasting lots of glass and modern architecture and a stunning view of the Pacific Ocean. Anise exited the car and walked toward the view, which looked superbly serene and postcard-perfect. She spun around, raised her arms, and proclaimed, "I'm on top of the world!"

Gregory smiled, his heart bursting because of her happiness. When he'd first seen this place his response had been the same, and he'd grown up with the ocean practically in his backyard. She looked at him and his heart melted. While far from a womanizer, he'd been with his share of women. He'd been in love. But he was experiencing a deeper feeling than he'd ever felt before. It pleased him. It unnerved him. There was just something about her.

Anise turned and ran back to him, all traces of her earlier sadness having disappeared. "Thanks for bringing me here," she said as she threw her arms around him. "It's just what I needed. Now I really feel like I'm in California!" She turned around, leaning against Gregory's solid chest, and felt something she'd never, ever felt before. Total peace. She could stay this way . . . oh, the rest of her life.

"Let me get our bags, babe," Gregory said, kissing the top of her head. "I hope you brought the thong bikini I suggested."

"You did not," Anise said, laughing as she pulled away from him.

"Oh, you didn't bring it? Then I guess you'll have to go nude."

"That can be arranged."

They went inside, and the house didn't disappoint. There were high ceilings, neutral colors, a glistening stainless steel kitchen, and a stone fireplace dominating the far wall. Everything was luxurious, obviously expensive, but yet understated and homey.

Anise walked around the impressive living space, awed at the amazing views that could be seen from every angle. She couldn't imagine living like this. She could barely believe she was here now! "Is this yours?"

"No," Gregory said, once again coming up behind her. For some reason he felt bereft without her touch, an unexpected development he'd ponder in his alone time. "Belongs to a friend of mine."

"If I had a house like this, I'd never leave."

"You would if you were this guy. He's from a wealthy family in Saudi Arabia. Beauty like this is all he's ever known."

"How'd you meet him?"

"I operated on his son. He credited me for saving the boy's life. Granting me use of this place is one of the ways he's thanked me."

Anise cocked her head to look at him. "How does that feel . . . saving someone's life?"

"Gratifying, very gratifying. Every time I bring somebody back from the brink, it feels like one more step toward paying the debt of not being able to save my dad."

"Gregory! How could you blame yourself? You were just a kid."

"Guilt doesn't make sense, just like his death didn't." He disengaged his arms from Anise and walked to the glass doors that nearly reached the ceiling. They slid back soundlessly, bringing the outside indoors.

"I know how you feel," Anise said, her somber voice matching his obvious pain.

"I know you do."

"Watching my mom suffer and feeling helpless to stop it was one of the hardest things I've ever had to do."

He came up and wrapped his arms around her.

"I'm sure that neither one of them would want us to suffer now."

She leaned back against him, once again feeling total peace in his arms.

Gentle waves slapping against the ocean shore filled the silence. They swayed back and forth, as if to a lovers' soundtrack that only they heard.

Gregory turned her around and kissed her. She kissed him back, wet and hungry, while running her hand up and down his back.

"Umm," he moaned, pulling back. "If we get started with that now, you won't see the outside of this house for the rest of the day."

"That's all right with me," she replied.

"You say that now, but you'll thank me later. It's paradise out there." He looked down at her wedge sandals. "Did you bring tennis shoes?"

"Yes."

"Good. Put them on. We're going for a walk." He took their overnight bags into the master suite. When he walked out, Anise was standing by the patio doors, scowling.

"What's the matter?"

"Oh, nothing."

"That frown you wore didn't look like nothing to me."

"I was just thinking about The Creative Space, and some news I heard."

Gregory's heart flip-flopped as a bad feeling arose. "The Creative Space?"

"That's where I have my studio, and where I work. I told you about it the other night. You must have already been asleep."

"What about it?"

"The lease is up and we might have to move. But I don't want to spend this beautiful day talking about work. Let's go outside!"

"All right, baby. Let's go." Gregory's voice was calm but his insides churned. *How am I going to tell her that I may be the reason for the demise of her art studio?* Gregory knew that soon, he'd have to tell her. But he also knew that it wouldn't be today.

They spent the rest of the afternoon enjoying their surroundings. During a long walk on the beach they continued to get to know each other. Despite their differences, their connection continued to deepen around shared views on music, food, politics, and love for the outdoors. Gregory learned that Anise used to walk in her sleep and Anise learned that Gregory once sucked his thumb. Anise went into a depression after killing her goldfish and Gregory and his brothers had had a funeral for their dog named Trot. Both loved mysteries but abhorred violence. And both learned that their fiery personalities were tempered with compassion. By the time they returned to the house, hungry and ready to chill, the discomfort of both the past few days and hours before the walk had faded, much like the sun that was starting to dip toward the water.

They reached the house and went inside. Gregory walked into a small room off the hall. Soon the sounds of smooth jazz filled the house. "Are you hungry?" he asked, once he returned to the living room.

"Yes, I am. What's for dinner?"

"I don't know. Can you cook?"

"Does opening a can and heating the contents count?"

He made a face. "Uh, that would be a negative."

"Don't look at me like I cursed at you. Can you cook?"

"Enough that I won't starve." He headed to the kitchen, reached into the refrigerator, and pulled out a package. "What about steaks on the grill?"

"Sounds yummy."

"Can you handle a salad?"

"Sure."

Less than thirty minutes later they were sitting on the deck, facing the ocean. They'd eaten the simple yet delicious dinner and drank almost a bottle of wine. The sun continued to set, and the wind coming off the water produced a chill. Anise shivered.

"You cold, babe?"

Anise rubbed her arms. "A little."

Gregory stood, his eyes darkening as he watched her nipples pebble with the wind. "Come here."

The command was delivered in a low, firm tone that caused another shiver. Anise stood and grasped his outstretched hand. He pulled her with him, to a cushioned lounge chair facing the water. He guided her to it but before joining her, lit the circular fireplace that anchored the space. He went to a knob on the wall and turned up the music.

"Dinner was nice," he said as he joined Anise on the chaise and settled her into his lap. "But now I'm ready for dessert."

26

"Ooh, you are cold." He began to slowly rub his hands up and down her arms, even as the kisses started on her temple, cheek, and neck. She turned, lined her mouth up with his. The loving quickly went to another level as the kiss deepened, and Gregory found a nipple, and Anise rubbed her booty against his hardening shaft.

He exposed her breasts, watched as goose bumps formed on her creamy skin. The coolness of the air mixed with the heat coming off her body was a delicious combo with Gregory's fingers quickly turning her mind to other more important things. Like having him inside her—now.

Gregory must have had the same idea. He guided her up so that he could stand. Anise didn't need any encouragement or instruction. She pulled the tank top over her head and shimmied out of her shorts. Gregory undressed just as quickly, but when she raised her arms to pull her to him, he pulled back.

"You're cold, baby. Let's get in the hot tub."

Anise looked around. "Hot tub? Where?"

"It's on the lower level. You can't see it from here." He took her hand and led her to a set of steps, carved neatly and discreetly on the side of the house. They went down them, turned, and Anise almost gasped. Before them was a full-size infinity pool with a gently bubbling hot tub sending its invitation.

"This is incredible," she said, walking to the tub and testing it with her toe. "When did you turn it on?"

"The controls for everything in and around the house are on panels strategically located in the house and on the patio. I turned it on when we finished dinner. Is it too hot?"

"It's perfect." She stepped one leg and then the other into the rectangular tub, pausing for a moment before slowly sinking down into the bubbles.

Gregory watched, his eyes darkening with desire. She looked like a nymph, posed as she was and backlit by the moonlight. He was sure she had no idea how beautiful she was in this moment, or how much he wanted her. He looked down as his manhood hardened, thickened, and lengthened. Anise looked over at him, at it, and smiled. *Well, she may have some idea.*

He slid into the water and immediately pulled her back against him. Or tried to. Anise became playful, floating away from him in the large enclosure, her pert nipples teasing him above the water, along with her round mound when she turned over to swim away.

To no avail. In two swift movements, he'd reached her and grabbed a leg. "Not so fast, beautiful." She twisted and turned. He laughed at her halfhearted attempts to break free. "You can run but you can't hide." The friction of the struggle only served to heighten their awareness of each other. He touched his lips to her nipples. She shivered. He floated them over to the benches and kissed every inch of exposed skin. His hands reached beneath the water, found her nub and stroked it slowly, keeping the same rhythm as their swirling tongues. Anise followed suit, reaching down to find Gregory's hard, swollen manhood. Wrapping her fingers around it, she began to massage up and down the length of him until what seemed to be the impossible happened—he grew even more. He slid up from the second tier step to the first one, his rock hard flagpole now clearly visible above the bubbles and steam. Anise slid down until she was floating in the water, stayed in her position with hands gripping Gregory's hips. The combination of night air blowing across her exposed booty and the hot water swishing against her heat was an incredible turn on, and Gregory's glorious dick before her made her mouth water. She raised up just enough to take it into her mouth and then went to work: nibbling, sucking, licking the length of him. He groaned as she found and fondled his sac. Her laugh was guttural, knowing; she felt like a powerful goddess slaying the giant with her touch. He raked his fingernails over her back, then reached beneath the water and fondled her breasts. Her nipples hardened instantly; her body screamed for the next level of love.

Anise didn't want to play anymore. No, she wanted to get very serious. Standing up, she pushed him back against the padded rim, straddled him and in one fell motion drew every inch of him inside her. He groaned. She moaned. And then the dance began.

Oh, wait. He's not wearing a . . . umm. Too late to think about protection. Gregory had grabbed her hips and was now easing in and out with a slow and steady rhythm. She placed her hands on his shoulders, and balanced herself on either side. Clenching her inner muscles, she slowly rocked back and forth, moved up and down, lost in the throes of ecstasy. He bent his head to those dark, wet nipples, beads of water dripping off them, waiting to be caught. He obliged, pulling her nipple into his mouth, swirling around it with his tongue. He enjoyed his woman riding him like a stallion, but that only worked for so long. Gregory was a Morgan

Man and as such, at the end of the day, he had to take control.

And he did.

While still deep inside her, he stood up in the Jacuzzi and walked them to the chaise. There, after gently putting her down, he turned her around. Instinctively she gripped the arm of the chaise and hung on for the ride that was sure to follow. Gregory did not disappoint. He grabbed hold of her buttocks, buried himself deep within her, and began to drill. The cold wind on her skin and the hot rod within made Anise shake all over. Before long the pace increased and the stars both lovers saw at their simultaneous release were not those in the sky.

"That was amazing." Anise collapsed onto the chaise, as limp as a noodle.

"It was good for me, too," Gregory replied. He bent down and kissed her temple, something that Anise noted he did often. "Let's go inside."

Moments later, they were snuggled against each other in the massive platform bed that anchored the master suite. "You're an excellent lover." Anise lazily ran her hand up and down his chest. "You must have had a lot of practice."

"Are you inquiring as to my love life?"

"Actually, yes. I . . . we got carried away and didn't use a condom."

"Damn. You're right. Sorry about that, baby. But don't worry. I'm clean."

"Are you . . . seeing someone else right now? It's okay if you are," she hurriedly added. "We haven't defined whatever it is that we're doing. I just want to know."

"The last serious relationship I had ended some time ago and since then I've been very careful to be protected when I'm with someone casually. When I say casual, I'm not talking strangers, but friends I've known and have . . . an understanding."

"Like the girl who called the other night? Lori?"

A slight hesitation and then, "Yes, like her. But the past few months have been very busy; I haven't been with anyone, including her. What about you?"

"There's an ex back in Omaha that I dated off and on since high school. When I found out about my mom and moved back there, we briefly got back together. I was so devastated; wanted to forget my reality and dim the pain. It didn't work. I didn't want to be with him; didn't want to be anywhere or with anyone but her."

"So did you break up with this guy or what?"

"Yes." Anise figured her answer was truthful, for the most part. She'd told Joey in no uncertain terms that their relationship was over. Because she'd not answered one of his e-mails or taken any phone calls, his attempts to reach her had also gotten less. "I realized that when it came to coping with my mom's transition, sex was a Band-Aid, not a cure. No matter what, I still felt sad."

"I know the feeling." Gregory pulled Anise closer to him. "Are you happier now?"

"Ecstatic." Anise yawned.

"So can we put a name to 'whatever this is that we're doing,' as you called it?"

"What do you have in mind?"

"Well, since I'm not one for juggling a lot of women . . . how about 'exclusive'?"

Anise was surprised at this suggestion but didn't hesitate in responding. "I like that."

"Good."

"Gregory?"

"Yes, baby."

"I'm glad you're Aunt Ree's neighbor."

"I'm glad Boomer barked."

27

"Good afternoon, Dawn!" Anise was all smiles the next day as she entered the office. "Looks like someone enjoyed their afternoon off. What did you do?"

"Absolutely nothing, which just happens to be one of my favorite pastimes. What did you guys do?"

"Went to the beach."

"I thought it looked like you'd got some sun. Which beach?"

"Malibu."

Dawn whistled. "Nice."

"It was. That unobstructed ocean view is so beautiful. I'm so jealous of the people who get to see that every day."

"Yes, but they pay the price. Mud slides, fires . . . you couldn't give me a house up there."

"Geez," Anise said, picking up a pile of mail from the in-box and sorting it where she stood. "I'm glad

I didn't know that before I went yesterday. I would have been all paranoid."

"Don't pay me any mind. I'm probably just jealous. Here, you might as well have a look at this before you file it."

"What is it?"

"Our official notice to vacate."

Anise almost snatched the papers out of Dawn's hands.

"Don't say anything yet. They've already given us an unofficial heads-up, but those are the official papers informing us that we are to be free and clear of the building in forty-five days."

"Who are 'they'?"

"The Rosenthal family."

"But I thought that's who started the gallery!"

"Lydia started the gallery. Black sheep of the family, from what I now understand. I guess she had brothers who never were in favor of what she did with this building, but by the time they found out about it the lease was ironclad. They've probably been counting down to the day when they could throw us ordinary people out. I hear the brothers are pretty highbrow, if you know what I mean; their idea of true art is probably Picasso and Monet."

Anise plopped in her chair, with a dozen thoughts vying for attention. "What does this mean? Where are we going to go? How can they just throw us out like this?" All of these questions came out in a rush with no air between them.

"Trust me, I'm just as upset as you are. One of my friends on the board wants to protest it, try and get a grass roots effort going to maybe block the move. But she's in the minority. Most of them don't want to ruffle the Rosenthal feathers. They think that if they play nice that the family may make one of their other properties available."

"Is that an option?"

"Maybe. But these last ten years have been difficult, what with the economy tanking and all. Donations are down and the rent went up. I think many on the board are ready to dissolve the center and either join up with another gallery or art organization, or dissolve and regroup on a smaller scale."

"Dammit!"

"I know. Me, too."

Anise became quiet, pondering this new dilemma as she separated papers to file and others to shred. Then, as a thought popped into her head, she turned to Dawn. "Do we know what they're planning to put here? Maybe we can appeal to them to go elsewhere and with no new tenant, maybe prolong our stay."

Dawn shook her head. "I don't think so. From what I hear these new tenants are coming here expressly at the request of the Rosenthal brothers. A medical building, research center of some sort."

Anise froze. *No. Couldn't be. LA is way too large for two small dreams to collide.* "Research center?"

"Yes. I guess before Mr. Rosenthal died, the father, he was well cared for by the doctors at UCLA. As a way of giving back, they are going to donate this building as part of some grant they're spearheading to do medical research."

"Mind if I take ten?" Anise asked, rising from the chair without waiting for an answer. "I need to make a call."

"You going to the coffee shop by any chance?"

"I can."

"I could use a latte."

"Okay. I'll be back."

As soon as she was outside, she dialed Gregory but got voice mail. "Gregory, it's me, Anise. Give me a call as soon as you get this message. I have a quick question." She ended the call and pocketed the phone. *And I hope the answer's no.*

28

Gregory ended the call with his accountant in a very good mood. In spite of the nation's recent economic woes, his portfolio looked healthier than ever. Unlike a few of his peers, he'd bypassed day trading and other quick money schemes for tried and true markets. The only exception he'd made to that was investing in a chain of Asian nightclubs, through one of his brother Troy's connections. Fortunately, that had been a great gamble as the company had now opened twice as many clubs as they'd initially envisioned. Gregory smiled. His money looked good. His chances at the grant looked good. The woman now sharing his bed looked good. *You're on a roll, brothah. What can go wrong?*

Looking down he saw the name of a caller that somehow he'd missed. *Anise.* And immediately into his head came the answer to what could go wrong: their relationship, if he didn't think of a deft way to handle this touchy situation of his research center taking the place of her art center. "Dang it! What are the chances?" he asked the empty room. Los Angeles, with its eight million residents and he ventured as many buildings—what was the likelihood that they'd potentially be at odds over the same building? His chances at winning the lotto were probably better.

Knowing that to avoid calling her back was simply delaying the inevitable, he punched redial.

"Hey, Greg."

"Hey." Silence. "I was on with my accountant and see that I missed your call. How are you?"

"That depends on your answer to a question."

"Okay."

"Is the research center for the grant you're getting going to be in this building, The Creative Space?"

A pause and then, "That's what I've heard."

A longer pause. "When were you going to tell me?"

"When I knew for sure."

"We just received our notice to vacate the building so I'd say the decision has been made for quite a while. Are you sure you didn't know this, and just didn't tell me?"

Silence.

"Gregory?"

A sigh and then, "I knew."

"How long have you known?"

"Not long. I was definitely going to tell you; was

just waiting for the right time and place. I know you have deep feelings for the center, and hoped that when we did talk about it things could be discussed rationally, without argument."

"Well, I can tell you right now that if you're planning on moving us out of this building, arguing is the least that we'll do."

"Whoa, baby. Are you saying we'll go fist to cuffs?"

"Try and take this building and I'll beat your ass like a calypso player on his favorite steel drum!"

Gregory's smile could be felt through the phone. "My baby's gone gangster!"

Even Anise had to laugh at how tough she sounded. "Just so you know, it looks like we're now out of the realm of possibilities."

"What do you mean?"

"We just received our *official* notice to vacate the building. The Creative Space is supposed to be packed and moved before the end of August."

Gregory sighed. "Out of all the buildings in Los Angeles, Santa Monica even. I can't believe the coincidence that the one they'd choose for this project is the one that you're in."

"Isn't there something you can do, Gregory? For us, this isn't just another building, it's like a monument to art!"

"Babe, they haven't even named the grant's recipient. And even if it's me, I don't know that I'd be able to change the minds of the main funders of the program. It's their building and, from what

I'm told, their specific desire is to use it for medical research."

"If they respect you enough to offer you millions of dollars, then they should respect you enough to house your research center where you want it; maybe there at the hospital or . . . anyplace else!"

"I wish I could help, Anise, really I do. But even if I get the grant, my hands are tied."

"How do you know?" He heard her voice rising. In anger, he supposed. "You haven't even talked to them; you haven't even tried!"

"They've already served notice, Anise, probably already have contractors lined up, plans, spent money. Unfortunately I think this conversation is happening way too late."

"Perhaps, but if one of their recipients comes to them with, say, an alternative space, perhaps you can change it. Aren't there vacant rooms or buildings there at the hospital, or at the university where you can set up . . . whatever it is you need to do your research?"

"I could ask you the same question. Isn't there some other place you can draw?"

"This isn't just about me. It's about an institution, Gregory, one that has been around for fifty years!"

"Look, I've got to go to work. While I'm there, I'll ask around, see if I can find out anything about how your building was selected for the research center and if something can be done about it. But don't get your hopes up. I'm not sure there's much I can do."

"You seem like the kind of man who can do anything he puts his mind to, who can always get what he wants."

"I'll remember that you said that; in fact, I'll immediately put your words to the test."

"Okay," Anise said slowly, the tone reluctant at best. She was still upset, and that was putting it mildly.

"I invited you to my mother's friend's retirement party. You never accepted my invitation. Are you coming?"

"If you can change whoever's mind about taking away the art center, then I'll think about it."

Gregory heard a tinge of smile in her voice and grabbed on to it with every ounce of optimism that he had. "Oh, you're my contingency date? What if I don't have the answer by then, because I don't think I will? The Saturday after the fourth, that's the date of his party. Are you coming?"

"If I don't, then what are you going to do? Call your friend-with-benefits, Lori, to go with you?"

"Maybe."

"Go ahead. At least you're honest." A few seconds passed as Gregory imagined that cute scowl she wore whenever she was peeved. "I might go, emphasis on *might*. Is this a formal affair?"

"Absolutely."

"You mean you may be responsible for my losing

both a job and a place where I work for my livelihood, and you expect me to spend even *more* money where you're concerned by buying a dress? Then you would really owe me."

"Oh, so I'd owe you, huh?"

"Yes," Anise responded, her voice curt, her mood not conciliatory in the least. She acknowledged that he was trying, but still wasn't ready to give Gregory a "get out of jail free" pass. "And you'd better be prepared to take care of business."

Gregory's voice dropped to a silky near whisper. "No problem, baby. I always pay my debts."

29

Anise returned to the office that she and Dawn shared, no less upset than when she'd left.

"Where's my coffee?" Dawn asked, as soon as she'd turned into the room.

"Oh, shoot, Dawn. I got so wrapped up in my conversation that I totally forgot. I'll go back and get it for you—mocha latte, right?"

Dawn dismissed the suggestion with a wave of her hand. "Don't even worry about it. I probably don't need it anyway."

"I'm sorry. Needless to say the news about the center closing has me upset."

"You're not alone, sister. I just heard from a board member. They are seeking legal counsel to possibly get an injunction against our moving."

"So we're planning to fight this?" Anise asked.

"It looks that way but it also appears that the board is pretty much split down the middle. Half of them would rather leave this landmark and lease a lesser expensive building. The other half are true lovers of not only art, but the history of this center. A couple of them are old enough to remember the space in its heyday. They are the ones leading the charge to not go quietly, if we go at all."

The board . . . of course! Why am I just now thinking about this? Anise turned to her computer and finished typing the thank you letters to TCS patrons. Gregory might think that his hands were tied, that it was too late to save this treasured institution. But Anise was pulling from words learned a decade ago, while drawing eighteenth-century naval ships in Miss Miller's history class. Anise was feeling like John Paul Jones. "I have not yet begun to fight." She smiled as she finished one letter and went on to the next. *What he said!*

Anise got home, changed clothes, and walked Boomer. She'd decided to delay her call until she could be on her aunt's comfy couch, relaxed, and not trying to have a crucial conversation while navigating LA's rush-hour madness. Now sitting comfortably on the sofa, dressed in loose white cotton shorts and a white tank, she reached for her cell phone.

"Jessica, it's Anise."

"Anise, we really have to stop meeting like this."

"What do you mean?"

"I literally just got off the phone with one of my fellow board members. I told him about you, and how you'd just recently relocated to intern at The Space."

"Dawn said you guys also discussed a way that we can stay here, perhaps get the lease renewed?"

She heard Jessica's exasperated sigh. "That's what we've been doing for the past year, long before Dawn or anybody at The Space knew it might be closing. Lydia, the woman who spearheaded the lease fifty years ago, is now eighty-three and not in a position to fight with her younger brothers and headstrong nephews. You know what The Creative Space has meant to my life and career, so you must know how hard I've fought, how hard all of us have tried to negotiate an extension to the lease. But according to our insiders, this is as much a sibling rivalry decision as it is a business or economic one. The brothers never forgave Lydia for making such a monumental decision all those years ago and the youngest one in particular is showing his muscle."

"I can't believe that all of my dreams can go up in smoke behind some sibling rivalry bullshit!"

"It doesn't have to be that way," Jessica responded, her voice soft. "We are checking into whether or not we have any legal recourse against having to move. But I'm not all that confident on our being able to fight this. The lease is clear: after fifty years the building goes back into the custody of the owners. If that happens, Anise, all of your dreams can still come true. We will find another building. The Creative Space will go on."

"What about the magic of the building we're in?" Anise countered, surprised that tears were forming in her eyes. But then again, with as much as she'd lost in the past several months, The Creative Space was the one solid hope she'd held on to. "All those stories you told me? Spirits of all of the past brilliant artists evident all over the walls? We can't take their paintings with us, can't transport those striking murals from off the wall. We can't transfer five decades of the energy that went before us, can't replicate Andy Warhol's conversations in the corner or Charles Bibbs's impromptu sketch on the receptionist desk. Okay, maybe we can take the desk but we can't take the moment!" Anise stopped, took a breath. "The first day, Jessica, when I walked into The Space, I felt it, too, all of those wonderful energies you told me about, all the reasons why you've made it your mission to maintain the legacy. And now, that's also my dream. To keep this legacy alive."

"You know what, Anise? You remind me of a feisty, idealistic young lady I knew about twenty years ago."

"Who?"

"Me."

They enjoyed a few seconds of silence, Anise

rubbing Boomer's head as he came up beside her. "So what should I do?" she finally asked.

"Keep following your dreams, Anise. And remember that I'm here with you, every step of the way."

They hung up, and Anise continued to think about how she could hold on to all that she desired, maintain The Creative Space legacy, and keep the man who'd made her heart go boom. To try and be successful at all three was a daunting prospect. Honestly, she didn't know if she could pull it off. But Anise decided to go ahead and give it the good old college try. What did she have to lose . . . besides everything?

Anise checked her emails and was surprised to see a Facebook message from her online friend, Art-n-Sol. Since friending him they'd communicated almost every day, but it was always either through instant chat or comments on each other's pages. This was the first time he'd sent a private message. As Anise clicked on the email to open it, she realized that unless it was Art or Sol, she didn't even know his name. One sentence into reading his communication and her question was answered.

Anise, this is Edward, a/k/a Art-n-Sol. I was hoping to catch you before I logged off FB, but I never saw you online. This is going to sound crazy and I hope it doesn't make you think I'm loony but for some reason I just couldn't stop thinking about you today. Guess I just want to know that you're okay. Please reply so I don't have to bug you. I don't want to come off like a stalker! ☺

Interesting. Without hesitation, Anise went straight to Facebook. Aside from her astrological fascination she didn't consider herself the woo-woo or spiritual type. But she also thought it a strange coincidence that on the day that brought news that threatened to change the world as she knew it, she'd be on the mind of her online friend. Even if there wasn't anything to it, she thought that maybe Art-n-Sol, Edward, would be a person with whom to bounce off ideas, get a neutral opinion about what was happening with The Creative Space. Of course she planned at some point to talk with Aretha. But Edward was an art lover and from their conversations also seemed smart and level-headed. The more she thought about it, the more she became very interested in his opinion.

Anise clicked on the chat box icon. Edward was online. She clicked on the chat box and typed.

ArtbyAnise: Hey

Art-n-Sol: Hi! It's good to "see" you. Hope you didn't think my message was too weird.

ArtbyAnise: Not too ...☺

Art-n-Sol: I know it's crazy but sometimes I get these vibes about people and ... I don't know ...

for whatever reason you were really on my mind today.

ArtbyAnise: Thanks. I'm okay.

Art-n-Sol: You sure?

ArtbyAnise: Yes, but I did get some news today.

Art-n-Sol: Bad?

ArtbyAnise: The Creative Space may close.

Art-n-Sol: WTF?

ArtbyAnise: My sentiments exactly.

Art-n-Sol: What happened?

ArtbyAnise: Lease expired. Owners want the building.

Art-n-Sol: That sucks.

ArtbyAnise: Tell me about it.

Art-n-Sol: I'm sorry, Anise. I can feel your soul through your paintings, and your love for art. This must be heartbreaking.

ArtbyAnise: Yes.

Art-n-Sol: I don't have a building or anything but . . . if you need anything, or if there is something that I can do, I'm here for you. Please don't hesitate to ask.

ArtbyAnise: That's sweet of you, Edward. But I'm a stranger to you.

Art-n-Sol: No. You're not. To know your art is to know you. One second passes. Ten. Fifteen. Anise?

ArtbyAnise: I'm here.

Art-n-Sol: Did I say something wrong?

ArtbyAnise: No, Edward. You just said the nicest thing I've ever heard about my work.

Art-n-Sol: Not just your work, Anise. You are beautiful, too.

ArtbyAnise: How do you know?

Art-n-Sol: I've seen your Facebook pictures.

ArtbyAnise: People can post anything online. That may not even be me.

Art-n-Sol: LOL! It's you.

ArtbyAnise. You're right, it's me. Look, I gotta run.

Art-n-Sol: Nice chatting, as always.

ArtbyAnise. Yep.

Art-n-Sol: Until tomorrow . . .

With Aretha spending the evening with her gentleman friend, the Williams home was quiet. For Anise, it was too quiet. She placed her iPod in the dock and scrolled to a favorite playlist. Soon the sounds of Outkast, Mystical and Ludacris filled the upstairs guest room.

Later, as Anise waited impatiently for sleep to come, she realized two things. One, the conflicting position with Gregory had taken a bit of the bloom off of their romantic rose. Two, Edward's words had left an indelible impression on her. In this moment it was those words—to know her art was to know her—that filled her heart.

30

Gregory's brow furrowed as he pulled into his garage. He was still thinking about his earlier conversation with Anise and was frowning because one, he felt he had no real power to change the outcome of the research center location for her; and two, he felt he cared way too much about point number one.

He exited the car and headed for his back door, his mind in turmoil. Placing the research center—his research center if he won the grant—in the building now occupied by Anise's beloved space, would bring his lifelong dream into reality and at the same time end what she'd held as a longtime goal. He still didn't understand the building's significance. *Couldn't an artist draw anywhere?* But there'd been no mistaking her anger. She'd joked about kicking his ass but Gregory knew the statement was only half in jest. The truth of the matter was that if his center was the reason that The Creative Space was no longer in its iconic building of origin Anise would be furious . . . or hurt . . . or both.

And then a thought crossed his mind. At the end of the day, both he and Anise wanted the same things: to fulfill their dreams. Maybe instead of thinking that they were on opposite sides, they could approach this dilemma from a partnership standpoint, and come up with a solution together. As he removed his clothes and turned on the multihead jets in his custom-built shower, he felt the closest to a solution than he'd felt all day. *Now, this sounds like a plan!*

After more than ten minutes Gregory turned off the water and exited the shower, more relaxed than when he'd gone in, but still a bit keyed up. "Maybe a beer will help." He pulled on a pair of his favorite linen drawstring pants and headed downstairs barefoot and shirtless. Bypassing the minibar in the dining room on the way to the kitchen, he paused in front of a bottle of seventy-year-old Scotch. *Crème de la crème,* Dr. Meyers had told him, after sharing this gift. *And smooth as a baby's bottom.* Gregory wasn't much of a drinker, but he felt that tonight was as good a time as any to see what all of Aaron's hype had been about. Anything to uncoil the muscles in his neck.

He'd just poured himself two fingers of the amber liquid when his doorbell rang. Gregory's head shot up. *Who could that be?* It was a very rare moment that either Troy or Michael would show up unannounced. And there's no way his mom would drive over from Long Beach without calling. That only left one choice. *Anise.* He smiled, set down the whiskey, and walked to the door.

"Hey, you," he said, once he'd opened it.

"Hey," she replied, walking into his embrace.

Their bodies were flush against each other, lips so close that breath mingled together. He could see the fast pulse on her neck; she could feel his rapid heartbeat against her chest. They stayed this way for a moment, as the world melted away around them.

"What brings you over unannounced? Not that I mind," he quickly added.

"I started not to come over when my call went to voice mail but since you're right next door, I took a chance. Figured if you were busy you just wouldn't come to the door."

"You must have called while I was in the shower. But I'm glad you came over. I've been thinking about you."

"Good, I hope."

"More specifically, I've been thinking about our situation."

They reached the living room where Anise plopped down on the couch. "Yes, me too. Mostly I've been thinking how great it would be if the research center got placed somewhere other than where The Creative Space currently resides."

"I wouldn't have a problem with that." He walked

from the dining area where he'd been standing into the kitchen. "Would you like a glass of wine?"

"Yes, that sounds good."

"Red or white?"

"Whichever you want."

Gregory set his glass of whiskey aside. After retrieving wineglasses from the cabinet and chardonnay from the refrigerator, he returned to the living room. They both remained silent while he opened the wine and poured a liberal amount into the glasses.

They did talk. Not that night. No, that night was all about lovemaking. And not the next morning, when Anise rushed off to walk Boomer before going to work and Gregory caught another forty winks before his shift. Later that night they talked. And decided to call a truce and not talk about the future of The Creative Space. At least until they knew if Gregory had even gotten the grant.

The next day, Anise headed toward Venice Beach to check out an apartment that had been advertised on Craigslist. During the drive she was aware of how ever since the day she'd talked to Gregory and Edward about the building conflict, both men had been on her mind. For totally different reasons. Even though they'd called a truce, she still waged an inner battle on how she should feel about him and the role he'd play—albeit indirectly—if his research center was housed in the building that was now The Creative Space. Mental pro and con arguments could continue all the way until he opened his door. One look at that talented mouth, toned body and eyes dripping with sensual sincerity and Anise was toast. But when his arms weren't around her, and his stiff manhood wasn't buried inside her and they weren't talking on the phone . . . her thoughts would drift to Edward: sensitive, supportive and though basically a stranger, one who seemed to most understand her when it came to The Creative Space. Fortunately for both of them, there was something between her and any thought she may have to take the online pseudo-relationship from the Internet to real life. Yesterday, when Anise had joked that Edward might actually be a fourteen-year-old computer geek living in Europe, his response held no humor. He admitted to her that he was in a long-term relationship that he wanted to end, but that his girlfriend was battling an illness and it wouldn't be right to walk away now. Anise completely agreed, even as his confession made him even more endearing. So they would continue to be online pals.

Listening to her GPS, she eyed a homeless man sleeping near the curb as she turned right into a residential neighborhood. During a recent conversation, Dawn had told her about the proliferation of homeless people in and around the beach cities. "Guess if I had to sleep outdoors, I'd head west, too," she'd said. "And sleep to the sound of crashing waves."

She pulled up to a single-level stucco home and stopped. Looking at the paper she'd written directions on, she noted that—as the owner had said—there was a driveway with a narrow sidewalk alongside that would lead to the garage turned guest house behind the dwelling. It wasn't fancy by any means, but the yard was nicely landscaped, there was a large bird-of-paradise near the sidewalk leading to her potential new home, plus the entire backyard was fenced in. And the best part? She would be within walking distance to the beach!

Fifteen minutes later and Anise had put some of the life insurance money she'd received the week before to good use. After seeing the fully updated, small yet functional and shabby chic abode, she'd agreed to pay three months in advance plus a deposit to make up for the fact that while she was covering someone's maternity leave, she was technically unemployed. Thankfully her landlord, a retired army vet turned beach bum (his words), was also a dog lover and would have no problem with Boomer's presence. Of course, having a pet had increased the amount of her deposit, but overall, she was pleased at the progress she was making on the things she needed to do to get settled into LA. She and Dawn were getting along famously and after putting in her four hours—or any time there was downtime—she was in her small yet functional studio at the end of the third-floor hallway. She especially liked that hers was a corner studio with huge windows facing the south and east. Her natural light was the rising sun, and since unlike her name, Dawn did not like to rise early, Anise painted during the early morning hours and worked in the afternoon. So far she was in various stages of progress on half a dozen paintings and a definite theme was developing. In addition to her signature look—a liberal use of black, white, and subtle earth colors with splashes of bright color in unexpected places—she was pulling from her new surroundings. So far, her paintings were of nature juxtaposed with something resembling nature: Tibetan singing bowls surrounding a faraway sun, calla lilies brimming out of a saxophone. She hadn't planned on the musical theme. But a love for all types of music is something that she and her mother shared. Somewhere deep inside her, the memory of Carolyn lived on. The good thing was that more and more those memories came with a smile, not tears. And that, no doubt, was due to her new location and, even with their squabbles, also due to her new man.

Anise looked right, left, and right again before easing into the busy Sepulveda traffic. After a couple weeks of trying to navigate public transportation, Aretha had taken her to get a rental car. Now, since she'd received the insurance money, it was time to buy a car. Even so, she still planned on bussing it when convenient. *Doing so will add years to my life,* she thought, honking at a car that almost cut her off just so he could turn right at the very next corner. *These fools out here drive like loony tunes! It's a wonder they all don't end up in emergency.*

Emergency. Gregory. Even with the turmoil in their relationship, he was the first one she thought of, the first one who popped into her mind when it came to sharing the news about her new place. But her aunt had opened her heart and her home and graciously welcomed her into both. Now that Anise was striking out on her own in the city of angels, ready to spread her wings of independence, she decided it only fitting that Aretha be the first to know. Gregory would be the second.

Gregory was home, all right, but he was not alone. His good friend Lori had dropped by unannounced. That in itself wasn't a problem. What was a problem was how she was acting: strange, possessive, and more flirtatious than usual. Gregory knew why. Troy had run into Lori and her twin sister Lisa a few days ago, and that Gregory was seeing someone had come out in casual conversation. While Lori's keen interest had quickly sealed Troy's lips, the proverbial cat was out of the bag.

He may have been born during the day, but it wasn't yesterday. Lori had come by his house for one reason—to spy. During the whole time he was in between relationships, Lori had never tried to exchange her friends-with-benefits card for a wifey-with-a-ring upgrade. What was it about some women who seemed to find men already in a relationship the most attractive?

He had to give her credit. She'd employed some pretty good skills when doing a casual sweep of the downstairs, but now, since they were in his master suite on the pretense that "during her last visit she thought she'd lost an earring," her skills were not so tight.

"Maybe it's in your closet," she said, after getting on her knees to look under the bed and giving him a not-so-subtle view of her firm backside. "I don't remember wearing them since leaving here last."

"My housekeeper is thorough," Gregory countered, forcing sincerity into his voice. "If it were here, she would have found it." Following her into the closet where she fingered his clothes, he added, "Unless you think it hopped up into one of my pockets, I doubt it's among my suits."

"I was just admiring your tailor's work," Lori glibly replied. "You know I love your style. Both with clothes"—she stopped just before him, running a perfectly manicured finger down the front of his shirt—"and without." Placing her arms around his neck, she leaned in for a kiss.

He didn't oblige her, and didn't miss the frown that scampered across her face when he removed her arms from around him. Now was as good a time as any to cut to the chase. "What's really going on, Lori?"

"That's a good question. It's been a long time since you turned down good sex."

He raised an eyebrow. "That's what you're offering?"

She slithered over to the bed, sat, and leaned back on her haunches. The silky fabric of her skirt rode up as she scooted back on the bed. She wore no panties. "Are you turning this down?"

At the sight of a beautiful woman showing her bare assets, Gregory could normally be counted on to rear his randy lower head. But in this instance, Big G was decidedly at ease. *Hmm. Must be those marathon sessions with my insatiable new neighbor.* He walked over to the bed, reached out his hands. Lori hesitated a moment before lowering her legs, taking his hands and sitting up. In her eyes, he could see a myriad of emotions: surprise, confusion, wonder, and . . . *dammit* . . . love.

"In all the years we've known each other, you've never been the jealous type. And I've never been one to try and hold you down. I thought that we were like two branches cut from the same tree, giving each other pleasure while we pursued our dreams. No more, no less."

"It's been that way," Lori admitted, her voice low and . . . *trembling*? "But I must admit that I've missed you."

"What happened to the director?"

"Producer, Gregory, executive producer." She shrugged. "He's still around. But I'd drop him in a heartbeat if I thought you were serious about settling down."

"Whoa! Who are you and where is my no commitment, one-track mind, career woman?"

"Who's the new girl?"

"Ah, here we go." Gregory leaned casually against the closet doorjamb. "Now we're getting to the real reason for your visit."

"I was surprised to hear about Jackie's friend's special night. And not having been invited. It's been a long time since I wasn't your backup date."

"Things change."

"Who is she?"

"Her name is—" A knock interrupted. "Excuse me."

Gregory's face was in a scowl as he headed to the door.

31

"I found a place!" Anise sang, as soon as Gregory opened the door. She waltzed inside, past the kitchen and into the living room, oblivious to the strained look on Gregory's face.

"Really?" He followed behind her, glancing at the staircase as they passed it. "Uh, where?"

"Venice, not too far from where I'll be working, temporarily, four months or so. Nothing grandiose or anything, but enough for me and Boomer." She sidled up to him and wrapped her arms around his waist. "And the occasional overnight guest."

Had Anise been more observant, she would have noticed the erratic heartbeat playing against her chest. As it were, she was too busy noticing the disheveled woman coming down his staircase, shoes in hand.

She broke the embrace and stepped back to look at Gregory. Her face was a mask. "Excuse me for interrupting. I should have called." She shifted to step around him but he reached for her arm, holding it in a firm grasp as he turned around.

At the sight of Lori, his eyes narrowed. She'd mussed up her hair and taken off her shoes, and he knew exactly what Anise assumed had been taking place. "Lori was just leaving," he said, stepping closer to Anise. "She came over to look for an earring that she claims to have lost here, months ago. When I left her to answer the door, her hair was in place and her shoes were on. She has been a good friend of mine for a very long time, and it is totally unlike her to play these games. Lori, this is Anise, the woman that earlier you were asking about. Anise, this is Lori, my friend since childhood. Have a seat, baby, while I walk her to the door."

On the outside, he was as cool as ice in winter. Inside, he was seething. "This type of behavior is beneath you, Lori," he said, his teeth close to clenching, his voice deceptively calm. "I hope you found what you were *really* looking for."

"Listen, I'll call—" The sentence was cut off by the door in her face.

In the minute it had taken him to walk Lori to the door, Anise realized two things: one, she cared for Gregory way more than she should; and two, she didn't have the strength to care that much right now.

Gregory returned to the living room and wasn't

surprised that Anise had not taken his advice to sit down. "I'm sorry about that."

"Look, we just met. You don't owe me an explanation."

"Of course I do. I can only imagine what that looked like."

"It looked like I should have called first." She put up a hand to stop Gregory's response/excuse/lie—pick one. "It doesn't matter. Both of us are grown and neither of us are married, especially to each other. Without that commitment, I guess either of us are fair game."

"I thought there was a commitment. I thought we agreed to be exclusive. Have you forgotten so quickly?"

"There is absolutely nothing wrong with my memory, doctor. Looks like if anybody forgot, it's you." Anise let her hand run down his hard chest as she passed him on the way to the door.

"You're doing exactly what she wants and it doesn't change anything." The words sailed down the hall and slowed Anise's progress. "I'm not going to play her little game." Chin at a determined angle, Anise continued to the door. "I'm not going to be with her." Her hand reached for the doorknob. "You're the only woman I want right now."

She willed her hand to close over the knob and pull the door open. The seconds it took to try and talk herself into leaving were enough for the scent of Gregory's cologne to reach her. When he spoke, he was way too close for her to think straight. What was it about this man that entrapped her so?

"Let's talk, Anise." Silently, she turned around and leaned against the door. "Can you give me five minutes at least?"

Dang, why does he have to say it like that, like it matters whether I stay or go? And why does he have to look like a cute little boy who's lost his puppy dog? She walked to the bar counter between the kitchen and the rest of the space, sat on one of the stools . . . and waited.

Gregory took a breath and tried to reconcile his conflicting emotions. As an emergency room doctor, he went into each traumatic situation focused and prepared. He knew his team, which instrument to use, and what the end goal was. In short, except for the fact that God was the giver of life, Gregory was fully in control. Here, this clearly was not the case. He decided this honest admission was a good place to start.

"I don't know what's going on with her," he began, walking over to join Anise at the counter. "Lori has never acted possessive before."

"So you weren't honest before and the two of you *are* dating?"

"Not at all. I haven't been with her in a while. But as I told you before, I've known Lori most of my life. Our families lived on the same block and her sister, Lisa, dated my older brother, Michael. Lori and I messed around as teenagers and would see each other in between relationships. We'd also be each other's date if we didn't have someone to bring to an event. I thought we understood each other. Guess I was wrong."

"Wow, you men are a trip."

"Why do you say that?"

Anise slowly shook her head. "Here you are a medical doctor and everything. What does that take, about ten years of schooling? With all of that intellect you can probably save the planet, but when it comes to women you're as dumb as an ox."

Gregory's eyes narrowed. "I might resemble that remark but watch it, lady!" When that didn't lighten the mood the way he hoped it would, he rephrased. "Lori and I have been very open and honest about what we had—a friends-with-benefits situation. She has never pulled the kind of stunt she did just now and, trust me, she never will again. Not in my house."

"Oh, now you stand there with the authority to say what will and won't happen in your house. After your friend with benefits has left you looking a little stupid and a lot guilty when she came down the stairs looking like y'all had been screwing for hours!"

"You know what," Gregory said, standing abruptly. "I understand that you're upset, but you're also the one who came over uninvited."

"Like I said, I should have called." Anise got up.

"Fine, go ahead and leave. I deal with enough drama in emergency. I don't need this crap. I'm laying it on the line for you, pouring my heart out, telling the truth. And you're still tripping."

She was still walking, too . . . out the door.

"Go on. Get out."

"Your watching my back should be your clue that I'm doing just that." She made it to the door in record time and was upset that the springs on it were the kind that prevented it from slamming. She began to miss him even before she left his yard, and for hours after. Gregory would wonder when air would return to the room.

32

Anise was glad to be moving boxes. It gave her a way to uncoil the anger that, two hours after the showdown with Gregory, still roiled. *I can go? How dare he give me the boot out of his house!* And then there was the devil on her shoulder. *You were the one who first headed to the door.* In response to that thought, Anise lifted a box that was bigger than she was and dared her arms to not bear the load. She'd put off moving the heavier things from her storage unit to the studio but now it was a perfect way to vent anger, frustration, and heartbreak all at the same time. After leaving Gregory's house, she'd immediately gone there, retrieved several boxes of paintings, art supplies, and items labeled as "inspiration," and headed to Santa Monica. Hurrying from the parking lot to The Creative Space's back door, she opened it up successfully, barely, but stumbled as she neared the freight elevator.

"Whoa, shorty, let me get that."

The voice was deep and came from the side and a few inches above her. The heavy box was taken out of her hands and with it out of her line of sight she was able to see its source, the dreadlocked sculptor from the first day she'd arrived. She hadn't seen him again until now.

"Thank you." She pushed the elevator button.

"No problem." The elevator opened and he nodded for her to enter first. "It's not good for a woman to carry heavy boxes; you can mess up your back and female organs."

"Oh, really." Through no fault of Dreadlock, Anise had had enough advice from doctors for one day.

"That's the word according to Maybelle Humphries. My grandmother."

Well, that's just great. How can I be mad at a granny named Maybelle?

"My name's Truth."

"Truth? That's your real name?"

"Basically. My mama named me Luther but everybody has called me Truth since I can remember. On account of how I used to tell on everybody in the neighborhood."

"I'm Anise."

"That's your real name?" His chocolate orbs twinkled.

"Okay, I deserved that. My mother named me Shirley. It fit my grandmother, but not me."

And just like that, they settled into a simpatico

camaraderie that would only deepen in the months to come.

"So you're a niece, huh? As in one with an aunt and an uncle?"

"Ha, ha. I see that you moonlight as a comedian." Truth chuckled. "It's A-n-i-s-e. Like the spice."

Truth gave her an appreciative look. "I heard that."

"You sculpt, right?"

"I do some of everything."

"I saw you doing a piece the very first day I came here. Haven't seen you since."

"I was out of town. Partner of mine opened up an art gallery on the East Coast. I might be moving there." They reached the floor housing Anise's temporary studio. "I'm kinda surprised you're moving in here, with all of us having to be out soon."

"Dawn told me about that possibility but I'm hoping the decision isn't final."

"The fifty-year lease on this building is up. The owners have given us notice to move. Sounds final to me."

"Why would anyone want to move The Creative Space? It's almost like a historic landmark!"

"This is prime real estate. The owners probably want to tear it down and put up condos or something."

"Disgusting." They reached a closed door. Anise pulled out the key that Dawn had given her.

"Oh, you've set up in Trina's old spot?"

Anise shrugged. "Dawn didn't tell me who it belonged to. I was just happy to get it."

"It's a cool space to work, I'll give it that." They entered the studio. Truth set the box on the table. "So what are you . . . a recent college grad, new transplant, what?"

"I graduated from the KC Art Institute a few years ago, just moved here from Omaha."

"Cool. I'm from St. Louis."

"Midwest in the house . . . nice!"

"I figured you weren't from here; I never saw you acting all stuck up and whatnot. The women over here can be a trip."

"How long have you been here?"

"A little over two years. Have had my work shown in a few museums, and I'm working on a lead over in Leimert Park. Are you familiar with that neighborhood?" Anise shook her head. "It's pretty much the art scene for African-Americans, though it's not the thriving neighborhood it once was. Back in the day, I hear it was the spot for jazz and blues, even comedy. People like Robin Harris got started there."

"Who's that?"

"You don't know Robin Harris? The comedian?"

"Never heard of him, sorry."

Truth shook his head. "You've been missing out, girl. I've got his DVDs. If you like good comedy, you'll have to check him out sometime."

"I like the guys who did the Kings of Comedy

tour, loved Bernie Mac. But I haven't really been into that in the last couple years."

"Into what . . . laughing?"

"Yes."

Truth took a step toward her, his voice becoming soft and flirtatious. "Maybe we need to change that."

Anise looked up into the sparkling eyes set in a dark brown face, framed by thick, shoulder-length locks on a medium build body. Perhaps it was best that she get her head out of the clouds, stop thinking she could breathe at the same altitude as her wealthy, successful, gorgeous, highbrow, soon-to-be-ex-neighbor and his runway model so-called ex-girlfriend, and hang with a person where there was obviously more in common.

She tilted her head and offered a sexy smile. "Maybe we do."

33

Gregory sat in Troy's Leimert Park bachelor pad, hot under the collar with a cold beer in hand. As his brothers high-fived he looked on dispassionately.

"Did you see that?" Michael exclaimed, talking about how his client Huang Chin, the newest NBA darling from China, now playing with the Nevada Nighthawks, had just blown back Kobe's would-be three-pointer. The ball now nested somewhere between the tenth and eleventh row of the Staples Center's lower level. "My man is fire."

"You're not as excited about that block as you are about the dozens of would-be sponsors who just saw it," Troy commented.

"True that. If he ends the year as the team's MVP, it will pretty much seal the deal I've got going with EAE. That, my brothers, will make me a multimillionaire."

"What's EAE?" Troy asked.

"East Asia Electronics, the newest Asian

electronics outfit that is blowing well-known companies off the map. They are interested in a deal that will feature Chin in commercials all over the world, including Asia and Europe. This will set him up for life long after basketball."

"Looks like you'll be pulling in more paper than if the doctor here gets the grant. What do you think about that, Greg?" No response. "Yo, G!" Troy threw a wadded up piece of paper at Gregory. "I know you're not that interested in that soda commercial."

Michael concurred. "Please, bro has been looking at the screen for the past ten minutes and hasn't seen a thing. What's up?"

"I bet I know," Troy said, his voice teasing. "His new sweet had a run-in with Lori."

This got Gregory's attention. "What do you know about it?"

"You know Lori and Lisa have no secrets between them, and Lisa tells me everything."

"Yeah, now that Michael's married, you're her new 'best friend.'" Gregory encapsulated the last word in air quotes, showing how much he believed that's all they were.

"So, Michael," Troy continued, ignoring Gregory's taunt. "What do you think about Gregory's latest candy, Anise from Kansas—"

"Omaha," Gregory corrected, with a scowl.

"He says they're not serious. Says she's staying next door at his *neighbor's* house."

"Was staying; she moved over the weekend."

"I made the mistake of mentioning her to Lori, who promptly went over there and threw a hitch in the giddyup."

"Damn. You do know everything."

"Homegirl is hella jealous. . . ."

"Lori?" Michael asked, to make sure he was following this circuitous story.

"Right," Troy continued. "Went over to Gregory's house unannounced. Meanwhile sweet thing comes over for some afternoon delight—"

"Wrong. She came over to share some good news."

"Oh, is that what they call it in Omaha?" Gregory's scowl deepened. Troy bit back a laugh. "So Lori was upstairs, right? She came down looking all tossed up and you can just about imagine what his new sweet was thinking."

Michael looked at Gregory with compassion. "Dude, you've got to get on top of your game!"

"I don't have a game," Gregory said, not finding anything funny anywhere in the situation, though both his brothers' humored looks showed that he was alone in this position. "And I'm not seeing Lori. We haven't been together in a while when she came over on the pretense of looking for an earring she said she lost."

"Oldest trick in the book," Michael said. "Girlfriend was looking for panties in the closet and tampons under the sink."

"You know it," Troy said with a nod.

"Would she have found them?" Michael questioned Gregory. "Because that only happens if your game's not tight."

"As it stands, the entire issue is moot. Anise and I didn't exactly part on the best of terms."

"Deniece?" Michael asked.

"Anise," Troy corrected. "Like the spice."

"Well, you must not be too happy about that. Considering you've been a world-class grouch ever since walking through the door."

"I'm all right."

"Sure you are," Troy said, walking into the kitchen. "It's written all over your face." He came out with three fresh brews.

Gregory took his and downed half the bottle in one long swig. Troy and Michael exchanged glances. "Anything worth having is worth going after," Michael said, sounding like the typical older brother. "Do you like her like that?"

"I was feeling her a little bit," Gregory said, admitting yet again out loud what his heart had felt from the start. "I'm upset with the fact that she could walk away like that but I'm angrier with Lori for not only purposely creating this mess but then going and blabbing all over LA about it."

"Come on, man. You know how Lori is about her reputation. Trust me, Lisa is the only one who heard this story. And she probably told me because she'd want you to know that Lori is upset about what happened, too. Lisa said Lori told her she didn't know what she'd been thinking when she did that. At the thought of losing you permanently, something came over her and she . . . snapped. She says you're not taking her calls."

"She's right."

Troy sighed. "Sounds like a messy situation. That's not like you, bro."

"Tell me about it."

"There's never been a woman who's made you lose your cool before," Michael stated. "You know what happened to the woman who took me out of my zone."

"What?"

"I married her."

Gregory eyed his brother a moment before draining his bottle of beer. "I remember Daddy saying that sometimes love doesn't make sense. I sure as heck can agree with him now."

"Why's that?" Troy asked.

Gregory looked from one brother to the other. "I think she might be the one."

"Then one of these days," Michael drawled, stretching his long legs out before him, "you might just want to let her know."

34

I should call her. Every fiber in Gregory's being agreed with Michael. All, that is, except the ones making up his ego. Truth be told, he was a little unsettled by Anise's attitude and fire. That was usually his department. He thought back to the last time he'd chased a woman, the last time he'd even wanted to. When his mind searched through the past five years without a name jumping out, he stopped trying.

His last serious relationship had been what . . . two years ago? *Has it already been that long?* He thought back to when Katrina had given him the ultimatum that they either get engaged or get on with their lives—separately. Even though they'd been dating a year and a half, the answer was easy. There'd been a lot about her to make a union attractive: educated, cultured, easy on the eyes. But the nagging. The trying to change him. The competing with him for attention from that which he loved . . . medicine. After their first meeting, his mother had expressed doubts.

"She's low-temperance but high-maintenance," his mother had offered, when he'd asked for her impression. "She'll keep you happy in the short-term but the rest of your life? Take your time, son."

He was glad he'd listened to Jackie.

His countenance took on a determined look as he reached for the phone. Gregory Morgan wasn't going to stop until he got what he wanted. And right now, what he wanted was Anise.

She almost didn't answer. It had been two days since their little rumble and while Anise had missed him fiercely—*ridiculous*—and had almost caved and called him several times—*seriously?*—settling in to her new place and working had kept her mind occupied. Now, here he was and darn it if her heart didn't beat faster and her kitty meow. She was really going to have to do something about her body not following where her mind wanted to go. Like now, as her finger fairly itched to rub the screen and accept the call.

"Hello?"

"Anise."

Breathe, Anise. He's just a man. "Hi, Gregory."

"I haven't seen your rental car. How far away did you run from me?"

She heard the smile in his voice and willed herself to calm down. If he could play nice, so could she. Maybe . . . "Please," she replied, with a grin as well. "We both know that isn't true."

"How do you like Venice?"

"I haven't had a chance to really check it out yet, but I think I'm going to like it. There's only on-street parking but it's been doable so far."

"That's good."

The small talk ran out like water from an up-turned cup. Quickly. Anise decided to pet the elephant in the room. "Has your company been back? What's her name . . . Lori?"

"No. I've already explained that situation to you and don't plan to again." Silence. "I was hoping we could talk, sensibly, like grown folk. I miss you. I know it's crazy since we just met. I even miss your guard dog's bark. Didn't realize how quiet our neighborhood was until now."

"It is rather crazy, this attraction between us. I admit I feel it, too. But you're not the only one who doesn't do drama. I'm not going to compete with these West Coast skirts."

"You don't have to."

Anise heard a beep in her ear. "Hold on, Gregory." She switched over. "Hey, Truth. Let me call you back."

"Hey wait," Truth said. "I've got tickets to the Laugh Factory. Do you want to go?"

"Yes. I'll call you back." She swapped the calls. "Okay, Gregory. I'm back."

"Have you eaten? Want to go grab dinner, maybe listen to a little reggae?"

"Umm, no. I can't tonight."

A pause long enough for a cricket concerto.

"All right, then. I'll let you go. But call me later. I'd like to see you."

"Okay, I will."

He ended the call and sat back, contemplative, refusing to let his mind go to the phone call Anise had gotten during their conversation. He'd never been unsure of himself, never cared who else was in his woman's life. *Wait, where'd that come from? She's not mine. I just met her.* That's what he told himself, but in his heart, it felt that way. From the moment she'd dismissed him during her run to the moment he'd seen the spark of vulnerability in her eyes at the mention of her mom . . . he'd felt a certain responsibility. To her. To them. "This is crazy, man," he mumbled, reaching for a report Dr. Meyers had given him, determined to put his mind on work, where it should be. He'd just read the first paragraph when a nurse stuck her head into his office.

"Gunshot victim, Doctor Morgan. We need you. Stat."

Gregory was up and headed to the door before she finished. The familiar pump of adrenaline filled his veins, the laserlike focus immediately shutting out all thoughts. Well, almost. There was one final one before he turned the corner at a fast gait, heading to the emergency room doors. *If there is to be any drama in my life . . . this is the only kind I want!*

35

Anise sat at the tightly spaced tables in the comedy club. Bored. To Tears. Truth, meanwhile, was laughing like a hyena, as though every amateur comedian who took the stage was the next John Belushi or Richard Pryor. The kid with the red shock of hair and Buddy Holly glasses did a fart joke. Truth almost spewed soda through his nose. *Really? All of this for a fart joke? Are we twelve?* She excused herself and went to the bathroom, holding a conversation in her head the whole way. *This is what you get for trying to make a point. You know you miss Gregory and want to be with him. Two days away from that piece of goodness feels like two years.* There was no denying it; Gregory had reawakened her sexual fervor with a vengeance. By the time she'd squatted, rinsed, and dried her hands she'd made a decision: this date was done.

Returning to the table, Anise murmured, "Truth, I'll see you tomorrow." She had to lean down to speak into his ear because his head was almost between his legs as he guffawed at a man yapping like a dog. *Boomer could get up there and bark a better routine.*

"Wait." Truth held his side and took a deep breath to stop laughing. "Where are you going? The main act isn't for another half hour. You haven't even heard the funniest dude."

By which point I'll be dead, is what Anise thought. "I'm not feeling well," is what she said. A small white lie delivered without shame.

"Okay," Truth said, with the look of a boy who'd just lost his puppy. "We can go."

"Oh, no. Please don't think you have to leave. It's one of the reasons I drove myself—so that if I needed to bounce before you were ready, I could. I hope you don't think I've wasted the ticket. If you want, I'll pay you back."

"Okay."

With that, Anise turned and made her way through the dense crowd. Truth was cute and from what she'd seen, talented. But if a man was going to actually accept money for a ticket he'd initially offered as a gift, well, there was really nothing more to say.

Once she reached her car, a singular thought had become a mantra: *Call him. Call him. Call him!* She couldn't be sure but he'd probably assume that her plans tonight included a man. Just something about how he'd responded after she told him she couldn't get together. He hadn't become a doctor by not being bright. She looked at the clock: *11:30 pm.* It was a Tuesday night. This time not too long ago they were sharing a passionate kiss at Aretha's back door, while the rest of the night visions of his nakedness had danced in her head. And the next day . . .

That's it. I'm dialing.

Voice mail. After the split second decision to not hang up she left a short message and ended the call. Now it was her turn to wonder where he was, and if he was alone. Hadn't he said he was off on Tuesdays and Wednesdays? Had he called Lori after being turned down? Why even try and figure it out? she reasoned. The possibilities were endless.

Anise entered her home to Boomer's bark and wagging tail and for the first time since arriving in LA . . . she felt lonely. These first few weeks had gone by in a whirlwind: arriving, meeting Gregory the very next day, their instant connection, spending time with Aretha, getting hired and securing a studio at The Creative Space, connecting with Truth and Edward, and finally, arranging the items she'd had shipped from Omaha. Just now was she realizing the benefit of that harried schedule—it had left little time to think.

"Come on, Boomer," she said, opening the door. "One more time to do your business and then I guess it's off to bed."

She sat in the lawn chair she'd picked up after

passing a garage sale and watched as Boomer, who after making his mark on his new favorite tree, went in search of vermin unknown. The night was warm and quiet, a dim light attached to the back of the landlord's house cast a glow over the lawn and shadows against the wall. Here the walls were concrete instead of the wood and ivy surrounding Aunt Aretha's backyard, but still her thoughts went to when Boomer had barked and Gregory had come over to investigate. A wisp of a smile crossed her face. Yep, she'd fallen for a man faster than snow fell for winter. *Pathetic.*

Her phone rang. She raced back into the house to retrieve it, hoping—pathetically, she'd later admit—that it was Gregory returning her call.

No such luck. "Hey, Truth."

"Hey, Anise. They're taking a break before the headliner comes out. I'm calling to see if you're feeling better."

"Uh, yeah, I'm fine." *No I'm not. I'm a sex fiend craving a booty call.* And an ashamed one, too. Truth really was a nice guy. "How were the comics I missed?"

"Hilarious! The best guy so far came up right after you left, a cross between a young Martin Lawrence and an old Richard Pryor but before he had the stroke. He had this crazy joke about . . ."

Anise tuned out, immediately sorry that she'd asked him and all too aware of why she'd left him, in stitches no less, just thirty minutes ago.

". . . and then he told this other one about a man wanting to go to a zoo in the hood. Do you want to know why?"

Is this a trick question? "Why?"

"So he could see a ghetto bird!" And then Truth went into his annoying guffawing as though he would choke.

"Uh, I'm going to run, Truth. I just got up to let the dog out before turning in."

"Well, I hope you feel better. Nothing can start the healing like a good night's sleep."

"Thank you." No sooner had she gotten Boomer back into her little one-bedroom paradise than her phone rang again. She recognized the number and if her body was any indication, her nana did, too. "Hello."

"Hey, babe. I'm at the hospital and just saw that I missed your message. What's going on?"

"Oh, nothing. I just . . . uh . . ." *Wanted to come over and screw my brains out. . . .* "Thought about your invite." *Oh, Lord . . . where am I going with this?* "And decided to come to your mom's party." She squeezed her eyes shut, knowing she'd probably just placed herself in an uncomfortable situation. Aretha had told her that all the brothers were successful. She could just about imagine the crowd at this party: all weaves and silicone and red-bottomed shoes. But, oh well. In for a penny, in for a pound. "That is, if you haven't already asked someone else."

"No. I got called in to work and haven't had time to give it another thought."

"Oh. Okay. So you're at work? I thought you were off on Tuesdays."

"I am. Like I just said, I got called in."

"Oh, right."

"But the crisis has been handled. I'm on my way home." Silence. "Are you all right, Anise?"

"Yes." Said way too quickly.

"Are you sure?"

"Uh-huh." *Think, Shirley!* This sure enough had to be Shirley; Anise *Cartier* would not be so uncool. "I also had planned to, uh, go to my aunt's house. I left a few things and was going to stop by if you were home. But it's late and you're probably tired and maybe even still upset and—"

"Anise."

"Uh-huh?"

"Is this a booty call?"

There it was, all the cards on the table. All fifty-two and the jokers—full deck. Anise decided to play.

"A booty call?"

"You heard me."

"Yes. That's what this is."

"Good! I've been thinking about you all day and I need to . . . relax. Since I'm already driving, why don't you give me your address and I'll come to your place."

"Okay." She gave him the info.

"Do I need to stop and pick up anything, something to snack on, a bottle of wine?"

"Only if you want something. I'm fine."

"Then I'm on my way."

"Okay." Anise was so happy she could have jumped up and clicked her heels. Instead, she jumped in the shower. Sleep would have to wait because the doctor was coming over with a good dose of pleasure. She could hardly wait.

36

Fifteen minutes later and her phone rang.

It was Gregory. "I'm here."

"Okay. My place is behind the house you can see, so I'll come out." She slipped on her flip-flops and walked around to the front of the house, immediately spotting Gregory standing next to his car. He smiled and she swore his teeth were a pearlier white than that Mercedes. She wanted to run and jump in his arms.

They navigated around the huge bird-of-paradise bush and through the gate that led to the backyard, with Gregory taking in everything around him. "How in the world did you find this place?"

"Online."

"It's kind of dark back here. Do you feel safe?"

"I did until that comment."

"I'm sorry."

"I'm kidding. It's a pretty high wall for someone to climb over and with Boomer, I feel totally safe."

As if on cue, Boomer barked before taking on the important task of sniffing Gregory's shoe. For that, he got a pat on his big, furry head. "Good old Boomer."

Anise let them in and then stood in the middle of the floor and turned around. "Welcome to my home. Don't move. You can take in the entire tour from that spot: living room, kitchen, bedroom, and bathroom down the hall. The whole place would fit into your living room."

"Just about. Reminds me of my residency days. My apartment then wasn't much bigger than this. Besides, it's big enough for me to hug you and right now . . . that's all I want."

He hadn't said nothing but a word. Two steps and she was in his arms, feeling like it was exactly where she was supposed to be. A contented sigh escaped her lips as he rubbed her back and kissed her temple, a squiggle leaving her core and traveling down to her heat when his lips moved from there to her cheek and then her mouth.

And there it was. The kiss: hot, wet, demanding. Their hands touched and squeezed bodies while tongues worked to reacquaint: twirling, lapping, lightly touching. Then he nipped her lip and tweaked her nipple and it was as if a passion-filled cannon exploded. She reached for his belt, her hands fumbling with the buckle. He moved her hands, taking over, his eyes, dark with desire, boring into her. She stared back, licking her lips as she pulled the tank over her head and shimmied out of her jogging pants. Knowing where the night was heading, she hadn't put on anything underneath. There'd been no need.

Good thing, too, because Gregory was on a mission. In the time she'd undressed, he'd also removed his clothes. The ten steps it would take to get to the bedroom was ten steps too many. He dropped to his knees, right there in the living room, buried himself in her heat and . . . felt a big sloppy tongue precariously close to the family jewels.

Screech. "Stop, Boomer!"

Anise was already in the throes of pleasure, legs spread, nub wanting to feel more of his tongue. "What's he doing?" she panted, without opening her eyes.

"That big moose is gay!"

Okay. Eyes are now open. "What did he do?"

"Tried to lick my balls."

"He's a dog," Anise drily responded. "It's what they do."

"Well, since I'd rather you lick them, can we have some privacy?"

"Come on, boy," Anise said, finding the humor amid the heat. "Go hang outside for, oh, the next few hours." She let him out and then turned, walked to where Gregory stood, and reached for his pipe—soft as velvet yet hard as steel. "Now," she purred. "Where were we?"

"I think we were about to bury this treasure."

"Um, where were we going to hide it?"

He ran his hands between legs that parted of their own volition and flicked his finger over her waiting clit. "Somewhere near here," he murmured against her ear. With his finger, he continued to create a delicious friction between already slick folds as he outlined her ear with his tongue, walking them backward toward the couch without breaking contact. Once there he sat, placed her in his lap, and continued the oral artistry happening between them. His kisses were heady, her nerve endings strummed as he made lazy circles around her areola, until her nipples stuck out front and center—begging to be touched.

He wanted this, too.

Bending his head, with his close-cropped curls tickling her chin, he caught first one chocolate-colored nub and then the next between his teeth. Delicious bites, sending shock waves through her core, tightening the muscles of her heat, increasing the desire to have him inside her. She squirmed. He laughed, because he knew why she moved. Again, he slid his hand between her legs, this time burying a finger in her heat. And then another. Her hips ground against him, encouraging him to go farther, reach deeper, do more!

Okay, sweet thing.

He moved her off his lap and slid off the couch. In front of her, he kissed her taut stomach, lapped her belly button. He placed his hands on her knees and spread her wide, leaving her bare and vulnerable, exposed to whatever struck his fancy which— right now—was to initiate the most intimate of kisses. He leaned forward, his breath hot against her twat. He heard her quick intake of breath, felt her body freeze in anticipation. He smiled. *Yes. I know what you like.* To prolong the agony of ecstasy, he kissed one inner thigh before nibbling on the other.

"Greg."

His name came out on a whoosh of air, spoken with a quiet urgency that made his chest swell, proved the manly hold he now held, made him want to please her in every way. He slid on the condom, pulled her to him and joined them with one . . . long . . . thrust.

At first his strokes were light and tentative, and then bold and hard. His dick touching, searching, reaching past her feminine walls and into her soul. Grabbing her hips he poked and pounded, their gyrating hips in sync more than the boy band ever was. When the couch could no longer accommodate their positions, they moved the party to the bedroom. Amidst protesting scratches from outside they closed the door. Boomer was not invited.

37

For the next couple weeks, the two settled into somewhat of a routine. Anise spent her days at the center and most nights with Gregory. She became friends with a couple of the other artists who worked regularly at The Creative Space and occasionally they'd share dinner and drinks in the evenings. Sometimes Truth would join them, he and Anise now friends after "the talk," the one where she said that was all they could be. Slowly, Anise was building a life in LA. She hadn't expected an intimate relationship to be a part of it. And she definitely hadn't expected to be meeting a man's family, as she was about to do. On the Fourth of July, Gregory had worked and Anise had spent the day with Aretha, Bruce, and Bruce's extended family. Tonight, she would be meeting the Morgans.

"So this is your old stomping grounds," she said,

as Gregory exited the highway onto Long Beach's Shoreline Drive.

"Absolutely."

"It's pretty here."

"Yes, they've really built up this area the past fifteen, twenty years. I remember a time when it didn't look so nice. Part of the city still doesn't."

They reached the restaurant where she and Gregory would be joining his family for dinner. Gregory drove up to the valet and once they'd exited the car, took Anise's hand as they walked inside. He didn't miss the clamminess of its palm, nor the deep breath she tried to take on the low.

"Don't be nervous. My brothers will tease you and my mother will love you. I think you'll get along with Shayna, too."

"It will feel strange to see someone I've watched on TV."

"She's genuine and down to earth. You won't meet a mean-spirited soul—promise."

"Do I look okay?"

He gave her a quick yet burning once-over, noting how the simple design of her dress hugged her slight curves, and how the gleam of her skin competed against the cream-colored silk—and won. "You're going to be the prettiest woman in the room," he sincerely responded.

They entered the restaurant and, waving away the hostess, navigated their way to the front table. As they neared the table for ten, Anise saw two handsome men and knew immediately that they were Gregory's brothers. She also instantly recognized the track star and fashionista Shayna Washington, looking as attractive in person as she did on TV. A distinguished-looking gentleman with salt-and-pepper hair and a pleasant countenance said something to the woman speaking to him. She turned, saw Gregory, and rose from her chair.

"Gregory! Hello, baby."

"Hello, Mom." They each gave a hug and a kiss on the cheek. "Mom, I'd like you to meet Anise Cartier. Anise, this is Jackie Morgan."

"Pleased to meet you, Mrs. Morgan."

"The pleasure is mine, and please, call me Jackie. You didn't tell us that she was so pretty," she said to Gregory, with a nudge. "Now I understand why you've been chomping at the bit to show her off."

Any qualms Anise had about meeting the Morgans melted away within the first few minutes that she sat at the table. Michael immediately came across as the more serious older brother, while Troy, with his incessant teasing and constant flirtations with his gorgeous date, had that devilish and spoiled quality that the youngest in the family often possessed.

"Gregory says you're from Omaha," Jackie said, after introductions around the table had been made and pleasantries exchanged.

"Yes, ma'am."

"How do you like California?"

"I like it so far. I'm sure I'll like it even more this winter when it's snowing in Omaha and I'm here on the beach."

"I know that's right. I was born in Georgia but grew up in Los Angeles, so thankfully I've been spared from personally experiencing those harsh winters I've heard about." Jackie watched as Gregory and Michael laughed at something that was shared. "Is my son treating you well?"

At the thought of how well Gregory had been treating her, Anise's face grew warm. "You've definitely raised a gentleman."

"I tried. Boys are so rambunctious. Do you have children?"

"No."

"Do you want them?"

"Don't feel the need to answer that," Gregory interrupted, having turned from his brother to pay attention to Anise. "Mom is on a continuous campaign for grandchildren. That's Michael and Shayna's responsibility, right, bro?"

"Don't bring us into it," Michael said, with hands raised in mock surrender. "This is your hot seat."

"Y'all have been married, what, almost two years now?" Jackie said reprovingly.

Having effectively shifted the spotlight, Gregory egged her on. "Yes, bro, what are you waiting on?"

"Waiting for you to mind your business," Michael retorted.

Those who heard this joined in laughter. Gregory put his arm around his girl and she relaxed into his warmth.

This night, when they made love, it was slow and easy, the kind that suggested there would be months more, maybe years more, of grooving just like this. They stared into each other's eyes, felt the thrill of skin against skin, and took their time—leaving their hearts full and their bodies satiated. As she snuggled next to Gregory, content to grab the three or four hours' sleep she'd get before heading back to Venice, Anise had one simple thought—life could not get much better than this.

38

Gregory knocked and then entered via the unlocked door, thankful that his thoughtful mother had changed this Sunday's dinner time just so he could attend. "Mama!" He paused at the fireplace mantel and greeted Samuel Morgan, whose large framed picture dominated the wall, before following the sound of voices into the kitchen. There he found Michael sitting at the table with his tight-bodied sprinter wife, Shayna, perched on his lap.

"Hey, bro." Gregory gave his brother a fist pound and then kissed Shayna on the cheek. "What's up, Shayna?"

"Hello, Gregory. You're looking nice. What is it . . . different haircut?"

"We told you what it was," Troy said, coming around the corner. "Different woman."

"Where is she?" Jackie was right on Troy's heels. "Hello, son," she said, giving Gregory a hug. "Where's Anise?"

"At her place, I guess." He walked over to the counter and helped himself to a bowl of grapes.

"Why didn't you invite her over? Since you brought her to dinner to meet the family on Friday, I assumed she'd join us today. Wait, are you leading that nice young lady on? You did break up with Lori, didn't you?"

"Oh, man, do I have to sit in the hot seat so soon?" Though she knew all about their history, Gregory was in no mood to discuss Lori's antics and the fallout from said antics with one Ms. Jackie Morgan. "Anise had a good time at the party," he said, pointedly ignoring his mother's question. "Speaking of, where is Robert?"

"I was totally out of his favorite soda and he acts like he can't eat a meal without it. He went to the store. I'm sure he's on his way back." Jackie pulled a perfectly cooked standing rib roast from the oven.

Gregory whistled. "Thank God for Robert. Before his legs went under the dinner table all you'd cook was chicken and roast beef."

"That's not true," Jackie retorted.

"They say the way to a man's heart is through his stomach," Michael added.

Troy grabbed a handful of grapes and joined Michael at the table. "Yeah, but the man who said that probably wasn't thinking about Shayna's shortcut—serving nonstop fast food."

Shayna swatted Troy's arm. "Shut up. I cook." He gave her a look. "Sometimes." More silence. "When

I can. When my schedule allows it and we're not eating out."

Laughing, Troy continued to goad her. "When's the last time you cooked, Shayna?"

"Y'all leave Mike's wife alone," Jackie said. "And worry about your own. Oh, that's right. Neither one of you buggers have a wife. So y'all can't say a thing!" She looked at Gregory. "This new girl . . . can she cook?"

"I don't know, Mom," Gregory said, leaving out the fact that she sure could handle one of his appetites.

By the time Robert returned and they'd all settled around the dinner table, the conversation had meandered from track and field to the latest celebrity scandal seen up and close from Troy's position of bodyguard to Jackie bugging Michael and Shayna about grandbabies. It finally came back around to Gregory, but this time it was the boardroom, not the bedroom, that Jackie wanted to know about.

"It won't be long now," she said, after enjoying a bite of roasted potatoes. "How will you find out you got the grant, Greg? Will they call you, send a letter, have you come to someplace in LA?"

"Probably all of the above. And that's *if* I get the grant."

"No, it's not. It's *when*." Jackie said this with total conviction. "I know you think I'm crazy, but I've been dreaming a lot about your daddy lately. I think he's going to help you get that grant."

"He just wants his name on a building," Troy offered.

Gregory chuckled. "Probably so."

"He deserves it," Michael said.

The conversation continued but if asked later, Gregory would have had a hard time recounting the end of it. His mind kept wandering to Anise. And the crazy situation with her workplace space and his research center. And how their two worlds could continue to coexist if one took out the other.

"It's about time you came over." Aretha feigned chagrin as she opened the door for Anise and Boomer. The hug was all love. "I even missed this old dog. Hey, dog." She petted his head. "Wait, now. No jumping up on this suit. I just got it out of the cleaners." Aretha led the way into the living room. "Are you just saying hi real quick before seeing the doctor or is this a real visit?"

"I didn't come over this way to see Gregory. I came to see you."

"He must be working." She sat on the couch.

Anise joined her. "No, he's having Sunday dinner with his family."

"Why aren't you with him?"

"Because I'm here, spending time with *my* family."

"You want something to drink? Are you hungry?"

"No thanks, auntie, I'm fine."

"You look happy, Anise. I'm glad."

"I am, Aunt Ree. Like you said about your friend, Bruce. I might have a good one here."

"Girl, you're saying that like you're serious. Y'all haven't known each other much more than a month."

"I'm not ready to walk down the aisle or anything but . . . I like him."

"How was your holiday?"

"Wonderful. How was Vegas?"

"Luck smiled on me this time; I actually won back some of my money from Caesar." Aretha muted the television. "How was the party?"

"It was really nice."

"And meeting the family—how did that go?"

"Better than I expected. His mother, Jackie, is very nice and I liked Shayna, too. She wasn't snooty or anything the way I thought she might be."

"What about her husband? Is he as fine as he looks on TV?"

"Probably finer than that. He's Mr. Suave, Mr. Cool. But the real hunk is the youngest son, Troy. He's a walking heartbreak waiting to happen but I'm sure most women will take their chances."

"Well, girl, I'm glad you enjoyed yourself."

"I also heard some good news from home, from Omaha."

"Oh?"

"Yes. Bob called, my attorney. He worked out a settlement with the bank about the loan against the house, the one for the medical treatments not covered by insurance. He says the sale of the house should move swiftly now as he already has a real estate agent with prospective buyers lined up."

"That's great, Anise. That should ease your mind somewhat."

"It does." She placed her feet on the floor, her expression content. "I miss Mama something terrible—I always will. The situation at The Creative Space is still crazy. But for now, Gregory and I are still in our truce and I'm still working at my dream studio. So I really can't complain."

"Wouldn't help if you did," Aretha said. "If I were you I'd live in the present and enjoy my blessings. Tomorrow, with its bad news, piles of problems, fresh frustrations and endless irritations . . . will be here soon enough."

39

Gregory took a deep breath, tried to stay calm. This was the moment he'd waited for. He'd just received a call to head to a meeting in Santa Monica. The committee had made their decision. The recipient of the foundation grant had been selected and would now be informed.

Reaching for his keys, his breathing had slowed but his thoughts were whirling. *I have to have won it, right? Why else would they call me down there? Or maybe they wanted to deliver the bad news in person. Maybe they wanted a photo op with Drew as the winner and me as the runner up.* He stopped by to recheck the surgery roster and, not seeing his name listed, checked in at the nurses' desk.

"Paula, I need to run out for an hour or so. Is Dr. Meyers still in surgery?"

"Yes, but Dr. Fordham is available, and so is Dr. Johnson."

So Drew is here, huh? Does that mean he's already been

to the meeting, that they're giving the loser the information first, or that I actually may have this thing in the bag? The news only made Gregory more eager to get on the road.

"I'll keep my phone close in case of an extreme emergency. Otherwise, I'll see you in a bit."

Once in his car and heading down the 405, Gregory tapped his hands-free device. Soon a calming voice flowed in his ear.

"Hello, son."

"Hey, Mom. The grant committee just called me. They've made a decision and want me at their offices. When I left the hospital, Drew was still on duty. Do you think that means I've got it?"

"I've believed it was yours from the very beginning and that hasn't changed."

Gregory sighed. "I'm nervous, Mom. I want this so badly."

"That's understandable, Greg. This is life-changing. I'm pulling for you, and I know Sam is, too."

"I feel better. Thanks, Mom."

A short time later, he walked into the conference room. "Hello, everyone," he said as he entered, then went around the room, shaking hands.

After a bit of small talk the head of the committee, Dr. Dickens, asked that everyone be seated. Gregory looked around at the faces. Most were pleasant but unreadable. He thought he saw a gleam in Mr. Rosenthal's eye, but then again, they could have just been watery.

"Gregory," Dr. Dickens began, "thank you so much for joining us."

"It is my pleasure."

Dr. Dickens nodded. "As you know, it has been a thorough and sometimes excruciating process to select our recipient for this, the first Menachem B. Rosenthal research grant. And I'm sure you are aware that it was his wish, before he passed, that his legacy be one of research to the world of medicine in an ongoing and meaningful way.

"A field of over two-hundred and fifty entrants was narrowed down to fifty, then to ten, and then to three: you, Drew Fordham, and Ken Burrows. And while I am an alum of the esteemed university, I did not have anything to do with the fact that you all work at UCLA Medical. All of you have similar educational and work-related backgrounds and each of the areas that have been selected to research are important: the heart, the immune system and the brain. This made the selection process extremely difficult."

Gregory tried not to squirm. He appreciated the back story but really wanted Dr. Dickens to cut to the chase.

"Heart disease is a very real problem, especially in America," Dr. Dickens continued. "As you well know, it is the leading cause of death in our country and as such is deserving of all of our focus and attention so that we can try and get a handle on a disease that is taking far too many lives."

Did they drag me all the way down here just to tell me that I didn't *get the grant?* In his mind, Gregory imagined himself grabbing Dr. Dickens's collar and squeezing the truth out of him. The visual caused him to smile. And relax.

"The myriad of injuries that come under the umbrella of blunt force trauma," Dr. Dickens was saying when Gregory began listening again, "are vast and, in our opinion, under the radar of the at-large medical community. So while heart disease is prevalent, so too are the number of research groups working to expand the types of cures for it. We want to focus on the other: other causes of death, other major organs. And we want to focus on the brain. That is why, Dr. Morgan, it is with a great sense of pleasure and personal satisfaction that I say congratulations. Everyone on the board is just thrilled at what you've proposed to research: blunt force trauma with a special interest in brain in- juries. We know that the medical field will be made better by your work."

It was what he'd hoped for, but after the long intro not what he expected. Gregory was stunned and, coming as a bit of surprise to him, emotional. As soon as he heard the word "congratulations", he'd immediately thought of his dad.

"Thank you," he said, clearing the emotion from his throat, and looking around the room. "Thank you, all. This means more to me than you can pos- sibly know. I'm excited to get started."

"That's good to hear, Gregory, because we need you to dive right in. As you know, we have a building that will house the new research center. It is currently occupied, but the tenants have been given notice to evacuate. The building will be cleared out by August fifteenth and an extensive renovation will begin immediately thereafter. Until that time, we'd like you to join us as we meet with the architects so that we can be sure and include the special requirements you'll need during your research."

"That's The Creative Space building, correct?"

"Yes." For the first time, Mr. Rosenthal spoke up. "As you may know, my father's sister, Lydia, established a long-term lease with a group of artists fifty years ago. Much to the chagrin of my dad and uncles," he added, a bit under his breath. "It was always my grandfather Menachem's desire that the building be used for medical research, and we are grateful to finally be able to make his wishes come true."

Gregory sat, nodding, all thoughts of alternative locations for the building disappearing as rapidly as Anise's dream to remain there. His chest tightened at the thought of delivering this news. She wouldn't be happy, he knew, but she'd have to accept it. Life happened this way. One didn't always get what one wanted. He decided that when they spoke, this is what he would tell her.

40

Drew was livid. He'd just received the bad news. The phone call that he thought would change his life had come. But his life was not being changed for the better. *Shit!* He jumped up from his desk chair and began to pace the room. Getting that grant had meant everything to him, not the least of which was a way to show his father that he could make it without the family name or his old man's money. It was going to be the step up that he needed to get back in the medical community's good graces and make a name for himself. He'd planned it all out in his head. Get the grant. Do major PR on the center's work. Become an expert in the area of heart disease. Get on one of those news channels or maybe even on *Investigation Discovery*. In five years, the world would have known his name. But now, all of those dreams were swirling down the toilet.

He walked back to his desk and plopped down in the chair. *Damn!* Was there nothing that the golden boy Gregory Morgan wanted that he didn't get? In his mind, Ken Burrows had never been serious competition but from day one Drew had done everything he could to get Gregory eliminated from the list of potential recipients. When the list had been narrowed to three, Drew had stepped up his game.

I almost had him with the overdose. I was so close! Except it hadn't happened. Unbeknownst to him the intern he'd been grooming to follow his prescriptions without question had not been the one who'd gotten the medical chart he'd changed. By a stroke of his shitty luck of the past three years, Meagan had switched patients with veteran nurse Emma Byrd and gone on break. "The Byrd" as she was affectionately called because of her attention to detail. She'd noticed the incorrect amount of prescription painkiller with codeine at once and brought it to Dr. Meyers's attention. *Stupid old biddy. I should have given you the dose!*

His phone rang. After taking the call he turned to his computer and checked his emails. For the first time since hearing the bad grant news, he smiled. He opened the correspondence that had caught his eye and rapidly typed out a response. *If at first you don't succeed, then try again.* That a-hole

Morgan may have won this battle. But Drew was determined to win the war.

Anise waited an hour and then called Gregory. "I hear congratulations are in order," she said as soon as he answered, trying to remain calm and keep chagrin out of her voice. After all, this was the big day he'd dreamed about. That hers were now dashed really wasn't his fault. She thought these things but couldn't get her feelings to quite line up, evidenced in her clipped tone when she asked him, "Now it's official. When were you going to tell me?"

"How did you find out?"

"Does it matter?" Staying calm was going to be harder than Anise realized. "Dawn told me. She's the center's director. I would have preferred to have heard it from you."

"I just got out of the meeting not an hour ago, Anise. And while I admit you're special to me, the first woman I called was my mom."

This comment cut through some of Anise's anger. For a moment she saw her own selfishness. Right next to resolve. "I'm sure she's happy for you."

"Are you?"

"Honestly yes, Greg, I am. I know how much you wanted it. You say there was a meeting to make the announcement?"

"Yes."

"Did you ask them about relocating the research center; and keeping The Creative Space where it is?"

"There was no need to ask. It was the express wish of one of the donators that the building be used for medical research. I'm sorry, Anise."

She sighed. "I am, too, Gregory. And I might as well warn you. This might get ugly."

"What do you mean?"

"I probably shouldn't be telling you this but the center's board of directors has hired a lawyer to file a stay on our behalf. We're going to fight to keep this building."

"Seriously? You're going to fight knowing that I'm the person you're up against?"

"Aren't you moving full speed ahead with your plans knowing that it will put me out of a studio space and a job?"

"That's not the same, Anise, and you know it."

"Oh? How is it different?"

"You know what? I'm not going to have this conversation with you again. I've already tried it. There's no getting through. Just know that your willingness to block what you know is my dream says a lot about your feelings for me."

"This isn't personal, Gregory. If it were, I'd be the one with the right to be upset."

"I hope you find another studio," he said, after a pause. "Look, I've got meetings. I have to go."

* * *

Only a decade of discipline borne with scalpel in hand prevented him from slamming the phone down. That damnable woman could get under his skin like nobody he'd ever known. *Plucky Nebraskan.* As angry as he was, however, a part of him had to admire her will. And a part of him hated the fact that he was going to hurt her by defeating her cause. Because when it came to the research center versus the art center, Gregory had no doubt. He would win.

41

"Truth," Anise said, sticking her head inside the sculptor's studio. "Dawn has requested that we all gather in the lobby for a meeting." With the intercom down, it had fallen upon her to alert all the artists in the building.

"Any idea what it's about?"

"Unfortunately, yes. But she's asked that I not say anything. She wants to tell you guys all at once."

When they reached the lobby, there were about fifteen people milling around. Dawn saw Anise and walked over. "Is that everyone?"

"I think so."

"Okay, good." She turned to the group of artists, more like family, who'd formed a half circle around her. "As many of you know, a while back we received notice that we might have to vacate this building."

One of the artists murmured, "Oh, no."

Another one cursed.

"That's how I feel," Dawn said, sympathy evident

in her eyes. "Because that possibility is now reality. We have to move in thirty days, by August 30."

"A lousy month? That's all the time we have before we have to be gone . . . a few weeks?" The curvy Latina hadn't meant this to come out so frantic . . . but it did.

"I'm as surprised at this as you guys are. I really thought we'd be able to extend the lease."

"I can't believe anybody would close The Creative Space," Nancy said, wringing her paint-splattered hands. At sixty-something, Nancy was the oldest artist who used her studio regularly, seen as a mother figure by one and all.

"From what I understand, it wasn't an easy decision. But that's neither here nor there. I believe I have everyone's current e-mail address, but if you feel otherwise, please shoot me an update. I'm really sorry that I don't have more information, but felt it best to let you guys know about this as soon as possible so that alternate arrangements can be made."

Truth asked, "What's going on that they're asking us to move?"

Dawn told him. "But the board has decided to look into legal options for keeping the space that artists have called home for fifty years. In other words, kids, we're not going down without a fight!"

Spontaneous applause broke out among them.

Dawn held out her hands to quiet them. "I need

all of you to know that this is serious. We don't know what is going to happen. So even though we're receiving legal counsel, I suggest that all of you prepare to take your work and equipment elsewhere. If they do a counterclaim or this building gets tied up legally, the last thing you want is for your stuff to be held hostage."

"Who is trying to take the building?" Truth asked again.

Dawn looked at Anise, who took a step forward. "The owners of the building want to renovate this into a center for medical research. They've given a doctor a grant to do this research. It's a noble cause, and you guys should know that any of us who choose to fight to keep this building may get quite a bit of flak for doing so."

A normally quiet yet very talented artist, Kim Li, spoke up. "But we're going to fight it legally, right?"

"Yes," Dawn answered. "But Anise has also suggested that we do something more public to draw attention to what is going on, which is similar to what's happening in our educational system and elsewhere. Art is being cut out. It is often the first thing that is considered for elimination, whether because of budget, cutbacks, or in this instance, space."

Anise nodded and continued. "We want to stand up for artists everywhere, and we feel that because of the high-profile of the philanthropist giving the grant, this center will be receiving a lot of media attention—a perfect platform for us to push forward our message of the importance of art."

"We don't know what the public's reaction will be," Dawn said. "So during the next few weeks, while we're"—her breath caught, her voice wavered—"packing up our stuff and cleaning out our studios, think about what you want to do, if anything. Don't feel obligated. Only participate in this protest if you feel . . . compelled."

A few of the others asked questions while most just milled around, stunned. Sure, they'd heard about the notice, but none had given it too much thought. The Creative Space had experienced its share of ups and downs, mostly depending on the country's fiscal front, and somehow the center had always come out on top. This time, those involved didn't seem so sure.

Back in the office, Dawn's strong veneer crumbled much like her body as she slumped over her desk, head in hand. Anise felt as badly, fighting to hold on to her own tears. She felt she'd cried a river in the past year, all the more reason why the center was something she did not want to lose.

"Dawn, I need to tell you something." Dawn turned red-rimmed eyes in Anise's direction. "When I told you that I knew about the building owners, and about the research grant, there was more."

"What do you mean?"

"I didn't tell you all that I know." Dawn's brow

creased in confusion. "I also know who received the grant. I know the doctor personally."

"You do?"

"Yes."

"That's great, Anise!" Dawn's face brightened up. "That's excellent news. Perhaps you can talk to him and—"

"Already tried that and no, there's no chance."

"Are you sure? Maybe our attorneys—"

"I'm sleeping with him, all right?" Anise blurted out. Dawn sank back against the chair. "He's my aunt's neighbor. I met him my first day here. We've been dating since then. I called him as soon as I knew, and asked him. He says there's nothing he can do. That it's out of his hands."

"You must be heartbroken," Dawn said. "Here we're sad about losing where we work and where we create. But I'd imagine this situation is causing problems in your relationship."

"That is putting it mildly. Happy for him yet sad for myself. It's crazy."

More than crazy, Anise thought, as she tried to see a peaceful future for her and Gregory. But how could that happen, with them on opposing sides of a very important issue to both of them? With all of the focus on saving her work, she'd not given any thought to saving her relationship and her heart. But the very moment Dawn voiced this inconvenient truth, was the moment Anise realized Gregory had it.

42

This second July weekend in Long Beach could not be more perfect. It was eighty and sunny, with a cooling breeze blowing in from across the Pacific Ocean's sparkling waters. Seventy-five of retiring police officer Robert Donaldson's closest friends and former associates had come together at the Westin, with its nearby ocean views, to celebrate his accomplishments and his life. Couples and groups sauntered through the lobby; all suits and long dresses, light wools and silks.

"My man!" Michael came into the private dining room and slapped Gregory on the back.

"Hey, big bro!" Gregory stood to hug his brother and saw Shayna coming through the door. As soon as she reached her husband's side, he hugged her, too. "I thought you said you wouldn't be able to make it back."

"Couldn't miss the moment, Dr. Morgan." Michael

lowered his voice. "Mama threatened to beat me like I stole something if I didn't make it back."

"Ha!"

"Don't believe whatever he's telling you, Greg." Jackie entered the room, looking as proud as the peacock scarf that she wore over her navy suit. Robert was beside her, looking distinguished in a charcoal gray suit, and beaming as if Gregory was his own son. "He's got that look," she explained to Shayna as she leaned over and gave each of her sons a hug. "The one that says he's telling a whopper." She winked as Michael placed his arm around her. "A mother knows."

The small talk continued until Troy walked into the room. Then all sound—and for a second all movement—ceased.

"Look who I found hovering around the entrance, hoping for crumbs." Troy smiled as he dodged a swat from the beautiful woman beside him.

"Stop it, Troy." Lori left his side and walked over to stand with Gregory.

"Lori knows how much this all means to me," he said by way of explanation to the stunned family who were working hard not to appear stunned. "I knew she'd want to help me celebrate."

Jackie was nothing if not resilient. She found a smile, pasted it on quickly, and stepped forward. "Lori, this is a surprise. How are you?" She gave a genuine hug to the woman she'd known as a child.

"I'm fine, Miss Jackie. You look nice. I love that suit."

"Thank you, Lori. How's your mother?"

"She's fine—thinking about moving to Vegas."

"Really?"

"Yes. She's wanting to downsize and the housing market right now is fantastic."

"The next time you talk to her, tell her I said hello."

"Will do."

At the same time Jackie and Lori were talking, another conversation was happening mere feet away. It began with a single gesture: raised eyebrows and a look from Michael to Gregory.

"It's a long story," Gregory said.

"How long?" Gregory shrugged.

"You and Anise . . . ?" Michael made a slicing motion across his neck.

"Not if I can help it. But she's pretty upset with me right now."

"Man, I leave town for a minute and it looks like all hell breaks loose."

"Brother, you don't know the half."

"What happened?"

"I won the grant."

"I'd think she'd be happy about that."

"My win was her loss."

"I'm not following you, bro."

"It's a long story. Let's enjoy Robert's evening. Tomorrow, I'll fill you in."

Anise stood in the middle of her living room, trying to figure out how she was going to deal with the mess. When she'd rented the studio apartment, she hadn't planned for it to be her home, workplace, and storage space.

"This is impossible, Boomer," she said with a shake of her head. "I'm going to have to rent a storage space again. There's no way I can keep all of this here."

She walked over to the couch, pushed a pile of papers off the cushion, and sat down. And then it hit her. The feeling that had been nagging at her since Gregory's announcement. For the first time since her mother died, Anise felt alone. Really, truly alone. Not even Boomer's compassionate presence was enough to compensate for the lack of human companionship. After Carolyn died, Aretha was there. As soon as Anise had arrived in Los Angeles, Gregory was there. He wasn't there now. They hadn't talked since she'd told him about the artists' intent to protest. His absence was more overwhelming than Anise could have ever imagined.

She missed her mother.

And she missed Gregory. Since his grant announcement, they'd both needed space to process what had happened. Even so, he'd called last night and reminded her about Robert's retirement party. Pride had kept her from accepting the invitation. Hurt and misplaced anger kept her from doing what she wanted to do even now: pick up the phone and call him.

I should have gone.

One tear fell. Another quickly followed. She angrily swiped them away. "I'm not going to go there," she uttered through gritted teeth, jumping off the couch and picking papers off the floor. "I'm not going to feel sorry for myself. What's done is done."

Wanting a diversion she picked up her iPad and logged on to Facebook. After about ten minutes the instant message box popped up on her screen.

Art-n-Sol: Hello, beautiful.

ArtbyAnise: ☺ Hi, Edward.

Art-n-Sol: Where are you?

ArtbyAnise: Why?

Art-n-Sol: The event must be pretty boring if in the middle of it you're surfing Facebook!

ArtbyAnise: No. I'm home.

Art-n-Sol: On a Saturday night? Your boyfriend is crazy to leave you home!

ArtbyAnise: Just moved. My choice.

Art-n-Sol: Then he should be there with you. Especially now. How are you?

ArtbyAnise: I'm okay.

Art-n-Sol: Is it too personal for me to ask how he feels about the fact that your art center is closing?

Anise read the question twice. It was a good one. She believed that Gregory felt bad that her dream of interning at The Creative Space was being cut short but she honestly believed he couldn't care less about what happened in the art world. She didn't feel this was personal. She felt this was because art was her world, Edward's world, but not Gregory's.

ArtbyAnise: He feels bad about it.

Art-n-Sol: I read about what happened; that the owners are turning the building into one for medical research, and that some doctor named Gregory Morgan will be conducting medical research.

This was a surprise. Anise hadn't known the news had been made public.

ArtbyAnise: Where'd you read that?

Art-n-Sol: Huffington Post. Hold on, I'll send the link.

Anise received the link and immediately clicked on to open it. She scanned it while still instant messaging with Edward.

Art-n-Sol: I'm all for the advancement of medicine, but I can't believe that this Morgan guy was unaware of The Creative Space's history, and that his renovation is going to destroy fifty years of history. Or maybe he does know it ... and just doesn't care.

Anise was silent. *Should I tell him that I know Gregory?* She couldn't help but to snort at that blatant understatement. Yes she knew him intimately, but there was a large part of his life that she didn't know at all.

Art-n-Sol: Anise?

ArtbyAnise: I'm here. Just thinking.

Why shouldn't I tell him? He doesn't know me or Gregory. Might be good to get a nameless, faceless, unbiased opinion. She finished scanning the article and focused on the conversation. It made her feel good to talk to someone sympathetic of her position in all this. But she'd been raised by a wise and skeptical mother who right now would be telling her that it wasn't necessarily wise to share personal details with a stranger. *But what if he's not a stranger?*

Art-n-Sol: You're thinking about the center, and what you're going to do?

ArtbyAnise: That, but something else. I'm thinking that I don't really know who you are, your identity. And that if I did, I would want to bounce some things off of you, get your opinion.

Art-n-Sol: You know me. We've been talking for weeks.

ArtbyAnise: I don't even know what you look like.

Art-n-Sol: Would you like to meet?

ArtbyAnise: Sure.

Art-n-Sol: When?

ArtbyAnise: Now.

Art-n-Sol: Name the time and place and I'll meet you there.

43

Twenty minutes later Anise entered a Starbucks down the road from her home. She spotted Edward immediately, dressed as he'd described: jeans, T-shirt, baseball cap and thick glasses. He smiled as she neared him. *Hum, he's kind of cute, and taller than I thought he'd be.*

"Edward?" She walked toward him with hand outstretched.

He took her hand and held it. "Handshakes are fine for strangers, Anise. But I feel I've known you forever and I feel you could use one."

"One what?"

"A hug. May I?"

They embraced and walked to the counter, sharing small talk until they'd ordered and received their drinks. The place was busy for a Saturday night but Anise snagged a table in the corner while Edward waited for their drinks.

"One Vanilla Bean Frappucino for the lady," he

said as he placed the cool, frothy drink in front of Anise. "With lots of whipped cream. You sure you don't want anything with it, maybe a cookie or brownie bar?"

Anise shook her head. "No, I'm good." She took her drink and gave Edward a contemplative perusal as she sipped. "You don't look like I thought you would."

"How's that?"

She shrugged. "I don't know."

"Big ears, buck teeth?" Edward stirred his Hazelnut Macchiato and smiled.

"Not exactly . . ."

"Ha! That's exactly what you thought! At least I didn't disappoint in one area."

"What's that, the thick glasses?" She hadn't said it to be mean, only because she'd been trying to make out the color of his eyes behind them . . . and couldn't tell.

"See, you're an artist. I knew you'd have imagined a look!" They laughed. "So what's your last name, Anise?"

"Cartier."

"Anise Cartier."

She looked at him then, and tried to figure out what about him seemed familiar. After a while she realized it was probably just the fact that she was always studying faces and his was one of the more common in terms of profile and size.

They continued to talk and after about ten

minutes, during which time Anise found out that Edward worked in a family-owned business, Anise felt comfortable enough to broach the subject for which they'd met.

"This is really messed up for me, Edward."

"Because you're both working and painting at the center?"

She frowned. "How do you know that?"

"You posted it on Facebook."

"Oh, right. Yes, there's that. But there's more."

"Something worse than losing both your livelihood and where you practice your craft??"

Anise nodded. "I know the grant recipient, the man who will be moving his offices into The Creative Space building."

"You know Dr. Morgan?"

"Yes."

"How? I mean, is he a family friend or . . ."

"I dated him."

Edward let out a low whistle. "Oh, man." Anise sighed. "He had to have known that you worked there. And he still went after the grant, knowing that they planned to renovate the building?"

"That would have happened no matter who got the grant."

"Maybe, but still . . . that's a pretty low thing to do to someone you purport to love." Anise was silent. "What is he saying, now that his getting the grant is a done deal?"

"I haven't seen him since the announcement was made."

"It's probably for the best, Anise. He obviously doesn't recognize or appreciate your talent. Sorry to say this but he sounds like a jerk."

"It's not his fault. The owners are the ones who controlled what happened to the building. They are the ones who decided what would be housed there."

Then came the angel on her shoulder, the one she hadn't even noticed was there. *If it's not his fault, and things were not in his control, then why are you here talking to a casual internet friend instead of swaying in the arms of your lover?*

Before she could fully contemplate that question, the devil spoke up. *Because he dogged you, that's why. Relationships are built on trust and if he wouldn't consider your feelings on something this important then how can you believe that he'll consider them in other matters?*

Then finally, as if to make sure that she was fully and completely confused, Edward reached for her hand.

"Anise, it really doesn't matter what his reasons were. I don't think a man like that is right for you. I'm so happy we've met, and not just because of what happened with The Creative Space. I have something to share and I'm glad it's in person. Anise, I finally did it. I broke up with my girlfriend.

It was hard, but I can't live my life without having what I want."

"And what's that?"

"To take you on a real date."

"Edward, I really like you. But I—"

"Anise, please. I think we'd be good together. Promise you'll think about it, about everything I've said?"

"Okay," Anise answered, even as she thought of Gregory and their impossible situation. "I'll think about it."

44

Gregory gave the door a tap before he strolled into Troy's office. "You've really fixed things up around here," he said as his brother stood and gave him a shoulder tap. "Your offices look good." Gregory continued to look around. "Have you expanded?"

Troy nodded. "We've taken over the entire floor above us and we're getting ready to redo the lobby. Working with Hollywood, you have to have the look, know what I mean?"

"You've got it, brother."

"I'm on my way." He picked up a folder. "Have a seat."

"You said you have news?"

"Yes, I do. I wanted to tell you last night but your bringing Lori to the party was fireworks enough."

"We called a truce and are mending our friendship. Strictly platonic though—I was adamant about that."

"What's going on with your girl, Anise?"

"I haven't talked with her much; I'm giving her the space she seems to need. I do know that the organization that funded the grant has received the initial legal documents regarding the stay on vacating The Creative Space building."

"So, they're really going to go through with it."

"Looks that way. But the Rosenthals have a pretty savvy set of lawyers on their side. They told me not to worry, said that the lease agreement is clear and straightforward. There is no way they can stay in the building. Anise and that group are just delaying the inevitable, and bringing unnecessary drama to my front door."

"Maybe you should call her, man, so y'all can talk."

"And say what?" Gregory looked at his watch. "I've got a meeting with the architects and the board coming up. What do you have for me?"

"I wish I could say it was news that will make you feel better, but it's only going to make you even more upset."

"Great."

"I'd already requested the background checks on Ken and Drew when you were named the recipient of the grant. I just got back the information."

"And?"

"Ken Burrows has kept his nose clean his whole life. Middle class family who pulled themselves up by their bootstraps. His dad owns a string of used car lots. That's what put him through college."

"I'm not upset by hard work, my brother."

"Drew on the other hand . . ."

"What did he do, murder somebody?"

"Check this out."

Gregory took the sheet of paper from his brother and read aloud. "Prominent Doctor Gets Probation. Doctor Drew Fordham, Jr., son of world-renowned surgeon Drew Fordham, Sr. of Boston, Massachusetts, was found guilty of obstruction of justice and failure to cooperate with investigators regarding the embezzlement and gross misconduct case at Massachusetts Medical Center. Several former staff members, including the CFO, were found guilty and received prison sentences varying from one to seven years. The hospital board says they are determined to ferret out all corruption and will not stop until the hospital's reputation is completely cleared. Until that time, the investigation continues." Gregory looked at Troy. "Seriously?"

"It was actually worse than what you read. My sources say that Drew played a major role in the scam that defrauded insurance companies of millions of dollars by having false claims filed and performing unnecessary surgeries. His father's prestige and the family's old ties got the charges reduced so that he'd only have to do probation."

Gregory immediately thought of the patient who, if not for the astute eyes of Emma Byrd, would have died. "With that kind of baggage, how is he still even able to practice medicine?"

"That was a key part of the plea; that he'd only be forbidden from holding any type of administrative position within a hospital but that he'd still be able to practice as a medical doctor.

"I believe he was the one behind that situation you had awhile back, when you told me about the patient who could have overdosed."

"I just thought the exact same thing."

"You could have gotten prison time for involuntary manslaughter. That fool needs to understand how we do it on the west side. Just say the word and he'll get a lesson."

A slow smile spread across Gregory's face. "You always were the hothead. I appreciate the offer, Troy. I know you have my back. But no, I'm not going to stoop to that snake's level. Life has a way of working out. In due time, he'll get what's coming to him."

"In the meantime, what are you going to do about Anise?"

"What do you mean?"

"You can try and deny it, but I saw you last night, during the times when you thought that no one was watching. You may be upset with her. But you miss her."

"I just can't believe she'd do this."

"What, stand up for something that she believes

in?" Gregory frowned. "Hey, I'm not saying I agree with her, and when it comes to sides, I'm on yours. But it sounds like the girl is just doing what she thinks she has to do."

"But given her actions, where does that leave the relationship?"

Troy leaned forward. "That, my brother, is a question that only you can answer."

After a brief but productive meeting with the company who'd be doing the renovations for his research center, Gregory continued what would be a very long day by pulling into the employee parking lot at UCLA. So many emotions were going through him that it was hard to focus. The past forty-eight hours had seemed surreal. One thing he had thought about on the drive from Santa Monica to Westwood Plaza was the question his brother had asked him. Anise had asked for space, but that was only part of the reason he hadn't called her. The other reason was how her rejection had stung him. No matter the conflict, the special woman in Gregory's life would be on his side no matter what. That's what he'd seen with his parents and that's what he wanted. He hadn't told his brothers or anyone but before the battle over the building blew up their cozy relationship, he'd begun to think that Anise was that woman. Now, he wasn't sure. As he entered the doctor's lounge, he made a decision. The stalemate was going to end . . . and soon.

"Gregory!"

"There he is!"

"Congratulations, Greg!"

At once the small group inside the break room spoke their greetings. All except one—Drew—who sat stone faced looking at a medical journal. Or pretending to, as Gregory suspected.

"Thanks, guys." Gregory filled a cup with water and took one of the empty chairs. "I appreciate your support."

"We're happy for you, man." Doug, one of the ER doctors who worked the day shift, had started at the hospital shortly after Greg and while not close, there had always been mutual respect between them. "It couldn't have happened to a better, more qualified doctor."

"Thanks, Doug."

"When do you start?" another doctor asked.

"The building that will house the research center is being renovated, starting three or so weeks from now. The new construction is slated to be finished in roughly four weeks."

"Wow," Doug responded. "That's fast."

"We plan to be open by the first of the year, and have the ribbon cutting that first week if all goes as planned. Don't worry. You're all invited."

"We'll all be there," Doug responded. "Everyone here wishes you well."

"Everyone who matters," Gregory responded,

loud enough for Drew to hear and know exactly who he was talking to. "We all know how life works. Good or bad actions, they all come back at you. And when your actions have landed you on the bad side of fate . . . karma's a bitch."

45

Days after Gregory's announcement and still, other than the one rather terse exchange between them, Anise and Gregory hadn't talked. Granted, she'd been busy, planning today's protest with the other artists, but Gregory had never been far from her mind. She guessed the fact that she'd be protesting his center could be the reason.

"How do you feel?" Dawn looked at Anise, whose face showed worry and strain.

"I don't know."

"Anise, we'll all understand if you don't do this."

"How would that look? I was one of the main ones suggesting that we fight this, that we take our issue to the streets."

"Yes, but this is about more than the center. This is about you, your personal life." Anise remained silent, rubbing her eyes. "Have you talked to him?"

"Not much since after the announcement was made."

"Don't you think you should call him?"

"And say what? 'Hi, Gregory, it's Anise. I'll be protesting in front of your proposed center today. Good-bye.'"

"Yeah, that doesn't sound too good."

"Exactly."

"What do you think he'll do when he sees us—more specifically, sees you?"

Anise got up and reached for a poster board. She grabbed a marker and began to draw big, bold, black letters across the paper. "I guess we're going to find out, huh? In about two hours."

It was a full circle moment, and Gregory was savoring the experience.

"Do you remember your first day in ER, as an intern?" Dr. Meyers asked.

"Like it was yesterday." Gregory rubbed his chin thoughtfully, the years falling away as he went back in time. "I was introduced to you and Dr. Robinson—"

"Good old Bill!"

"Yes, indeed! He was the bad cop, firing questions at me left and right. I thought I was back in finals."

"But you impressed him. You remained calm, unruffled. And more than that, you knew the answers. . . ."

"Even expounded on his theory of basilar skull fractures and lessening subsequent disabilities."

"I thought you were one cocky son of a gun."

"Hey, he asked me!"

"That he did. I knew right away that I wanted you on our team here."

"And I knew as soon as I applied for the grant that if I got it, you'd be the first doctor I asked to join me."

"I'm honored, Gregory, I really am."

"I'm sure you'll want to think about it."

"I already have." Gregory didn't hide his surprise. "Ha! You're not the only cocky son of a gun in this building. I knew that if you got the grant to open the research center, I'd have to be the one to help you run it."

"I see."

"I'm your only logical choice," Dr. Meyers continued. "We've made a great team here for more than five years."

"That's very true."

"How many doctors does your budget allow?"

"Four doctors, an anesthesiologist, and two administrative personnel. For nurses, I'm going to pull from the school and use interns."

"Good choice." After a pause, he continued. "I haven't been by it lately, but that's a pretty big building as I recall. More room than I think we'll need, at least initially."

"You're exactly right. For the most part, the research activity and its corresponding rooms will be on the first floor. The second floor will house our offices along with several offices leased to alternative medical procedures that align with our work: psychotherapy, physical therapy, massage therapy, even some Chinese and holistic practices. There will also be a rather extensive medical library, a full kitchen, and a full bath complete with shower. The plans look pretty amazing."

"I'd love to see them."

"That's what I wanted to hear," Gregory said, clapping his hands together. "Because I am scheduled to meet the architects and some of the grant team members down at the space for our first walk through. I'd love it if you went with me."

"Gregory, I'd be delighted."

"All right, guys, listen up." Dawn looked around at the artists surrounding her. There were ten of them, poised and ready with signs containing messages they hoped would succinctly convey what those holding them wanted the world to know. "The new tenants are scheduled to be here in an hour for a walk-through. The media has been notified. We are going to conduct this protest quietly and peacefully. I want to reiterate there is to be no confrontation between us and the new tenants. I don't want any of us to talk to them, yell out questions, anything. There will be two groups of us—one directly in front of the building, one across the street—and we are to simply stand, in silence, letting our placards speak for us." She looked at each person around her. "Are there any questions?"

"What if we're approached by the media?" Truth asked.

"If someone from a television station, newspaper, or magazine approaches you and asks a question about what art means to you or what this center has meant to you, personally, then by all means feel free to answer. But all questions regarding the center specifically, including future plans, possible relocations, etcetera, should be pointed in my direction. Good question, Truth. Anybody else?"

"Are you sure I can't bop these bozos upside the head," Betty asked, "just one good time?"

Her comment lightened the rather serious mood.

"There will be no bozo bopping," Dawn said, making a fist for emphasis. "As much as we may disagree with it, the decision for us to leave has been made. We're protesting because that decision was made without our input, knowledge, or participation. Outside of what our attorneys will do in court, this is one of the few times our voices—in the form of our placards—will be represented. That and whatever we share with the media. Anise, thanks for the idea of having us all dress in black. I think we look bad-ass."

Gregory saw them as soon as he turned off Wilshire Boulevard. Before seeing the building, or the white banner across it announcing in big letters: SAMUEL MORGAN TRAUMA RESEARCH & HEALTH CENTER COMING SOON! The first group he noticed was across the street. Five people, holding placards and with looks ranging from solemn to defiant. They walked slowly, from the light at the end of the street up to the middle of the block before turning. Their messages seemed to shout from the stark white boards: ART: EDUCATE, DON'T ERASE; FIRED AFTER 50 YEARS; NO HEART FOR ART; NEW LEASE VS. ARTIST LEGACY; and perhaps the most provocative one, also being the simplest, the single word: NO!

"What in the world?" Dr. Meyers looked from one side of the street to the other. "Who is that?"

Gregory had found a place to park and was executing a perfect three-point turn. He turned off the key and responded dryly, "Looks like our welcoming committee. You still want to come work with me?"

"Absolutely! You forget I came of age in the sixties and seventies. Even threw a Molotov cocktail or two. It'll take more than a dozen or so card-carrying hippies to rattle my cage!"

Gregory wondered if the architects had already arrived and were in the building. And what about the consulting team? He squared his shoulders, adjusted his sunglasses, and together with Dr. Meyers walked toward the building's entrance.

That's when he saw Anise. His breath caught, but he didn't break stride. Anyone watching would have seen a handsome, successful-looking executive seemingly without a care in the world. In preparation for the meeting, he'd donned one of his tailored black suits and paired it with a black-striped shirt and matching tie. He placed a casual hand in one of the pockets, reading the signs of those standing in front of the building, his research center, as he approached.

A tall brother with long locks was nearest to him as Gregory neared the entrance. His sign read: LEAVE LYDIA'S LEGACY ALONE! Gregory had heard of her, Lydia Rosenthal, the sister who'd defied her brothers all those years ago and set up a group of her artist friends in the building and executed a legally binding lease before they could object. He only briefly scanned the other three signs as all of his attention was drawn to the one Anise held: ART HEALS THE WORLD. As angry as he should have been at her, his thoughts betrayed him. Thoughts like how she looked beautifully defiant in her skinny black jeans and black tee, hair pulled back in a simple ponytail, eyes hidden behind oversized

shades. A part of him wanted to walk over to her—
whether to shake some sense into her or kiss her
senseless he couldn't decide—but instead he
continued striding straight to the door, held it
open for the doctor, and went inside.

46

Anise could have died right there. Because God help her but the sight of him, looking both debonair and devilish in his suit and shades, made her weak in the knees. It was a supreme effort to stand there appearing unaffected when all she wanted to do was run into his arms and plead her case, let him know that it wasn't personal, that she wasn't choosing, that if she could she'd have her cake (art) and eat it (him), too. His stoic demeanor drove her crazy. *What is he thinking? Is he totally angry with me? Totally over me? Why haven't I called him? Anise, you are really screwing this up!* Five minutes ago, before his arrival, she'd been one-hundred percent sure of her actions and decisions. Now everything she thought she knew was in question. Was keeping this building, as iconic as it was, really worth losing a man as good as Gregory? She stood to lose her livelihood, the place where she painted and the best man she'd ever dated in life. At the end of the day, she now wondered, would it all be worth it?

Her thoughts were interrupted as she watched a camera crew walk toward her and the other protesters, accompanied by a smartly dressed woman, the reporter Anise assumed, who was talking on a cell phone as they drew near.

Reaching the group of protestors, she ended the call. "Which one of you is the spokesperson?" the woman asked.

Truth pointed to Dawn. The woman walked over to talk to Dawn while Anise observed that the cameraman was recording the messages on their posters. Once the reporter had talked to Dawn and Truth, she walked over to Anise.

"Hello. What is it about The Creative Space that has you standing here today, protesting its closing?"

"It's a California institution," Anise replied, removing her glasses. "The Creative Space is to artists what the White House is to America. Can you imagine someone telling the president that he has to get out so that they can turn that building into, say, a museum?"

"No, but there are those who would argue the comparison. Few would deem they have the same importance."

"Not anyone who's learned here, or taught here, or worked here. Not anyone who's felt the spirit of the other artists as they've created here. Not Lydia

Rosenthal." Anise looked into the camera. "And not me."

The reporter was visibly impressed. "Well said." She looked at the sign that Anise held. "How do you believe art heals the world?"

Anise lifted her chin as she gave her answer, the shiver going down her spine confirming what she thought she'd seen from the corner of her eye—Gregory's wide-legged stance and intense stare boring at her through the glass of the building's window.

After an hour-long tour through the building that would change from The Creative Space to the Samuel Morgan Trauma Research & Health Center in a few short months, Gregory steeled himself for confrontation. He'd listened intently as the architect brought the blueprints alive, pointing out in the real space what had been drawn on paper—the location for the lobby and waiting room, X-ray and examining rooms. It was hard to envision that what he now saw would become what was promised. Peeling paint and color-splotched hardwood bore the proof of decades of neglect. Clearly the building had seen better days. But a part of him had remained at that window, watching Anise's passionate response to whatever the reporter had asked her. Midway through the tour he'd made his decision. When he left the building, he wouldn't walk past her. They needed to talk, and that needed to happen now.

But when he walked outside, she wasn't there. He stopped, looked across the street where the other group of protesters continued to walk. Didn't see her.

"Looking for someone, Gregory?" Doctor Meyers asked.

"Yes, but I don't see her. Let's go."

They reached the hospital. Gregory changed into his scrubs and was immediately thrown into the orchestrated chaos of ER. A young man suffering a gunshot wound to the head had been wheeled in, barely conscious. Gregory was at once absorbed into the moment. Situations like this fueled his commitment to his profession; young men like the one he now treated inspired him to conduct the research that would save more lives. Cranial head wounds caused by gunshot were roughly ten percent of the more common types of head injury in the United States but they were often the most difficult in operation. Most victims who suffered these types of wounds died before even reaching the hospital. This young man was part of the lucky ten percent. Gregory knew that aggressive resuscitation was needed. After stabilizing the patient's blood pressure and oxygenation, he immediately ordered a CT scan to see the bullet's trajectory and exactly which parts of the brain had been hit. Depending on what the scan uncovered,

emergent craniotomy and clot evacuations might
be warranted. Simultaneously he worked to determine brain stem function. The team operated
diligently, their movements almost choreographed
like a well-oiled machine. Each person knew that
quick detection of potential problems was critical
and time was not their friend.

Several hours later, a weary Gregory walked into
the doctors' lounge and collapsed on the sofa.
They'd worked on the shooting victim for several
hours. For now he was stabilized but still very critical. Whether he lived or died was now up to a power
greater than him. There had also been five people
wheeled in from a multi-car accident, a construction worker who'd fallen off a three-story scaffold-
ing, and a baby suffering from what looked very
much like shaken baby syndrome. The work had
been nonstop and chances were he'd be lucky to
squeeze thirty minutes of downtime before being
called out again.

It was nine o'clock and the lounge was quiet.
Gregory reached for the remote and turned on the
television, just as a diversion, a way to calm down his
mind from the fast pace of the last several hours.
He'd only flipped through five or six channels
when a scene caused him to stop, sit up, and reach
for the remote.

He turned up the volume and heard, ". . . felt
the spirit of the other artists as they've created

here. Not Lydia Rosenthal." Anise looked into the camera. "And not me."

Gregory noted the fire in her eyes and the way she licked her lips after speaking.

"Well said," the reporter responded. "How do you believe art heals the world?"

"According to a recent study on visual arts," Anise said, looking confident and authoritative as she spoke, "the intrinsic pleasures and stimulation of the art experience connect people to the world around them and open them up to a new way of seeing this world. It creates a foundation to form social bonds and community cohesion, all essential to the world's overall healing. Recent studies have even gone further to suggest that physical healing can also be stimulated through the use of art, particularly visual art, by increasing the person's sense of well being, of wholeness, bringing about a positive outcome. Literally, art gives life. Art *is* life, and the importance of its impact on the world should not be underestimated."

"Spoken like a true artist. This painter, Anise, and many others are hoping that Los Angeles hasn't seen the last of The Creative Space. For Channel Nine News I'm Cynthia White, reporting."

Gregory lay his head back on the sofa, heaved a big sigh, and closed his eyes. *What am I going to do with you, Anise Cartier? How are we going to work this out?*

Soon, he would realize that he wasn't the only one asking this question.

After seeing Gregory for the first time in almost a week, looking handsome and proud despite the chagrin she also imagined he felt, something happened. Some of the anger faded, and in its place came memories of those early conversations about their dreams: hers for an art studio, his for a research center. Few of the protesters in front of the building would know the truth of why she'd feigned a coughing spell and darted into a nearby coffee shop for water. It had been because she couldn't bear to see Gregory again without speaking, couldn't bear this chasm that had come between them as quickly and as forcefully as their affair had begun. For the first time, in those few seconds that they shared air space, she saw the situation from his point of view. He'd achieved his dream, and she was protesting his victory. So she'd run and hid. Not something she was particularly proud of but she'd do it again.

Something about seeing him made her face the truth; that she felt bad about what had happened, felt horrible about the way she'd handled Gregory's good news. She still believed in the art center, still planned to do what she could to save it, but wondered if she could also save what she and Greg had. After arriving home and finding out that her landlord could indeed watch Boomer, she'd reached for her phone and scrolled to a familiar number. "Gregory, it's me," she'd said when she reached his voice mail, which she'd figured she would since he was at work. "I would like to talk about what's happened. Can I come over? I felt so many things when I saw you today and I . . . Listen, just please call me when you get this. Maybe I can meet you at your house when you get off work."

That had been almost two hours ago and Anise had watched the time tick since then. She'd canceled a get-together with Edward so she'd be available if Gregory called. She knew he got off around midnight and the later it got, the more nervous she became. *What if he doesn't call? What will I do then?*

Luckily, she didn't have to find out. At five after eleven, the phone rang.

"Hey, Greg. I'm glad you called." After he acknowledged that he'd gotten her message, she asked, "Can I come over?" She waited. "Now, if that's okay with you. I don't want to wait another day to talk to you. I shouldn't have waited this long. Okay, see you in a bit."

During her drive over, Anise tried to look at this crazy turn of events in an impersonal light. The bottom line was that both she and Gregory had goals and dreams. Her hope was that they could somehow have those, and still hold on to each other.

She reached his house in record time.

"Hey." She walked in, unsure of what to do, or

how he'd react. But when he opened his arms, she stepped right in and gave him a hug. A part of her wanted to stay right there, in his embrace, forever. It always felt so good to be in his arms. She hoped that after this conversation, there would still be a space for her within them.

"Can I get you something to drink?" he asked, when he broke the embrace and walked toward the living room.

"No, I'm good." She didn't wait for him to sit before beginning the spiel she'd worked on during the drive. "I want to start off by apologizing."

Gregory sat down. "For what exactly?"

"Good question," Anise said with a slight smile. "For the way I acted the other day, for starters. That was probably a huge day for you and instead of just being happy that you'd gotten what you wanted I was only focused on what I'd lost. I know that at the end of the day, you only have so much power when it comes to the building and what happens to it. Even though I've said this isn't personal, I clearly took it that way. And I'm sorry."

Gregory nodded, taking in what she'd said. "Wasn't quite expecting a group of protesters when I came to check out the space today."

"Yes, and then there's that. And while I wish that I'd called you, I won't apologize for that. It was an opportunity for us to push the cause for art in general and The Creative Space in particular. It's a platform that resonates with a lot of people and because some of the board members had been told that you would also be there, hinting that there might be some type of argument or altercation, we knew the media would come down."

"Oh, so your march was timed to my arrival."

"'March' is a little excessive. It's not like we held hands and blocked traffic in the street while singing 'We Shall Overcome.'"

"No, but it was a little intimidating to walk up on a group of people dressed in black and accusing us of ending their legacy and killing their dreams."

"Nobody said that about dreams . . . well, not exactly."

"Pretty much."

An awkward silence fell between them. Anise traced the lines on her jeans. Gregory looked at the ceiling, and then at her.

She felt his eyes on her and looked up. "What?"

"I saw you tonight. On television."

"Oh?" He nodded. "What did you think about what I said?"

"I thought it was interesting. But at the end of the day, Anise, I don't know what you and your group think to accomplish. The fact that the art center will close or be moved, and the research center will go into that space is a done deal. I wonder if your energy wouldn't be better used trying to find a new studio. You're going all out for The Creative Space when I thought that opening up your own gallery was your dream. My mom says that everything happens for a reason. Maybe you're losing that space because it's time to look for one of your own."

"I don't have the funds to do that right now."

"What about all of those people holding up picket signs? Maybe y'all could open up one together. If you ask me, that would be a more productive use of your energy."

"Well, I didn't ask you." The words were curt, but a wisp of a smile accompanied the verbal jab.

And then more silence fell.

"I accept your apology," Gregory said as he rose from the couch and walked to stand in front of where Anise was sitting. "And, for what it's worth, I'm sorry that so many of you are unhappy about losing the space." He reached out and tucked an errant strand of hair back behind her ear. "So where does this leave us?"

Anise looked up, her eyes locked with his. "I don't know."

"Well, while you're trying to figure that out will you do me a favor?"

"What's that?"

"Will you help me celebrate my birthday?"

"When is it?"

Gregory looked at his watch. *12:01.* "It's right now."

47

His request made her quiver, even as she thought back to the wonderful afternoon when the whole topic of birthdays had come up—during their third official date, when they were driving up to Malibu. What a wonderful time they'd had that day. Yet so much had changed in so short a time that the memory seemed from long ago.

Still, what he'd asked her made her forget about everything but this man. And this moment.

"Well?" he stood there, with a mere foot or two between them. His hands were by his side, his breath steady, his eyes searching.

"You want me to help you celebrate? After all that's happened?"

"Are you saying you haven't missed me?" He took a step closer. His voice lowered. "I wouldn't ask you if I didn't want it."

"Want what?" Her voice was barely audible as she took a step.

He reached out his hand and lightly ran a finger down her cheek. His smile was subtle as he studied her, while running his hand up and down her arm. "My spicy protestor. Come here." He closed the distance between them and took her in his arms.

It felt like exactly where she was supposed to be. Holding each other, she could feel his heartbeat just as strong as his arms. Could feel the beginning of a five-hour shadow. Could smell his subtle cologne. Unexpectedly, tears came to her eyes. The turmoil was still there—about the grant, the center, this undeniable yet impossible attraction between her and Gregory—but none of it mattered.

"I missed you," she whispered, kissing his cheek. A tear slid from her cheek to his.

He pulled back his head. "Shh, what's this?"

"I'm sorry. I know we've made it hard for you and—"

"Shh. We can get back to our differences tomorrow. Let tonight be about us." He stepped away just long enough for Usher to suggest that they take things nice and slow. Walking back, he took her into his arms. For the first time since Bob Marley, they danced, their bodies slowly beginning to say what words could not.

Anise initiated the first kiss. Raising her head from off his shoulder she kissed his cheek, softly, then his chin; then teased the corners of his mouth with her tongue before swiping it across his luscious lips.

In return, his arms slid from around her waist to cup her butt, even as the beginning of a hard-on pressed against her stomach. He turned his head and slanted his lips over Anise's, to take what she'd started to another level. He pushed his tongue deep into her mouth, touching hers; swirling and tasting, as if for the first time. Her nipples hardened, straining against the lacy fabric that kept them bound.

It was time to do something about that.

Anise stepped back and without breaking eye contact, began to slowly unbutton her blouse. The music had gone from Usher to Maxwell, giving Anise the idea to show him her butterfly.

"Come over here," she demanded, taking his hand and leading him to his couch. "Sit down."

She'd never been to a strip club or danced on a pole, but that didn't stop her. Feeling the music she slowly rubbed the blouse across her body before taking it off and tossing it on the floor. Sliding her hands over her nipples she rubbed them through the mesh-like fabric of her bra as she moved her hips back and forth in time to the music. *Pretty butterfly*. While playing with her breasts with one hand, she slid the other along her stomach and down to her heat. She placed it between her legs and slowly drew it back and forth against the seam of her jeans. Gregory's eyelids drooped. He spread his legs to make room for the third one that was now as hard as steel. Unsnapping the closure on her jeans, she outlined her lips with her tongue as she unzipped the jeans, then slowly lowered them over her hips, thighs and calves, until she stepped out of them and kicked them aside. She placed her fingers inside the elastic of her thong, giving Gregory teasing peeks at what was barely hidden.

Sidling up to him she asked, "Are you having a good time, birthday boy?"

He nodded, rearranging his stuff yet again. When she turned to give him a lap dance, he rearranged it a third time, pushing aside the wispy material covering her treasure and sliding it deep inside her with one long thrust.

Then he took over the dance.

After undoing her bra, he reached around and rolled her nipples between his thumb and forefinger, even as he continued thrusting up as she was bouncing down. The sounds of slapping flesh filled the room, along with love-making's fragrance. Greg directed them to a new position— Anise kneeling as she faced and gripped the back of the couch; Gregory behind her. He resumed their romantic rumba, pounding her relentlessly, teasing her clit. Just when she was about to go over the edge he stopped, knelt down, and let his tongue take over where his dick had left off. She exploded, and he drank her nectar like the finest of wines before lying her on the couch, covering her body with his, and enjoying his own climatic finale.

"Let's move this party to the bedroom," he said after they'd rested, before picking her up and mounting the stairs. They reached the room but instead of heading to the bed, Anise walked over to where she saw a pen and pad on the table in the sitting room.

"What are you doing?" Gregory asked.

"Living out a fantasy. The first time I drew you nude, I too wanted to be naked. Now I am."

"All right. Where do you want me?"

"Laying on the bed."

He complied, and then she sat on top of him, just above his now flaccid member. Before she could get a line drawn, he began teasing her nipples.

"If you don't stop, it's going to take me forever to do this drawing."

"Hey, wait. You said the next time you drew me—" He paused and kissed one nipple and then the other. "I'd have to pay for your talents."

"I did, didn't I?" Anise smiled as she remembered that dinner conversation. "Instead, consider this my gift for you. Happy birthday."

He pulled her close, thrusting his tongue into her hot mouth while she reached for his dick and began to massage it. She'd get to it eventually, but for right now, painting a picture of him—or anything else—would have to wait.

48

Anise stepped into her studio and dumped the load of cardboard boxes she carried. Two weeks had passed since the demonstration and aside from a couple news stories and articles written in a few magazines and the night she'd spent with Gregory for his birthday, not much had changed. The research center was still coming. The artists were still moving out. It seemed like just yesterday that she'd unpacked all of this stuff. And now, all too soon, it was time to pack it up again. She turned off the light, locked the door, and headed down the hallway to the office she shared with Dawn.

"Hey, girl."

"Hey there, Anise. What was that sound I heard?"

"Boxes hitting the ground. I don't want to wait until the last minute. I'm going to box things up a little at a time."

"You're probably doing the right thing. I think a part of me refuses to believe we're leaving. I keep hoping that I'll wake up and find this has all been a dream."

"It's a nightmare that's happened with our eyes wide open. I don't see the Rosenthal brothers reversing their decision. That family has been waiting fifty years to set Lydia straight!"

"Have you ever met her?"

"No, but I feel like I know her from all the stories I've heard. She is a cosmopolitan force to be reckoned with, definitely ahead of her time. From what I hear, she spends most of her time these days in Palm Springs."

"Did we ever hear anything more from the attorneys?"

Dawn shook her head. "There was no way to fight what was in black and white. After fifty years the property reverted back to the owners, who can choose to renew the lease or take the property back. We both know what they've decided."

Anise walked over and sat at her desk, but swiveled the chair around to face Dawn. "So . . . what are you going to do?"

"Thinking about moving. I've been in LA for fifteen years and am about ready for a slower pace. Or at least a different one."

"You're from Oregon, right?"

"Yeah, but I'm not planning to move back there. Beautiful part of the country but too much rain."

"Where to, then?"

"Maybe the East Coast. Or maybe Taos."

"As in New Mexico?"

"They have a wonderful artist community there and my roommate, who's also my bestie, makes jewelry. We've wanted a change of pace for the past few years and when we attended a jewelry fair there last summer, she really fell in love with the place, the people, and the surroundings. So . . . yeah . . . it might be time to pull up stakes."

"Ah, man. You're one of the few friends that I've made here and now you're leaving?"

"There will always be an open invitation to wherever I land." She shuffled a few papers around. "What about you? Any chance for you and that hot doctor you were dating? Damn, girl. When you told me that he was the man you'd been dating, I knew for sure that you were a born artist. Because anybody who'd give up *that* for a paintbrush . . ." The sentence hung unfinished as she shook her head.

The day after the protest, Anise had had a heart-to-heart with Dawn, telling her why she'd spent a large part of the protest away from the picket lines, trying to resolve her feelings. "We'll see. We talked a couple days ago. There's still something there but it may take a while to find our way back to it. Besides, he's really busy right now and I need to be. I need to find a job and Kim Li has asked if I want to share a studio in Leimert Park."

"Anise, that's fantastic!"

"Yes, but we need a third partner. Do you know anyone who might be interested?"

She thought for a moment. "I might ask Truth."

"No, Truth's moving back east."

"Really?"

"Yes, he wants to start an art gallery, too."

"Maybe I'll talk him into staying. He's good people, very even tempered. I wouldn't have to worry about him tripping out when it's that time of the month, you know?"

"You can ask, but his plans sounded pretty solid."

Anise peered at Dawn more carefully. Was it her or was a light shade of red creeping up Dawn's neck. *Hmm, what's going on here? Is it possible that . . . no, couldn't be.* Surely if he and Dawn had become an item, one of them would have told her.

"Do you need these letters right away? If not, I'm going to take fifteen and ask around."

"No worries. I don't have anything else for you after that and, unfortunately these days, the phone is barely ringing."

Truth's studio was the first place she stopped. "I hear you're leaving me. Were you even going to say good-bye?"

Truth turned around, his smock covered with smudges of clay, his hands covered, too. "What are you talking about?"

"Dawn says you're moving back east."

He turned back around, drawing lines into the clay, turning a lump of wet dirt into the image of a little girl. "Looks that way. I have a partner over there who might have a space. I'm going to go over and check it out."

"Good for you."

Truth didn't respond; he was focused on pleats in the little girl's skirt, sculpted to make it appear that the wind was blowing it. Done so well that anybody looking at it could almost feel the breeze.

Anise bypassed the elevator and took the steps. She came to Kim's open door and knocked on it. "Hey, Kim."

Kim turned around. "Hi, Anise."

"Any luck on finding a third person for the gallery?"

Kim's eyes brightened. "So you are interested?"

Anise smiled. "Maybe. The only thing I need is money."

"Girl," Kim said, putting down her palette, "let's start dreaming. The money will come!"

The women put their heads together and when Anise left Kim's studio almost half an hour later, her dream was still breathing.

49

When Anise got home, she called Gregory. The call went to voice mail. It was much this way over the next week; their playing telephone tag or catching snatches of conversation early in the morning or during Gregory's drive home. From what he told her, Anise knew that he had to be very busy—still working his full shift at the hospital and doing the prelim work for his research center.

But she missed him, and was delighted when her phone rang, on a Saturday, just after when his shift usually started: three pm.

"This is a surprise!"

"Hello to you, too," Gregory said, with a chuckle.

"You sound tired. Are you at work?"

"I'm on call today."

"Oh. How's that work?"

"If they call me, I go in."

"Cute. I figured that much!"

"Then why did you ask me, woman?"

"I meant do they . . . Oh, never mind. What are you doing? Besides getting smart."

"Nothing much, watching the game. Thinking about you. Thinking about the way I'd rather be spending my Saturday."

"Yeah?" Anise sat on the couch and placed her feet on the ottoman. Her voice lowered, became silky as she continued. "And how is that?"

"Let's just say it would involve lots of slow music and few clothes."

"Hmm, let's see. You want to sit for another nude painting? You still owe me one from the other night."

"I'll take off my clothes if you will."

"Done!"

"Ha! That would be a nice way to start." A comfortable silence ensued before Gregory said, "Anise."

"Yes?"

"Tell me about Shirley."

"Huh?"

"I've realized something over these past few weeks, during our . . . disagreement . . . and time apart."

"What's that?"

"I don't really know you. I mean, I *know* you, but I don't know all about you. And I want to."

His words and especially the sincerity with which he said them touched her in a way that she hadn't expected, and that hadn't happened before.

"I want to know about that little girl who grew up in Omaha. What was she like?"

"What was Shirley like? She was shy, and quiet, an only child who spent a lot of time alone. I think that's when she first discovered how much she liked to draw. Her mom was a teacher and at night, while she graded papers, she would give little Shirley a piece of paper and a box of colored pencils and Shirley could draw for hours, quiet and content, while she worked. For a whole evening. Interesting . . . it's been a while since I've thought about her, about me as a child."

"How old were you then?"

"I'd say no more than six or seven."

"What else?"

"I loved coloring books. I would color very neatly; even when I was really little I wouldn't color outside the line. Gosh, I couldn't have been more than four or five with the coloring books. I still remember my favorite one, Barney. I would sit in front of the television watching the show, and then try and color the pictures exactly."

"What about friends? Were there many kids on your block? Did you make friends at school?"

"Mom was very particular about who I played with and unfortunately few in my neighborhood qualified. They were—how can I say this nicely?—a little rough around the edges. One Christmas I'd gotten a teacher set with a board, markers, magnetic numbers and alphabet. My friends took it and when I tried to take it back we got in a fight. Okay, I'm revising history. They beat me up."

"Oh, no. My poor baby."

"Stop laughing."

"I'm not!"

He was.

"It was just as well that I had few friends because like I said, I was a quiet child. And I've always been an observer. I think people always assumed I was acquiescent. Quiet people are often misunderstood. But seldom are they stupid."

"What about the boys? I bet the girl they saw fighting isn't what they had in mind."

"Ha! No, and that was another reason the girls didn't like me. Because the boys did. I still remember my first crush. His name was Benjamin; we called him Benny. And I remember the first thing he ever gave me. A cassette tape of the Dr. Dolittle soundtrack."

"Oh, man. What a whack gift!"

"What? I loved that movie! And the cassette was bangin'! It had our favorite song on there."

"What? Something about talking to animals or something?"

"Montell Jordan's 'Let's Ride.'" She began singing the hook.

"I remember that! That song was nice."

"Uh-huh. Told you." A pause and then, "What about you? Tell me about your childhood."

"Don't think you're getting off that easy. I have a lot more questions. But I'll take a turn. What do you want to know?"

"How was it growing up in Long Beach?"

"Very different from your childhood from the way it sounds, starting off with the fact that I have two brothers. The three of us are only four years apart so the sibling rivalries were pretty strong. We loved each other like crazy but fought like mad. Mama would threaten us with the belt while Daddy would suggest letting us kill each other."

"Oh my goodness! He'd say that? What would you do?"

"It was pretty good psychology, actually. When faced with the prospect of that actually happening, we had to ponder: do we really want the other one to die?"

"That's cruel."

"It worked. Some of the time. There were lots of kids on our street and most of us lived there all our lives. We'd have block parties. It was like one big family, really. Especially on the holidays: Memorial Day, Labor Day, Fourth of July. And Christmas, oh, man. Everybody knew what everyone else got because we'd all be outside playing with it, riding it, or wearing it. Those were crazy days."

"When did you and Lori first become boyfriend and girlfriend?"

"You know what? Maybe this walk down memory lane isn't such a good idea."

"No, let's have it. You're the one who started us down this road."

"Okay, if you must know, she is the first girl I kissed. I think we were around seven or so. Michael caught us and threatened to tell. I had to do that boy's chores for a week! Until I caught him playing doctor with her sister, Lisa. Then we were even."

And so the conversation went, back and forth, for almost three hours. Gregory finally got the call to go into work and Anise took Boomer out for his walk. As she observed the beautifully landscaped yards, the fluffy white clouds, and the warm summer breeze, one thing was clear. She had a phone call to make. Edward was a good guy. They had a lot in common, had gone on a couple dates, and could hopefully remain friends. But when it came to who tugged her heart strings, warmed her with a single glance or touch and made her think of happily ever after . . . he was not the one.

50

"Aunt Ree, it's Anise!" Anise adjusted her hands-free device as she changed lanes and prepared to exit the freeway.

"Hello, stranger."

"I deserve that, and I'm sorry for not calling. I've been really busy."

"What's going on?"

Anise told her about the last days at The Creative Space, moving her things back to the apartment, and job hunting. "But I'm calling you because in the midst of all that, I've just received some good news."

"I can always use some of that."

"The house sold!"

"All right! That is good news."

"Yes, and it sold close to the asking price, so even after paying what's owed to the hospital, I'll have some money left to put into savings, and enough to maybe partner in the art gallery I want."

"Gallery?"

"Yes. Kim, an artist from The Creative Space, and I are planning to open one up. We just have to find a third person to partner with us."

"That is wonderful, Anise. Nothing would make me happier than if you'd get to do that. It's what I envisioned for you when you came here."

"Really?"

"Yes. Remember that night back in Omaha? That's what I shared with you—my hope that you'd be able to move out here and make a living doing what you love."

"We're not quite there yet. If we open a gallery, I'll probably still work an outside job, at least until my pieces start selling. I'd rather use my savings as a cushion than live off them."

"Getting yourself set up will still be a step in the right direction. Will you have to go back to Omaha for the sale, to sign papers or anything?"

"Yes, in fact I'm going to leave tomorrow. A friend of mine knows someone who works at the airport and got me a buddy pass—that's like a standby ticket. So I'm going to fly home tomorrow. I'll probably be gone a week or two. I'm going to try and make sure everything is taken care of because once I leave this time, who knows the next time I'll see Omaha."

"What about you and the doctor? How are y'all doing?"

"Better. As long as we don't talk about what happened."

"The fact that he got y'all's place shut down?"

"That's not quite how it was, Aunt Ree. He didn't have anything to do with us moving, directly. The lease would have expired no matter what was happening. But yes, we still haven't really revisited that territory. We have been talking, though. And that's been a good thing. We jumped into a relationship really quickly so it's actually been rather nice slowing things down and just . . . communicating. We've both been really busy so I haven't seen him much. But we talk every day."

"Well, that's good, Anise. If you're happy, I'm happy."

"I am, Aunt Ree."

"Who's going to watch Boomer while you're gone?"

"My landlord. His dog and Boomer are friends so it will be easy for him to keep him. Why, would you rather me bring him over there?"

"No, girl. A dog is a *man's* best friend. Diamonds are mine!"

"Aunt Ree! You're a mess."

"I know. That's why you love me."

"I absolutely do."

A little more than twenty-four hours later and Anise was in a rental car, driving down the familiar streets of Omaha, Nebraska. She called the attorney, made an appointment for the following day, and checked into her hotel. After unpacking her suitcase, she decided to go by her mom's house and to get something to eat.

It was a short drive to her mother's house but to get there she had to pass her old neighborhood and before she knew it, she found herself turning down the street where she grew up. Funny, but she couldn't remember the last time she'd been on this street. Ten years or more, she guessed. She pulled the car over, stopped, and got out. The house was still there and it appeared occupied. She crossed the street, stood on the sidewalk in front of the house. A flood of memories assailed her: sitting and coloring on the steps, playing hopscotch on elaborately colored numbers with imaginary friends, the bullies down the street. She looked up and it was as if she could see her mother beyond the screened porch, now painted black though it was white in her childhood.

She was drawn to that door and without thought she walked down the sidewalk to the steps, and up to the door. She hesitated only briefly before knocking once, and then again. A woman carrying a baby came to the door.

"Yes?" she said when she opened it, and none too friendly.

"Hi. I'm sorry to bother you. But my name is—"

"Shirley? Shirley Carter?"

Anise squinted, trying to recognize the woman. "Pat?" The older sister of the bully down the street. "I was expecting to see a stranger. I can't believe you still live on the block."

"Yeah. I was living over in the projects. But that was before I got married."

"You're married? Congratulations."

"Thank you. Me and him together got five kids. But he's a good man. He works. Bought this house."

"You own it?"

"Uh-huh."

"Wow, I can't believe you live in my old house."

"It's not old no more. The last people who lived here had it updated. You want to come in and see it?"

"I'd love to if you don't mind. I stopped by because it holds so many memories of me and my mom."

"Yeah, I heard about her passing. My condolences."

Anise stepped through the door but unlike how she felt when she turned onto the street, she didn't step back in time. The inside of the house looked very different. They'd torn down a wall and what used to be two separate rooms, a living room and a dining room, was now one combined space. The kitchen was just beyond it, but the wallpaper had been replaced by a light gray paint, which paired well with the black appliances. The closest to the room of her childhood was the bedroom, but her white wrought-iron princess set had been replaced with a bunk bed and a crib. True, she had once lived here. But this was no longer her home.

"How's your sister doing?"

"Jean?" Anise nodded. "She's all right. She lives in Kansas City."

"Wow, small world. That's where I went to college. Did she move up there to attend school?"

"Girl, please. You know Jean. She ain't changed. Only school that child has been to is the one of hard knocks."

"Funny, but I was just talking to someone about growing up here, and how she beat me up."

"I don't remember that."

"She probably doesn't either." After catching up a bit more, Anise thanked Pat and said, "Take care of yourself."

Five blocks and two turns later Anise stopped at the elementary school where she attended and her mother taught. As she looked at the now empty playground, she could almost hear the sounds of yesterday, could remember recess when she got to see her mother from time to time. She'd always wanted her mother to be her teacher, but they would always put her in a different class. Again, as if compelled, she got out of the car and walked to the playground. The swings were no longer there but she could still see the grooves where they once stood. She walked to what looked to be a newly painted half basketball court and then over to a set of benches, also new.

"Things are so different here, Mommy," she whispered. "I guess that's life though, huh? Things change. People change. We move on. That's what I'm doing, too. You probably know that the house sold. I meet with Bob tomorrow. Once we finalize this transaction and I leave, I don't know when or if I'll come back here. I don't really have a reason to. Like Aunt Ree said, your spirit is with God, and wherever I go. Right?"

A group of boys came around the corner, acting rowdy and talking loud. One of them was bouncing a basketball.

Anise smiled, stood, and walked to her car. A week and a half later she left Omaha.

Things change. People change. We move on.

When she turned her phone back on after arriving in Los Angeles, Anise's mother once again seemed to give her a message; proof that she was indeed with her wherever she was.

The call was from Kim.

She'd found a third partner, and the papers were all ready to be signed. They had the space.

Things were changing in LA as well. The place once known as The Creative Space had been totally gutted. New windows, wiring, floors, walls, lighting—new everything had been installed. Gregory had no idea he'd love this part of the process, had never even considered being involved with the construction of his center. But to see his baby come from nothing, from a shell of a building to what it was now, was amazing. And to see his staff come from just him and Dr. Meyers to a team of seven, even better.

He took one last look around before leaving the crew to their work, then headed out into the Santa Monica sunshine. He'd just reached his car when his phone rang.

"Michael!"

"Greg."

"What's going on, man?"

"Nothing much. What are you doing?"

"I'm just leaving the research center."

"How's it looking?"

"It's crazy how fast they're renovating that place. It's starting to look like a workplace."

"You know that all work and no play makes Jack a dull boy."

"That's what they say."

"That's why I'm calling. I've got floor tickets to the Lakers game."

"I'm there. What time? I need to go home and change."

"Don't bother with that. You're already in Santa Monica so you might as well come here. I'll find something in my reject pile that you can wear."

"Gee, thanks. Have you eaten?"

"I figured we could go early; grab something at the center."

"Sounds like a plan. Hey, wait. What about Troy?"

"He'll be there, working."

"Cool. I'm on my way."

A short time later, Gregory and Michael strolled into the Staples Center, where even though it was early, there was already a crowd. Michael called Troy and a few minutes later he came strolling toward them, dressed in his signature black, with black sunglasses. Even inside. Even in the dark.

The brothers exchanged fist pounds and shoulder bumps before Michael spoke. "Can you take a little break, bro? Gregory and I were going to grab something to eat at the Bus Stop. I've got a taste for sushi but Gregory wants a turkey sandwich."

"Fellahs, fellahs," Troy said, putting an arm around each of them and walking them in the opposite direction. "Haven't I taught you two anything about how we do it in the big leagues?"

"Oh, here we go," Gregory said with a groan.

"He's getting ready to regurgitate one of my lessons," Michael drawled. When it came to arena suites and plush box seats, this successful manager of several superstar athletes was a regular.

They neared an already crowded suite and Troy turned to them with brightly-colored wristbands. "Here, put this on and don't take it off unless you have no plans to come back in here."

"I don't need that," Michael said, waving away the fluorescent red band. "Everybody working at Staples Center knows who I am."

"That may be, but because of the beef between Mr. President and that hothead rapper Dark Knight, and the public threats he's made towards my client, my men have strict instructions. No one gets into the suite without a wristband. Even you, big brother."

Michael nodded as he accepted the band. What his brother said made sense. Mr. President was the hottest hip-hop artist in the game right now. And Dark Knight's penchant for drama was as well known as his number-one hit singles. He and Gregory exchanged glances. It was going to be an interesting night.

They walked in and two things were immediately evident: food and ladies. Knowing which one he preferred at the moment, after exchanging pleasantries with the host Gregory headed straight to the buffet. He fixed a plate and found a seat next to the window, where he could see the crowd. Taking a bite of his filet mignon taco, he saw the usual: beautifully dressed women mixed with those wearing jeans, kids waving banners and other memorabilia and die-hard fans dripping in purple and gold. He was just getting ready to take another bite when someone in the seats below him and to his right caught his eye. He was mostly seeing the back of the man's head so he had to wait until he turned to the courts to be sure but when he did, there was no doubt. *Drew Fordham.* As big as LA was, and even in a crowd of thousands, his caution radar had still scoped that dude out. He continued to watch casually and what really began to intrigue him wasn't so much that Drew was there but who he was with, someone who looked totally unlike a person that image-conscious Drew would hang around: stringy hair covered with a Lakers cap, Lakers T-shirt, khaki pants and thick black-rimmed glasses. Gregory didn't know why but the picture somehow looked incongruent.

Before he could ponder the image further, his phone dinged with a text message. He hurriedly responded.

What? You're here? You're back in town?

An hour later he was in a town car, headed over to a guesthouse studio in Venice. Troy could hang with the big boys if he wanted to. Right now, Gregory preferred the company of an out-of-work artist and her oversized dog.

51

Since returning from Omaha, Anise and Gregory had been together almost constantly; in fact, she'd spent more nights at his house than she had at her own. He'd even broken down and gotten Boomer dog bowls and a pillow for him to lay outside. But today, her cuddly was hanging out with his baby-sitter, Aretha. And Anise was hanging out with a cuddly cutie as well.

"You know what?" Anise said, as they exited the highway and entered Long Beach's Shoreline Drive area. "I really like Long Beach. I think I could live here."

"It's got a cool little vibe."

"Do you think you'd ever move back?"

"No. The next time I move it will be to an ocean view property though, someplace like Pacific Palisades or Palos Verdes."

"Are they as pretty as Malibu?"

"I think each area of California has its own

beauty, and each of these areas has stunning views. I have friends who live in both cities. The next time I'm invited over, I'll take you with me so you can see what paradise looks like."

"I'd like that."

"Would you like to live near the ocean?"

"Maybe close enough so that I could see it but far enough to outrun a tsunami."

"Ha! Good point."

They turned into Jackie's gated community and were soon inside her high-rise condo, with unobstructed floor-to-ceiling views of the marina on one side and the Pacific Ocean on the other.

"Hello, come in," Jackie said as she opened the door and gave first Gregory a hug and then Anise. "Anise, it's good to see you. For a minute there, I—"

"Mom," Gregory carried just the right amount of warning in his voice.

"What? I think it's great that the two of you were able to work out your differences, that's all." She ignored Gregory's frown and placed a hand on Anise's shoulder. "Come on and have a seat. Would you like something to drink?"

"Whatever you're having."

"Gregory, will you be a dear and get all of us some of that freshly brewed iced tea in the refrigerator?" She turned back to Anise. "I hope you don't mind that it's just going to be the three of us today."

Gregory came back from the kitchen. "Where is everybody?"

"The tea, Gregory?" He frowned, but returned to the kitchen. He might have been a renowned ER doctor at UCLA Medical but in Jackie's house he was whatever she needed, which at the moment was a server. "And wipe that frown off your face, son." She winked at Anise.

"I love those flowers," Anise said. "What kind are they?"

"The only ones I know are the orange and purple, which is bird-of-paradise, and those red ones with the yellow tubelike thing, which are called anthuriums. And the only reason I know that crazy name is because those are one of my best friend's favorites."

"They are gorgeous."

"Robert brought them for me. Thanks."

Gregory came around the corner with a tray carrying three glasses of tea and a saucer of lemons. He set the tray down on the table in front of the ladies. "It's already sweet, Anise." He kissed her temple. "Like you."

"Ah." Jackie beamed. "That's so nice."

Gregory sat down. "So where is everybody, Mom? I can't remember the last time we weren't all here for dinner."

"Me either. It seems like something came up at the last minute for everyone but y'all." She saw Gregory's eye narrow. "I did not plan this, son, though I am happy to spend some time with just the two of you. I knew that Robert wasn't going to be here last night. He has an army buddy in town and they're out fishing. Michael called this morning saying that Shayna wasn't feeling well and that he was going to stay home and take care of her. Then it wasn't a good half hour before Troy was calling saying he was taking an impromptu trip with some friends to Palm Springs."

"It's all good, Mom. I like having you all to myself." Gregory leaned over and kissed his mother's cheek.

"You always were the one who would spend time with me, even though you and Sam were so close." She turned to Anise. "After his dad died, Greg would keep me company on Friday nights. I'd pop popcorn or make chicken wings and we'd rent a movie or watch Jay Leno. Remember, son?"

"Yes," he said with a smile.

"You seem like the good son," Anise said to Gregory before asking Jackie, "Who was the troublemaker, Michael or Troy?"

"Troy," both Jackie and Gregory said at once, and then laughed.

"Without a doubt that youngest one gave me my first gray hairs."

"Michael was the entrepreneur," Gregory offered. "He always had one business going while keeping an eye for the next big idea."

"They were all so different," Jackie said. "Yet tighter than the Three Musketeers. At one time, when they were around nine, ten years old, Michael and Gregory could almost pass for twins."

"Really?"

"I kid you not. Hold on, I'll be right back."

Jackie left the room and returned with two worn photo albums.

"Oh, no, not the pictures from back in the day."

"What, you don't want Anise to see when you had braces? Or when you were trying to look like Kid 'n Play?"

"You wore a fade! Oh, please, Jackie, let me see!"

For the next hour, the three looked at pictures and reminisced about old times. They ate dinner and then shared more stories during dessert. As Anise looked at photos and learned more about Gregory, an idea began to form in her mind. When he excused himself to go to the bathroom, she proposed it to Jackie.

"Do you think he'll like it?" she asked.

"I think that is a lovely idea, Anise. I think you should do it, and I'll be glad to help."

52

Anise blew an errant strand of hair away from her face. After almost eight hours of nonstop transporting, moving, hanging, and arranging, she was sweaty, hungry, and her feet hurt. But none of that could take away from the day's excitement: opening her art gallery! Well, not totally hers but close enough for jazz. She, Kim Li from The Creative Space, and YaYa Senghor, the Senagalese sculptor and painter that Kim had met online had pooled together their resources and renovated a small yet classy two-room showroom in Leimert Park, in the rear part of a popular coffee shop. The owner of the shop was even going to allow them to place their work on her café walls to increase their exposure and drive traffic back to the shop. The fifteen percent commission per painting was a small price to pay to have a place where her work could be permanently displayed. On top of that, the owner's son was a Web site designer who'd given her an excellent deal on redesigning her Web site. As of noon yesterday, anyone who wanted to see her work could check out almost her entire collection at ArtbyAnise.com.

"Where do you want these sculptures, Anise?" Truth's muscles bulged under the weight of the three-foot-high figure he carried of a man hugging his son.

"We're going to feature your work on that raised dais over there." Anise pointed him in the right direction and watched him place this particular piece front and center. She would have loved for Gregory to be here to help her, and to attend tonight's opening, but it was rare that he had a weekend off and this one was no exception. As it was she was happy that Truth was here. She knew that some of his work was still in an LA storage facility and when she'd offered to sell it on consignment at the gallery, he jumped at the chance. Having to wrap up some business anyway, he'd come back from Philly to help her, where he and a friend were trying to set up something a bit like she'd once envisioned. They wanted a place that would serve as an art gallery during the day and a spoken word/alternative music scene at night.

Truth finished bringing in his art and joined Anise, who was standing in the middle of the floor, looking around. "These stark white walls make the pictures really pop."

She nodded, still eyeing the room critically. "I

wish we'd been able to get those recessed lights installed. That would have really added dimension."

"Yeah, but those sconces aren't a bad alternative. And the live plants are a nice touch."

"Do you think there's too many pictures on the wall?"

Truth shook his head. "I think that everywhere the eye lands, there is something to see." He nodded to a small space near the door. "What's going there?"

"Our music. We found a one-man band on Craigslist. He'll be bringing keyboards and swears he can sound like a four-piece band."

"Nice." Truth's phone rang. Anise noticed his countenance change as he read the screen. "I have to take this," he said, backing away.

"Girlfriend?" She took his shy smile and silence as an affirmative answer. She knew that at one time he'd been interested in seeing if they could take things to another level. *So a business isn't the only thing poppin' in Philly, huh, Truth? Good for you.* She noted one of the partners, Kim, walking in the door with the catering company. *Excellent.* That was the last thing she was waiting on before going to Aretha's to shower and change. She told Kim she was leaving and then headed out the door.

Fifteen minutes later she was knocking on her aunt's front door.

"Hey, Anise!" Aretha stepped back so that she

could enter and gave her a hug. "How's everything coming together?"

"There were a few glitches but overall, very well." She filled her aunt in on the day's happenings. "I only have about an hour to get ready. You and Bruce still coming, right?"

"I wouldn't miss it, girl. What about Gregory?"

"He couldn't get off."

"Oh, darn. That's too bad."

Anise shrugged. "It is what it is."

"Do you want me to call Bruce and see if we can get there early? If he's not ready I can ride with you and have him meet me there. I hate for you to have to do all this by yourself."

"Thanks, Aunt Ree, but that's okay. My partners are there, plus a friend of mine who's also an artist has come back from Philly for the opening."

Aretha's brow rose. "Hmm, a friend, huh? Coming all the way across the country—he sounds like more than that!"

"Gregory doesn't have anything to worry about. Truth does these amazing sculptures, mostly out of clay, but we're also showing one he's done from glass and another from wood."

"Sounds talented."

"He is." Anise looked at her watch. "Oh, goodness, Aunt Ree. Let me get in the shower. Time is flying by."

Forty-five minutes later a freshly showered Anise parked her car in the lot near the coffee shop and headed toward the door. Her heart dropped a little because even though it was a Saturday night the streets were fairly quiet, empty parking spaces were plentiful, and only two of the ten tables inside the shop were occupied. With a lift of her chin and a deep breath, she reached for the doorknob and went inside. Whether there were two people in Artfully Yours, or two hundred . . . it was showtime!

Okay, counting her, there were ten. If you didn't count her, the two other partners, Shawn, the caterer, and the musician setting up his keyboard . . . there were four. But they were here! *I wonder if Edward will come?* Since getting back with Gregory and telling her internet friend that she was only interested in a platonic relationship, their daily chats had all but vanished. But he'd been her support when she really needed it. He'd believed in her dream and encouraged her to keep believing it, too. That's what she reminded him when she sent him a personal invite. *I hope he shows up.*

She looked at her watch. 7:15. Considering that the showing was from seven until ten, she figured she'd wait an hour before panicking. That decided, she walked over to the table laden with champagne flutes and hors d'oeuvres. The rest of the catering staff had obviously arrived as evidenced by the organized chaos happening in a small room just beyond the table. She noted how classy Kim looked, standing a few feet from the table, in her little black dress and five-inch heels as she stood talking to a well-dressed Asian man. It made Anise glad that she'd decided to forego her first choice in what to wear—a black dress—and choose the skin-tight maxi with abstract print and dolman sleeves.

"Here we go!" she said as she approached them, raising up her hand for a high five.

"Yes!" Kim smiled. "Anise, I want you to meet my brother, Jie. Jie, this is Anise."

"Nice to meet you."

They shook hands.

"I like your work," he said.

"Good. Just pick out the one or twelve that you like. I'll give you a good deal."

By nine o'clock Anise was glad to see that there was a nice crowd milling around the room. The champagne was flowing, the music was playing, and several pieces, including one of her more expensive ones, had already sold.

"I might have a buyer for *Father and Son,*" Truth said, nodding at the large clay figurine that had garnered much attention.

"Really, Truth? That would be awesome!"

"Sure would, considering I need rent next month."

"Oh, man. You shouldn't have come if your money was funny. We could have worked out some way for me to get your stuff out of storage. I would have sold it even if you weren't here."

"It's all good. I had to come anyway to handle some business. Besides, when you blow up and have your art in celebrity homes, I want to be able to say I knew you when. What about you? Sold anything?"

"Yes. One of my larger pieces. So thanks to the buyer who left before I could thank him or her, I can cover rent a few months myself."

"Congratulations," Truth said, turning to give her a hug.

She put her arms around his neck . . . and was promptly pinched on the butt. "Truth!"

"What?"

"I felt that!"

"Felt what?"

Someone pinched her again. She whirled around, her hand ready to slap the audacity out of whoever was feeling her behind. "What the—Gregory!" Agitation turned to exhilaration as she hugged him. "What are you doing here?"

53

Gregory leaned down and kissed her cheek. "I got a doctor to cover me for a few hours; couldn't miss your big day."

"I'm so glad you're here! I have someone for you to meet." She introduced Gregory to Truth. "Come on, let me show you his sculptures. They're amazing." She and Gregory began walking to the other side of the room.

"Didn't I see Aretha?" he asked.

"Yes, she and Bruce got here about twenty minutes ago."

"Have you seen Troy?"

"No. Is he coming?"

"I told him about it. You know he lives in Leimert Park, not too far from here."

"If you told me, I forgot."

"When I said the name, he knew exactly where this place was. Told me he'd try and stop by."

"That would be great. I'd love to get my work into the homes of some of the clientele he guards."

"That would be terrific."

They continued to meander around the room, stopping at one of Kim's exquisite watercolors. "Guess what?"

"What?"

"I sold a painting."

"Really? Baby, that's great!"

"One of the more expensive ones, too. I'm so happy. And now that you're here, my evening is perfect."

"No, the evening is perfect because I've arrived."

Gregory and Anise turned around. "Troy!" she said, walking over to give him a hug. "Thanks so much for coming."

"The newest and most exciting grand opening happening in my neighborhood? You know I couldn't miss this!"

There was something else that Troy hadn't missed. He wasn't quite sure what it meant but he'd gotten a gut feeling and was definitely alert. Having planned to only stay a half hour or so, Troy now knew he'd be here until the event ended. He reached for his phone and texted the honey he'd planned to meet up with afterwards before rejoining his brother, now alone, as Anise greeted more guests.

"This is nice," he said to Gregory. "Looks like a success."

"I couldn't be more proud," Gregory said. "And relieved."

"Now you can stop feeling guilty?"

"Exactly." Gregory noticed Troy scoping out the intimate gathering. "Man, if I didn't know better, I'd say you were on the clock."

"Security personnel are never totally off duty," Troy replied. "Checking things out, keeping people safe, is what we do."

"Well, chill out, man. You're at an art gallery. I don't think you have to worry about danger tonight."

Troy chuckled. "You're probably right. I'm going to go over and grab a glass of bubbly. You want one?"

"No. I'm going back to the hospital after a bit."

"They've probably got something non-alcoholic."

"I'll take that."

Troy strolled over to the drink table, barely aware of the female eyes that followed him across the room. There were two members of the catering team, a man and a woman, chatting behind the table.

"Good evening," he said. "Do you have anything non-alcoholic?"

"No."

"Yes."

They'd both spoken at once.

"I didn't think we had any of the sparkling juice left," the young woman said.

"Yes, we do. It's in the back." The man smiled at Troy. "I'll get it and bring it over to you, sir."

"It's not for me. It's for the man standing over there." He pointed at Gregory.

"Okay. A sparkling juice coming right up!"

Troy took the flute of champagne from the server's outstretched hand. He turned to walk back over where Gregory now chatted with an Asian couple. But just as he did so, something caught his eye that caused him to turn back toward the table, just in time to see the man he'd spoken to about the juice, go out the back door. Without thought or hesitation, Troy placed down the flute of champagne and headed out the front door. He didn't know why, he just did it. Because of that something in this gut.

Once outside, Troy casually scoped the perimeter. Nothing looked out of the ordinary. He walked down the sidewalk and turned right, so that he could get a better look at the sides, front and back of the building. As he neared the coffee shop he slowed his pace, wanting to be able to look in the window without being seen. When he did, he saw the young caterer talking to another man. They exchanged something and then the caterer hurried back through the door that led into the art gallery.

Troy took a moment to study the man still sitting at the back table before returning to the art gallery through their front entrance. He retrieved another flute of champagne, walked around, and tried to figure out why he was getting this strange vibe from the caterer dude. Both of the guys were young, in their twenties. *Maybe the man was copping some 420 for after work, or a little ecstasy for an after-hours rave party.* Troy had been young once and while he'd never been too interested in drugs, he knew the culture, knew how it worked. *Maybe his boss was watching and he took the opportunity of getting the juice as one to score some drugs as well.*

"Greg is right," he mumbled to himself. "You're tripping." He downed the champagne and walked over to one of the art pieces, determined to shake off this discomfort and have a good time.

The second Troy made this decision he heard the sound of breaking glass. What he saw upon turning around almost stopped his heart. The man for whom he'd take a bullet was sprawled on the floor.

"Gregory!"

54

Before Troy covered the short distance to his brother, Anise was already by Gregory's side. Meanwhile, Kim and Truth had jumped into action and were ushering the patrons into the other room to give Gregory privacy from the curious gawkers.

Anise was panicked. "Baby, what happened?"

"Drink . . ." Gregory muttered. "Hospital."

"I've already called 9-1-1," Troy said, kneeling opposite Anise. "Hang on, man. We'll get you to UCLA."

"Closer," Gregory mumbled.

"All right, all right," Troy said, bending down closer to his brother. "Just hang with me."

"No, nearest . . . hospital," Gregory whispered. His eyes fluttered.

Troy's eyes widened. "Stay with me, bro!"

"Gla . . ." Gregory was moving, motioning, trying to do something that neither Anise nor Troy understood.

"Don't try to talk, Greg," Anise said, trying to be helpful. "The ambulance is on its way."

"Glass," Gregory persisted, frowning with the effort it took for him to talk and stay conscious. "Get . . . glass."

"Water?" Anise asked.

Gregory pointed feebly at the shattered glass of the champagne flute before he lost consciousness.

The paramedics arrived just in time.

Two and a half hours later a sore, exhausted yet still alive Gregory recuperated in a private room at Inglewood's Centinela Medical Center. The doctor had given a preliminary diagnosis and the nurses had finally left the room. For the first time since the drama began, Troy, Gregory and Anise were alone.

"Look, bro. I know they put that tube down your throat and it's sore. So don't try and talk but I need you to listen. Then nod your head once for yes and two for no. Okay?"

Gregory nodded once.

Troy then shared with both Gregory and Anise the bad feelings he'd gotten earlier in the evening; about the weird vibe coming off of the server and how after asking for a non-alcoholic drink, he'd seen the same guy over in the coffee shop exchanging something with another guy there.

"That's when it happened," Troy exclaimed, the picture becoming clearer as he repeated it to

Gregory and Anise. "I'd bet my company on it. He got something and put it in your drink. I knew I felt something," Troy said, his eyes narrowed, his stance determined. "And I was right. It was the caterer, Greg. Did you recognize any of the catering staff?"

Greg nodded twice.

"You guys hired them, Anise. How were they referred?"

"I'm not sure, Troy. I was working during much of the actual planning for the event but I believe she went through a planner she met online. I'm just not sure."

"The guy in the coffee shop looked shady, too."

"What did he look like?" Anise asked.

"On the slender side," Troy said, his mind's eye recalling the details, probably around five-eleven, six feet. He had reddish-brown hair stuffed under a baseball cap and wore these black, thick-ass glasses."

Anise's head whipped up. "That sounds like my friend, Edward. But no, couldn't be. I don't believe there's any way that he would have been that close and not come to my opening."

Troy pulled out his phone and opened a memo pad. "Okay, Anise. I need you to tell me all about this friend of yours. Start at the beginning."

* * *

Less than two weeks later, Troy was knocking on Gregory's door.

"Here's the man!" Gregory said once he'd answered the door. He and his brother shared an embrace. Since the scare on the night of Anise's grand opening, they'd hugged more often, every time they saw each other in fact.

"Finally getting your color back, I see," Troy teased.

"Brother like me doesn't lose his color," Gregory retorted.

"You didn't see yourself on that gurney. I tell you no lie, man, you were as white as the sheet!"

"Whatever, fool. Can I get you something to drink, some water . . . a beer?"

"Water's fine. I can't stay long."

"What did you come over for then?"

"My company and our investigator partners have just concluded the investigation into what happened to you that night. More specifically, we were able to identify Edward Durkovich—the guy who knew Anise through Facebook and who you believed you saw at the Lakers game with that asshole Drew."

"What did you find out?"

"I found out that you're right. There is a connection. Edward's sister dated Drew's younger brother. At one point, Drew helped him get a summer job at his parents' country club. Obviously they kept in touch. I believe Drew put him up to becoming friends with Anise so he could keep tabs on your whereabouts without raising suspicion, and then paid him to put a near-lethal dose of something in your drink."

"Can we prove it?"

"According to the investigator, we don't have enough that would hold up a case in the court of law. But don't you worry about that. We have our own court of justice, and punishment will be meted out."

"I knew he was capable of a lot of things, but I never thought he'd stoop this low."

Troy snorted. "Well, he did."

"I don't want you going off half-cocked," Gregory warned. "If you're involved with anything happening to Drew, the connection will be made and it will come back to haunt me."

"You underestimate me, brother. I'd never do anything to jeopardize your reputation. Especially with the high profile you've risen to given the grant. But trust me, we can't let this crap go unanswered. One way or the other, Drew Fordham is going to be dealt with."

Gregory sighed. "Tell me what you found out."

"Because Anise met him online, the first thing we did after positively identifying him was go after his IP address. We were able to confirm that he indeed was the one who'd been corresponding with Anise. There's one other person that for the past few months he's talked to quite regularly."

"Drew."

"Exactly." As often happened when he was hyped, Troy stood and paced the room. "I figure it went down like this: You got the grant. Drew got pissed."

"He wanted revenge."

"He wanted to make sure that even though you received the grant, you didn't get to stick around and enjoy it."

Gregory looked at his brother, his brows creased. "You really think he was trying to kill me?"

"Hell, you're the doctor, man. Whatever he gave you sent you to your knees after one small flute-full. What do you think?"

"I think we've got a renegade doctor who needs to be dealt with."

The brothers bumped fists.

"What do you want to happen?" Troy asked.

"I think it would be a good idea if he left town."

"He's out of here, brother, believe that. I'll talk to my guys. It's as good as done."

55

Shortly after Troy's visit, Gregory was almost back to one hundred percent. To celebrate, he told his brothers that he wanted to get on the court and make them look bad. Both Michael and Troy were more than ready to take him up on that challenge and readily agreed to meet at the athletic club. They wore old T-shirts and stretched-out shorts, but anybody looking at the three men walking onto the athletic club's basketball court would have assumed that they were successful. One simply could not fake the kind of swagger that oozed from the Morgan brothers' pores. More than once, when either guarding or hanging with one of his pro baller friends, Troy had often been mistaken for a baller himself. And more than once, he'd chosen not to correct the willing female. Even without the designer suit and Rolex watch, Michael looked like he could easily swing a million-dollar deal, and scrubs and surgical tools aside, Gregory looked like a healer.

The three were unaware of their collective sex appeal as they bounced the ball among them before taking it to the board. But all of the women who'd seen them had noticed. And some of the men.

"Stop acting like taking a shot is an executive decision, Michael," Troy taunted. "Pass the ball!"

"Stop whining like a girl," Michael replied, posting up and sinking a three-pointer with ease.

Gregory shimmied to his left and caught Troy off guard, taking the ball he'd rebounded after Michael had shot. "Let's settle this on the court, boys."

"Three-way," Troy said, referring to the twenty-one-point game they'd made up when their mother demanded that they all play together if they couldn't take turns without arguing.

"Ball," Michael said, giving Gregory a nod to throw the ball. "Today, the oldest goes first."

"How you figure?" Troy asked. "If anything the youngest should start."

"Both of you need to take it down a notch." Gregory walked toward the brothers. "We're going to determine who starts the way we always do— shooting from the top of the key. First one who makes the basket gets the ball. If we all make it on the first shot, then we keep shooting until the tie is broken."

"Listen to the voice of authority," Troy said. "Getting that grant must have confused you, son. That center is the only thing you're running. I own the court." As he said this, however, he lined up behind

Gregory, who'd taken and made the first shot. He too sank his shot, nothing but net.

"Yes, he got the grant but almost lost the girl," Michael said. He aimed, fired, and missed. "Damn!" Throwing the ball to Gregory, he asked, "But that's all resolved, right?"

"Everything's cool. That's what we doctors do," Gregory said. "We fix things."

"Oh, man, careful with the crap talking," Troy said. "I didn't wear my doodoo boots." They laughed. "He's buying her affection, Michael."

"How's that?"

"Let's just say the next time we go over to Gregory's house, his walls will be covered with Anise's art."

"Don't listen to him, Michael. Of course I'm going to support her, but so far I've only bought one piece. She doesn't even know it yet. It's getting a custom frame." Gregory shot the ball and missed. He passed it to Troy.

"Told you the oldest was going first. You two have known me all your life and still refuse to believe I'm always right."

"Whatever, dog. Troy, did you buy anything the other night?"

"No."

"Well, I expect that to change. In fact, I expect to see her artwork in both your homes and offices."

"Is that so?" Michael asked. "Um, when is the last time you came to one of Shayna's track events?"

"When is the last time you invited me?"

"I agree with Michael, Greg. When is the last time you supported one of the women I'm dating?"

"I try and stay out of the strip clubs, son. I've got a reputation to protect."

Gregory dodged the ball that Troy threw at his head. And then their game of three-way began.

After forty-five minutes of serious hoops the brothers took a break. As was often the case this time of day, they were the only ones in the gym.

"What's the latest on that situation," Michael asked, as he uncapped a bottle of water. He and his wife Shayna had been doing track meets across the country. He'd kept up with most of the family business, but not all.

"You'll have to ask Troy," Gregory said. "I figured the less I knew, the better."

Troy wiped sweat from his face and chest before draping his lean frame across a couple bleachers. "Neither one of you has to worry," he said. "Me and my boys would never do anything against the law. But let's just say that a couple of my law enforcement friends have very persuasive personalities. They've had a chat with good old Drew. Told him things could get messy if all of his little shenanigans—which are all documented and can be proven—saw the light of day."

This got Gregory's attention. "Documented? I thought that's why we didn't take this to court. Because it couldn't be proven."

"Drew doesn't know that. And like I said, my guys are very convincing. So don't be surprised if you read about his resignation in the paper."

"I had second thoughts about him leaving," Gregory intoned, as he rubbed his head.

"Having him leave the city is much more civil than what I had in mind," Troy replied. "Trust me on that, bro."

Michael plopped down next to Troy. "Sounds fair to me, Greg. He could have gotten worse."

"Much worse," Troy agreed.

"Next question," Michael said.

"Last question," Gregory corrected. "I'm ready to put that unfortunate incident behind me. I'm tired of talking about it."

Michael nodded and said, "Are we going to tell Mama?"

"No." Gregory's reply was quick and decisive.

"Best she doesn't know," Troy agreed.

"I hear you. But you know how she is; she has a way of finding out stuff that even the FBI hasn't mastered. If she gets wind of anything—"

"She won't," Troy interrupted.

"If you say so."

"We do," Gregory said.

"Then I guess since you dodged a funeral, all that's left for her to do is start planning the wedding."

"Your logic is whack, son," Gregory said, throwing the ball at Michael, who ducked. "But I could see being with Anise for the rest of my life."

56

Gregory went to the kitchen and opened a beer. Then he went into his home office, sat behind the desk, and fired up his computer. For a moment he just sat there, fingers poised over the keys. He still couldn't believe she'd talked him into it, but he'd agreed to take Anise's advice and look up the correlation between art and healing. In all of his years of schooling, residency and beyond, he'd never heard of these two modalities being teamed together. But the thought that he and Anise could work together for a common cause, after enduring and overcoming conflict, was appealing. So here he sat.

He typed "healing arts" into the search engine. Sites dealing with psychology, massage, hypnotherapy, nutrition, and holistic health popped up. *No, that's not it.*

"Let's try healing with art." He typed those words

into the search engine and was rewarded with a myriad of Web sites. He began clicking on ones that looked interesting, finally finding a site that sounded similar to what Anise had shared with him:

Scientific studies tell us that art heals by changing a person's physiology and psyche. Through exposure to art, the body-mind changes from one of tension to one of deep relaxation, from one of fear to one of creativity and inspiration. The visual arts and music can modulate brain wave pattern and alter the production of neurotransmitters, and can also affect the autonomic nervous system and endocrine system.

Art and music affect every cell in the body instantly to create a healing physiology that changes the immune system and blood flow to all the organs. Art and music also have an impact on a person's perceptions of the world. The arts change attitude, emotional state, and pain perception. They create hope and positivity and they help people cope with difficulties. They transform a person's perspective and way of being in the world.

In fact it is now known by neurophysiologists that art, prayer, and healing all come from the same source in the body; they all are associated with similar brain wave patterns and mind-body changes. Art, prayer, and healing all take us into our inner world, the world of imagery and emotion, of visions and feelings. This journey inward, into what used *to be called the spirit or soul and is now called the mind, is deeply healing. For healing comes to us from within when our own healing resources are freed to allow our immune system to operate optimally. This contemporary perspective is now recognized to be crucial to the health of the body and mind. We go inward on The Creative Spiral together through art and music.*

"Interesting." Gregory clicked on other sites that dealt with the history of art as a healing modality, techniques of self-healing, and authors who'd written books on the subject. For more than an hour he perused the Web, with the link of one site often leading him to two or three others. By the time he shifted gears and began checking e-mails he'd made a few phone calls and a decision. After finishing up on the computer, he again reached for the phone.

"Anise, Gregory."

"Hey, baby."

"What are you doing right now?" Gregory interrupted.

"Working."

"How long before you can get away?"

"Why? What's going on?"

"I want you to come over."

"Are you taking me to dinner? I haven't eaten all day and I'm starved."

"If you'd like."

"Okay, I'll be over in about an hour."

Actually, it had taken less than an hour. Just as Anise was about to turn into the alley, her aunt's car was coming out. She waited until Aretha's car was beside hers and then rolled down the window.

"Since we talked earlier and you didn't mention coming over, I take it you're not here to see me."

"I was going to call and come over before I left the neighborhood."

"Girl, don't mind me. You know how I like to tease."

"Yes, I know."

"You are glowing again, Anise. I'm glad you and Gregory were able to work out your differences. Because if you'd decided to leave that sweet thing, I was going to bring out my cougar suit and pay that sexy something a visit. 'Hey, neighbor,'" she said all girly like.

"Aunt Ree, please. I don't need to get that visual in my head."

"Ha! All right, baby, Bruce is waiting for me. Y'all have fun. Stop by and see me in the morning."

"If I'm still here," Anise responded. "I don't know if I'm spending the night."

Aretha gave her a look, cocked her head to the

side. "Girl, you won't be going anywhere tonight. So I'll see you in the morning. Stop by."

She stepped on the gas. Anise laughed at how Aretha didn't wait for a response. *Probably because she knows she's right.* "Lord have mercy, a cougar," she mumbled. "Aunt Ree, you're a mess!"

She parked her car and walked up to Gregory's back door, chiding herself for feeling butterflies. Yes, they'd just seen each other at her opening but since his overdose, they'd put lovemaking on hold.

"Hello."

"Hello."

Four months and counting, and this man could still take her breath away. "Where's your shirt?" she asked, as much to gain control of her emotions as to find out why he wasn't fully dressed "I thought we were going out to eat."

"Where's my hug?"

She went into his outstretched arms and as they wrapped around her she sighed in spite of herself.

"What are you hungry for?"

His voice vibrated against her ear, causing places on her to vibrate as well; stirring up another kind of appetite. "Doesn't matter. As long as the food is good."

"All right. I'll be right back." Gregory hadn't been upstairs for more than a minute when he called out, "Baby, come here."

"What do you want?"

"I don't want sex if that's what you're thinking."

Well, damn. Now that he doesn't want what I wasn't going to give him, I'm offended!

"What do you want then?"

"Just come here, woman!"

Resisting the urge to stomp up them like a recalcitrant child, she moseyed up the steps just to make him wait. Rounding the corner and heading into the master suite, she was all ready for more smart retorts.

"Now, what is so important that you— *Aaaaaaaah! My picture!*" She wasn't even aware that she'd screamed, or that it came out two octaves higher than her normal speaking voice. She turned to look at him, in shock. "*You* bought my picture?"

Gregory crossed his arms and leaned against the doorjamb. "I did indeed." The satisfied look on his face said that her reaction was better than expected.

"Oh my God, it looks perfect over your fireplace and with your color scheme." She walked over to the mantel, staring up at her art as if it were a foreign object. "All this time I've wondered who bought it, wondered why they didn't at least come up to meet me or let me know which one they'd liked as the others did." She continued to gaze at it, noting how the deep blues of the ocean waves picked up the navy in his comforter and the pillows on his love seat, and how that splash of red orange in the waning sunset would be a perfect match for a fall night's fire. It was her most expensive piece. And he'd bought it. And given it a place of prominence on the walls of his master suite. "Wow."

When she turned, there were tears in her eyes. "Thank you." Spoken softly. Sincerely.

He walked over and once again took her in his arms. "You're welcome." He put space between them so that he could look in her eyes. "I get it . . . Okay? I listened to what you said and . . . did some research and . . . I want to talk to you about putting some of your work in my center."

They went out to eat. Gregory saw a different kind of passion in Anise, the passion of loving what she did and, as she discussed which pieces she felt would best affect his research participants, a passion for helping others. Just like him. But in a different way.

They were almost finished eating when Anise reached across the table for his hand.

Noticing her troubled expression, Gregory asked, "What is it, baby?"

"I've been thinking about something." A few seconds passed before she went on. "I owe you an apology."

"Aw, baby. Let's not rehash our conflict over the building. We've put that behind us."

"Not that. About Edward."

Gregory's brow creased in confusion. "Edward? You don't need to apologize for him."

"But what happened to you is my fault, in a way.

If I hadn't been so trusting, and hadn't friended him on Facebook, he wouldn't have been able to poison you at my event!"

"Baby . . ." Gregory leaned over, brushed the tear that ran down Anise's cheek away from her face. "You couldn't have known his ulterior motives. You take people at face value, believe what they tell you. I'm not saying you're gullible, but you're not jaded or hard or suspicious of everyone who crosses your path either. Drew was determined to undermine me and tried many things to sabotage my career before you met Edward online. I hope what happened doesn't scar you or make you lose that innocent quality. It's one of your most attractive qualities."

A look of anger began to replace Anise's sad countenance. "When I think of all the things he said—how much he loved art, how he wanted to support me. And now to know it was all a lie? A front so that he could get close to me and, in turn, get next to you? Acting like someone's friend when you're not is the ultimate betrayal. It makes me want to find something lethal to put in his drink!"

"There you go again, being gangster. I like that about you, too. Your kindness isn't weakness and one would be a fool to mistake it to be so." He leaned over and kissed her. "Thank you for caring about me, baby. But nothing that happened to me is your fault. Except that I'm so happy."

They went back to Gregory's and made slow, passionate love.

The next day, when Anise did knock on Aretha's back door, her aunt opened it and with a smile, simply said, "Good morning."

57

"Dr. Morgan, please report to the break room. Dr. Morgan, please report to the break room."

Gregory looked up as he heard his name. He was in the locker room, removing all but the essentials out of his space. Yes, he'd still be coming to the hospital to perform surgeries a few times a month, but he knew that initially most of his time, and his focus, would be on the research center. If he'd stayed in the locker room a half hour longer, he would have gotten to witness Drew Fordham doing the very same thing—moving on.

Gregory passed the nurses' station, noting that three of the four seats were empty, and then by the file room. The clerk was gone. Just as a thought began forming in his head he turned into the break room and heard one word:

"Surprise!"

His colleagues and coworkers stood there, all grinning from ear to ear. A large cake sat on the table and balloons saying "Congratulations," "Good Luck!" and "Way to Go!" vied for space near the ceiling. A couple of wrapped presents sat next to the cake. Dr. Meyers began singing "For He's a Jolly Good Fellow."

Gregory blushed.

"Shucks, guys," he drawled, hiding how touched he was behind humor. "You didn't have to do all this."

"We wanted to," Betsy said, a nurse he'd worked with since his college days. "Even though you suck as a doctor and none of us like you, it just seemed like the right thing to do."

That effectively released the lump that had formed in Gregory's throat at their kindness and allowed him to relax and take it all in. "Betsy, you're going to have to stop holding your tongue and being afraid to say what's on your mind."

"We don't want you to forget about us little people," the anesthesiologist chimed in.

"Yes, when Dr. Gupta is interviewing you on CNN," said another.

"Or Anderson Cooper," yet another one offered.

"We want you to remember who gave you balloons," Betsy finished.

Dr. Meyers laughed. "And cake, don't leave out the cake."

Gregory walked over to the table holding the large cake. It was decorated with the image of the plaque that would hang on his new office door:

"Gregory Morgan, MD" and beneath it, "Samuel Morgan Research Center."

"This is really special, you guys. Thank you."

Various responses rang out.

"But don't think you're getting rid of me this easy. I'm going on vacation, not giving my resignation. I'll be back here regularly, still doing my thing in ER."

"Yeah, yeah, yeah," Betsy said. "Just cut the cake. I got you red velvet . . . my . . . uh, I mean your favorite."

The joking around continued as cake was cut and punch was poured. At one point, Betsy pulled Gregory to the side of the room. "I heard something from a little birdie about your friend Drew."

Gregory was all ears. "Oh, yeah?"

"Word is he's a sore loser."

"Tell me something I don't know."

"He's been bad-mouthing you to whoever will listen."

"Hopefully not many will."

"Well, if you ask me, I'd say the best man won."

"Betsy, I'm glad I'm on your good side."

"You've pretty much been there since you tried to pinch my rear as a fresh-faced intern."

"I did not."

"I know, that was wishful thinking and one of the reasons I can't stand you." She turned to leave, then turned back and winked. "But I love you to death."

* * *

Farther north, in Venice, California, Anise was on the phone talking to Aretha and she too was in a celebratory mood.

"When Jessica phoned and said *the* Lydia Rosenthal had seen my work in a catalog and was interested in some pieces, I almost passed out! Having my work hang in her home will be such an honor. Heck, I'm almost tempted not to charge her, but to say it's a gift."

"Honey, you've worked hard to get where you are and your work is worth every penny. So if I were you, I'd get that little temptation right out of my mind."

"I guess you're right, Aunt Ree," Anise said with a laugh.

"So you said you'll get to meet her?"

"Yes! Jessica, that's my mentor and friend from Kansas City who is friends with Miss Lydia, she's coming to town next week. Together we'll go down to Palm Springs for a private showing."

"That's wonderful, baby. I'm so proud of you. What about your Web site? How's that coming?"

"We've almost finished photographing the pieces. It was supposed to be updated next week, but with Gregory on vacation and his center about to open . . . there's a lot going on."

"Whew, I still can't believe how touch and go it

was with you and Gregory for a minute. I thought at one time I'd have to put you guys in a ring and serve as your referee."

"Thank goodness that everything worked out for both of us. So, Aunt Ree, I think you can put away the gloves."

58

The day of the dedication had arrived, the Samuel Morgan Trauma Research & Health Center was about to open, and Gregory was experiencing too many emotions to identify a single one. He stood on the sidewalk along with Anise and his family and, no doubt, his dad. The mayor and city council of Santa Monica had come out for the ribbon cutting along with friends and colleagues from UCLA Medical Center, friends of the Rosenthals, and media. Later in the day, scores of other medical personnel, potential patients, and curious citizens would join in the open house. The day was overcast, but not even rain could dampen Gregory's spirits. This was the dream he'd held in his heart. And now, it was reality.

Anise held on to Gregory's arm as she peered at the small group of protesters across the street.

Neither Dawn nor Truth was there—both had moved out of the city—but she still saw a couple faces that she recognized. The snarl on their faces said they recognized her as well. She only hoped that they wouldn't yell out and ruin Gregory's moment, or that a rock wouldn't hit her in the back of the head. Normally not one for cheering men in blue, Anise was glad to see that a small but well-equipped group of police were close by as well.

The mayor climbed the short flight of steps and turned to face the crowd. "Good afternoon," he began in an official sounding voice. "I am here to read this proclamation." A single tear rolled down Gregory's cheek at the mention of Samuel Morgan's name. After a slew of "whereas" and a few "therefores" thrown in for good measure, the mayor pronounced it Rosenthal-Morgan day in Santa Monica.

"You did it!" Anise said, squeezing Gregory's hand. "I'm so proud of you."

Jackie turned and hugged her son. Her eyes were bright with tears. "I love you, baby," she eked out, trying to avoid an all-out boohoo. "Sam's here," she also whispered.

Anise and Jackie hugged. "Is everything ready?" Anise asked her.

"Just keep an eye out for me," Jackie replied with a nod. "I'll give you a sign."

Troy and Michael walked over to congratulate

Gregory and soon after that he was engulfed by the well-wishing crowd. After a few more speakers and many more congratulations, Gregory cut the ribbon and the group walked into the brand-spanking-new building. Anise looked around in awe; it was as if The Creative Space had never existed and this modern architectural wonder of chrome and glass, marble and mahogany had always been here. She thought she'd feel nostalgia, perhaps melancholy. But nothing, not the spirit of the artistic loft and seemingly even that of the artists who'd worked there, remained. The lobby area was bright and open, with plush tan carpeting beginning where the marble ended. The sitting area to the left of the entrance was at once colorful and serene, and throughout, Anise's artwork provided energy and beauty. People oohed and aahed and nodded their appreciation as they walked from lobby to offices, from examining rooms to the break area, complete with a full, stainless steel kitchen. Upstairs was the lab and X-ray rooms, gleaming with silver this and chrome that. They munched on hors d'oeuvres and sipped sparkling fruit juice. Anise moseyed around the two-story edifice and sometimes discreetly watched Gregory in his element as the doctor. Once, when she walked near him, she heard him using words that sounded foreign as he explained a certain procedure or technique. He was such an ordinary-who-was-anything-but-ordinary guy that this was one of the few times where his skill and intelligence actually hit her. This wonderful man with whom she spent nights healed people, saved lives. She thought of the fight she'd put up to block him getting the building, and felt ashamed. Yes, she'd apologized, but it would probably take a while for the guilt and contrition to totally leave her. And when she heard how his mentors and colleagues praised him she found herself all agog.

"Anise," Gregory said, bringing her out of her musings as he walked her way with a distinguished-looking gentleman by his side. "Here's someone I want you to meet. My mentor, friend, and second dad, Dr. Meyers."

"Nice to meet you," Anise said, as the kindly-looking doctor placed her hands between his.

"The pleasure is mine," Dr. Meyers responded, as his blue eyes twinkled. "I hear you're responsible for this beautiful artwork gracing these walls." He swept his hand across the room. "Impressive, very impressive."

"Thank you."

"You know, I attended a seminar recently that mentioned art and the creative process as a healing technique, especially in brain injuries."

"Why, yes," Anise responded, clearly impressed.

"You might want to talk to Gregory here about using your art and the practice of art therapy with some of his patients. You two could work together, like a team."

Anise got excited. "Dr. Meyers, that's exactly what I've been trying to—"

"Don't get all excited, love. He's yanking your chain." At her somewhat confused expression, he continued. "I told Doc here all about *our* plans to integrate art as a healing modality into our research. It is something that he mentioned early on, when he was defending your position in not wanting the Creative Space closed down."

Now it was Anise's eyes that were twinkling. "Why, Dr. Meyers, you came to my defense? Even before the deal was done and keys had been exchanged? Well, please, would you allow me to personally describe my paintings to you, and their meanings?"

"Anise, I'd be most interested." He turned to Gregory. "If you'll excuse us."

Gregory nodded and continued circulating until he observed an elderly man who had taken keen interest in one of the larger paintings Anise had done. This one showed a profusion of flowers, all muted in color, but outlined in brilliant shades of vibrant reds, oranges, yellows, and lime green. He stared at it so long that Gregory walked over and stood next to the man.

"It's an extraordinary painting," he offered, staring too at the picture before him.

"Absolutely amazing," the old man said, his

voice a bit shaky and full of awe. "Staring at it kinda makes you feel peaceful, doesn't it. And it's so life-like! Looks like you could lay down on the grass in that meadow and go right to sleep!"

Anise and Dr. Meyers were just returning from the second floor when she caught Jackie's head nod from the corner of her eye. "It's been a plea-sure speaking with you, doctor, but if you'll excuse me, I think Gregory's mother needs me."

"No problem, dear."

As casually as she could, Anise walked over to Jackie. "Did they deliver it?"

"Yes, and I have Troy and Michael keeping Greg busy."

"Do they know?"

"Not a clue. I just told them to keep him busy. Come on."

They walked down the hall and, after grabbing one of the maintenance men, dashed into Greg-ory's office, closing the door behind them and pulling the blinds.

"Where do you want it?" the man asked, pulling out the small stepladder he'd brought with him and laying a hammer and picture hook on the desk.

"What do you think, Jackie? On this wall where I now have my abstract interpretation of the Hippo-cratic oath?"

"Hmm, he does like that painting, has mentioned it to me before."

"He'll like this one better," Anise said with a nod. "Yes, there," she said to the maintenance man. "I'm sure of it."

The man made quick work of replacing one painting with the other and once it was up the ladies covered it with a black cloth.

Jackie turned to Anise. "Are you ready?"

"Yes," Anise replied, nervous squiggles clashing in her insides. "Let's bring him in."

Jackie walked around the center until she found Gregory. He was talking to a group of reporters, but when he finished, she grabbed his arm. "Son, can you come here for a minute, please?"

"What is it?" he asked, his voice low yet demanding.

"Anise has something for you."

"Something like what?" Gregory gave his mother the side eye. She knew he didn't like surprises.

"You'll see," was Jackie's noncommittal reply. Once they'd reached his office and walked in, Jackie closed the door.

Anise looked at Gregory. "Your mother wasn't the only one who wanted to put a personal touch on your space, Dr. Morgan. So did I. In fact, we worked on this together. I hope you'll enjoy." She walked over to where the painting was hidden by a black draped cloth. With one pull of the cloth the painting was revealed: a real-as-life portrait of

Gregory's dad, Samuel Morgan, and on the canvas next to him, a picture of a scrubs-wearing MD, the shipyard worker's son.

For a moment, Gregory stood as still as a stone. Then slowly, his eyes glued to the painting, he walked toward it. For this masterpiece, Anise had used acrylics, causing the colors to pop and the faces to almost come to life. She'd perfectly captured the crinkles around his father's eyes when he smiled, just like in the photo that Gregory remembered. The mole on his chin and the gray at his temples, the sparkle in his eye and slightly uneven teeth. It was as if at any moment Samuel Morgan would turn his eyes, look at him, and say hello. And next to him, Gregory, in his green scrubs, mask pulled down, stethoscope around his neck. She'd painted Gregory looking in the same direction as his father, as if they were both seeing the same thing. He remembered the photo Anise had worked from, remembered the nurse taking it one day after he'd just come out of surgery, remembered her sending him the digital image and him sending it to his mom. She'd commented that she'd received it and that she really liked it. Now, he knew just how much.

He knew something else. He knew that his heart was bursting for the woman who'd done this for him, the woman who'd captured with the deftness of hand in one single portrait, all of what this whole building meant to him.

"This is, umm . . ." He cleared the hoarseness from his throat and fought back tears. "Just beautiful, Anise." The tightness in his chest prevented more words from coming out except, "Thank you."

He hugged her. "I love it."

"I'm glad."

"I love you."

Anise was even gladder about that! "I love you, too," she said softly, and kissed his cheek.

59

"No one has ever done anything like that for me. Ever."

It was around five o'clock, an hour after the dedication had ended. At Gregory's suggestion, he and Anise had walked the three short blocks to the ocean's edge to watch the sunset. They rested against a concrete half wall, Anise shielded from the light breeze by the curve of the stone and Gregory's arms around her.

"What made you think to do that?"

For a while, she said nothing. She watched seagulls literally float on air. Watched a few bikers bike, a few skateboarders skate, and a homeless man stretching his blanket out under a tree.

"You know that day at your mom's house when she brought out the photo album?" Gregory nodded. "That was such a good day. I had so much fun. Your mom telling stories to go with the pictures. You and your mother teasing each other. All of the love. That's the day I fell in love with your family"—she turned to face him—"and even more in love with you."

She turned back around. "That evening, after dinner, when I was helping your mother in the kitchen, she shared with me how close you were to your father; how out of the brothers his death affected you the most. She told me what I already knew, what you'd already told me, about how the way he died influenced your becoming a doctor. About how you want to save other people's lives because you couldn't save his." Together, they watched as the sun began its descent into the ocean, changing from bright yellow to orange to a fiery red. "Later, I had the thought to paint him for you. And give you the picture. It was your mother who thought maybe it belonged on your wall. In the office that he inspired."

"Anise." He breathed the word as if it were life-giving, stroking her cheek with one lone, strong finger. "My Anise. I cannot put into words how big that gesture was, nor how perfect, nor how much it means to me. It says a lot about how much you know me, and how you pay attention to who I am. You have made me one very happy"—he kissed her nose—"grateful"—he kissed first one cheek and then the other—"and now horny"—he gave a surreptitious grind against her to prove whether that was a gun in his pocket or whether he was just happy to see her—"man."

They stayed that way, quiet, reflective, until the sun had dipped into the ocean, until even the thin red line had disappeared. Anise shivered.

"Let's get you back inside where it's warm," Gregory said. They hurried back to the research center to retrieve Gregory's car, then called ahead to one of their favorite Thai restaurants and ordered dinner to go. Once back at Gregory's house, he pulled on a pair of drawstring pants and she wore one of his oversized shirts, with two buttons fastened and nothing beneath. They put in a movie and ate from the cartons while sitting in bed. They laughed and teased, and simply enjoyed being together. And when the food was gone and the movie was over, Gregory pulled Anise into his arms.

"Umm, you're too good to me," he murmured, nibbling on her ear as his hand eased inside the stark white shirt she wore and tweaked a ready nipple. Anise's head rolled back, exposing her neck. Gregory took this as an invitation and placed small nips and warm kisses all the way down. She could feel him hardening beneath her but when he rolled her over it wasn't to thrust himself inside her as she had hoped, but to give her a massage.

He began at the top of her head, massaging her scalp—slow, firm circles—then moved his hands down until his thumbs lined up with the nape of her neck. He pressed and rotated his thumbs until he could feel the muscle loosen, before continuing across her shoulders and down her back, each cheek of her buttocks, her thighs and shins. He turned her back over and began the massage from the tips of her toes, pulling and circling them much like the pedicurist did before massaging the balls and sides of her feet, her ankles, her calves, outer and inner thighs, her pulsating nub. The friction of his fingers against her heat was so relentless and unexpected she came in an instant and cried out her release. He lay beside her, pulled her into his arms, and kissed her gently, tenderly, over and again.

"It's your turn," she whispered, reaching for his sex, ready to give as good as she'd gotten. She outlined the perfectly shaped mushroom tip and her mouth watered at the ideas that came to mind as to what she could do with it. But his hand stayed hers, before pulling it away and entwining their fingers.

"You don't have to do anything but lie here," he whispered. "When you're just being who you are I'm satisfied. Just holding you, squeezing you, pleasing you . . . pleases me."

He continued to caress her arms, to rub her back, to kiss her wherever his lips could reach. In time, he turned until they were spooned against each other; she nestled against his chest, her head comfortably placed in the crook of his arm. They hadn't had sex, yet Anise felt as satiated as she'd ever felt, the lovemaking more beautiful than she'd ever known.

Just as she drifted off to sleep, she heard it. So faint she thought it could have been imagined, but no, there it was again. His lips so close, warm breath against her neck.

And the words, "I love you." Twice.

60

It was Sunday brunch at Jackie's and the house was full. In addition to the Morgan family and Robert, there was Aretha, Bruce, Bruce's daughter and son-in-law, and their son, Dante, Troy's latest arm candy, Jackie's best friend, Mary, and a few of Gregory's friends who'd flown into town for the dedication. It was crowded. It was boisterous. It was Jackie in her world.

"Everybody, listen up. Brunch will be served shortly and everyone will have to fend for themselves. We're going to place the platters here"—she placed her hand on a beautifully carved mahogany piece—"and serve buffet style. Get your drinks now and claim your place at one of the three tables we have set up. If you don't know somebody well, sit next to them. Let's make everyone feel welcome and spread the love around!"

A cozy buzz ensued as the ladies carried out large bowls of vegetables and one of fluffy rice pilaf to go with Jackie's meat trio of lemon-pepper baked chicken, blackened salmon, and barbequed ribs. A large mixed salad and array of dressings anchored one end of the buffet with a tray of baked potatoes at the other. There was a quiet chaos as everyone (meaning mostly the men) jockeyed to get their plates filled first and get their preferred choice of meat.

"Stop acting like I didn't raise you," Jackie admonished Troy, who'd pushed his brother Michael so that he could get next to the ribs.

"Did anybody bless the food?" Aretha asked.

Dante piped right up. "Good bread, good meat. Good God, let's eat!"

"There you go, boy," Bruce said, slapping his grandson on the back. "It don't take all day to praise the Lord!"

Everyone found a spot to graze and for a while, tinkling silverware against bone china and the occasional grunt were the only sounds heard. Slowly, however, conversation resumed and that several were going on simultaneously was no problem at all. Following Jackie's request, Anise found herself sitting next to a man named Cameron, a general practice doctor and one of Gregory's best friends. Along with how life was lived in New York

City, she'd learned that he was married to a dancer and that they were expecting a child.

"Did you and Gregory grow up together?" she asked.

Cameron took a drink as he shook his head. "We met in college. First day."

"That's pretty cool."

"Yes. Well, someone had to take care of him."

"Ha!" She took a moment to savor a rib. "So tell me something about your best friend that I don't know, but I should."

To Anise's surprise, Cameron turned serious. "They don't make them like Gregory too much anymore. He works too hard and loves the same. Never was much of a player and, trust me, he had the whole field at his feet. If you hurt him, you should know that he has friends who will hunt you down like an animal."

Anise's eyes widened.

"Just kidding."

"Don't be scaring my woman," Gregory said, walking up to the table and taking the place that little Dante had vacated. He leaned over to Anise. "Don't listen to his lies."

"I don't know, babe. He had some pretty good things to say about you."

"Oh, then listen to those!"

"Ha!"

And so the afternoon continued, with lots of laughter broken up by a serious moment or two.

Robert and Bruce chatted like old pals and once Mary and Aretha started talking, a date with a slot machine was quickly set. People ate until their stomachs hurt and then, when Jackie brought out the dessert choices of sweet potato cheesecake and three-berry cobbler, they ate even more. In the midst of it all, Anise caught herself being the observed and the observer, enjoying herself even as she took it all in. Growing up it had been her and her mother, that's all. This big, boisterous family was a new experience, one that she thoroughly enjoyed. Even as she laughed at the brothers' antics and their mom playing referee, she was struck with what could become quite the uncomfortable dilemma. She might break up with Gregory, but his family would have to stay. His new girlfriend would just have to deal with it. Bottom line.

"All right, family, I've got to get moving," Troy said, standing and stretching his lean, six-foot four-inch frame; a move not missed by the lovely at his side. What was missed by most was the look that passed between Michael and Gregory. They both knew what was on Troy's mind, something that if told would make their mama blush. "I know I already said it, but I'm proud of you, man," he said, giving Gregory a hug. "Hey, man, pass my number to Shayna's track mate," he whispered to Michael, as they bumped shoulders.

"You're a mess, man," Michael said with a shake of his head. "Get out of here."

"Bye, Spice," he said, leaning down and giving Anise a hug. "Take care of my brother."

A slow procession of leavers continued after that, most of them taking doggie bags: Gregory's out of town guests, Michael and Shayna, then Aretha and her crew. When Gregory mouthed a "let's go" to Anise, only Mary, Robert, and Jackie remained.

"I guess it's about that time," he said, rising from his seat.

"Oh, no. Y'all leaving?" Jackie asked. "You want me to fix you two containers of food?"

"I couldn't eat another bite," Anise said, holding her stomach.

Jackie gave her a look. "You say that now but you'll be cussing come midnight."

"Fix us one, Mama. Put some ribs and chicken in it, and some of the salad and rice."

"I'll help you, Jackie," Anise said.

Jackie returned from the kitchen with a Styro-foam container into which Anise placed a couple pieces of chicken and several ribs. "Thanks again, for everything. You have a wonderful family. I had a great time."

"You are welcome anytime," Jackie said, placing the vegetables and rice in the container alongside the meat. She then wrapped a couple rolls in aluminum foil and placed both items in a plastic bag. "And Gregory doesn't have to bring you, either. You're family."

61

Once good-byes had been said, and they'd made it to the car and started down the road, Gregory asked Anise, "What about a drink to end the night?"

"That sounds good."

"Okay. I'll take you to one of my favorite places in Long Beach."

A short time later, Gregory turned onto Shoreline Drive and then into Shoreline Village. He parked the car and came around to open the door for Anise. When she exited, he did not step back, but rather pinned her against the car and gave her a hot, wet kiss.

"Wow, what was that for?" she asked, when she regained her senses.

"It's so you'll have some idea what's going to happen later."

They reached a set of wooden steps and climbed them to a building that was very in keeping with the area's marina theme. "Parkers' Lighthouse, huh?" she asked, as they entered.

"Yes, and it's too bad you're full," Gregory said, as they took another set of stairs to the magnificent nighttime water views on the second floor. "Because they've got some of the best seafood around."

They were seated and given menus. "This is nice," Anise said, looking around. "Why is it one of your favorite places?"

"Don't get mad but . . . this is where I brought my first date."

"Gee, thanks."

"See, I told you not to get mad. Now picture this. Cool brother, rolling in his first ride that I bought myself with money I earned at the age of seventeen." Gregory made a show of puffing his chest.

Anise giggled. "What kind was it?"

"Baby, it was a cherry red, eighty-nine, tricked out Trans Am with white walls, all around and a set of twenty-twos. Brothah was styling! She was twenty, had graduated three years earlier, so you know I thought I was the man! My friends told me that neither Pizza Hut nor McDonald's would be a good look for date night, so I asked one of my teachers where he took his wife, and he told me here. Needless to say, she was impressed."

"What happened?"

"I wasn't the only one impressing her. Shortly

after we started dating, she got pregnant. The child wasn't mine."

"How do you know?"

"Because I'm not Caucasian and her child clearly shared this heritage. Not only that, but the father stepped up to the plate. They're still married, the last I heard."

"All's well that ends well, I guess."

He reached over and took her hand. "No doubt. Because look at life. I still ended up with the best girl."

"Ah. You say the sweetest things." She leaned over and kissed him.

"Only when they're true."

The waiter came over to take their order. "You sure you only want drinks?" Gregory asked Anise.

"Positive. I'll just have tea."

"Make that two." The waiter left and Gregory stood. "I need to use the restroom, baby. Be right back."

Anise looked around the rustic yet cozily appointed space. The view was indeed stunning. And she liked the fact that while there were a good number of people in the room, it didn't feel cramped or crowded. Gregory had said it was one of his favorite places. She liked it, too.

"I'm back."

"That was fast."

"Just because it's long doesn't mean it has to take

long." He gestured as though he'd hit a drum. "Badda bum badda bing."

"That was bad, Gregory."

"Ha!"

"Hey, what is that big boat out there, the one outlined in lights?"

"That's not a boat, baby, that's a ship. The queen of ships; I think second only to the *Titanic* at the time it was built. That's the *Queen Mary*."

"Oh. It's beautiful."

"I grew up here and have never toured that ship. In fact, there are several sights around town that I haven't visited but are worth seeing."

"We'll have to change that."

"For sure."

The music that had been playing softly beneath the chatter was turned up. Anise cocked her head and smiled. "Gregory!"

"Yes?"

"They're playing our song!" She began bobbing her head and snapping her fingers to the beats of Bob Marley.

"They are indeed. Wanna dance?"

She looked up. "Here? Now?"

"Sure, why not?"

"Because nobody's dancing!"

"Come on," Gregory said, rising from his seat. "I want a legitimate excuse to rub on your booty."

"Greg!"

He led her to an open area near the bar where

they began to dance. Most eyes were on them, some smiling, others openly curious. Gregory took it all in stride. Anise felt like a fool.

"Come on, Gregory," she mumbled, between gritted teeth. "Everyone is staring at us."

"That's what happens to beautiful girls. You get looked at."

"Whatever." Still the compliment kept her on the dance floor. She closed her eyes and got into the music, soon forgetting the discomfort she'd felt just seconds before. Until she heard Gregory's voice. Away from her. On a mike.

"Anise Cartier."

Her eyes flew open and only by sheer will did her mouth not follow suit. She stared at him, saying nothing.

"Anise Cartier, could you come here, please?"

She looked around, as if she were searching for someone else by that name. Amused faces looked back at her and one woman nodded her encouragement. "Go on," she seemed to say.

Anise walked over to where Gregory stood.

"Anise, from the moment I met you, you captured my heart."

Said heart began pounding. Furiously.

"You're everything I've ever wanted in a woman: strong, smart, talented, and beautiful. And you like Bob Marley, one of my favorite musicians of all time." The crowd chuckled. "I know this is happening quickly, but everything we did happened fast."

He reached inside his pocket.

No, he couldn't be.

He stepped away from the mike and went down on one knee.

Oh my goodness! Yes, he could!

"Anise Cartier, will you marry me?"

Anise's hands went to her mouth. She was in shock, didn't know what to say. The sound of Bob's voice faded as the song ended. Now whether or not she could be loved would be entirely up to her. It was as if she could hear her own heartbeat, as if time and everything else stood still. She looked down into the kindest, most sincere, most beautiful eyes she'd ever seen and heard Cameron's voice. *They don't make them like Gregory too much anymore.* Tears came to her eyes as she opened her mouth. "Yes, Gregory Morgan. Yes, I'll marry you!"

The audience cheered as Gregory picked her up and twirled her around. He set her down and kissed her, long and lovingly as the chance onlookers continued to applaud. Other couples hugged or kissed each other. Love was contagious! The bartender cranked back up the music. This time, when they began dancing, the impromptu dance floor was full. Indeed, there was enough pleasure to go around.

Zuri Day turns up the heat with three sexy page-turning tales of unexpected love and introduces the Morgan men, three fine brothers who have it all—except what their mama wants most for them: wives. . . .

Meet Michael Morgan

In the world of sports management, Michael Morgan is a superstar. But his newest client, Shayna Washington, may be his most lucrative catch yet. The record-breaking sprinter with the tight chocolate body has a talent and inner light Michael knows he can get the world to sit up and notice. He's certainly paying attention—and suddenly the sworn bachelor finds his focus changing from love of the game to true love. . . .

**Pick up *Love on the Run*
wherever books and ebooks are sold.**

Meet Gregory Morgan

When artist Anise Cartier leaves Nebraska for LA, she's finally ready to put the past and its losses behind her. She's even taken a new name to match her new future. And she soon finds a welcoming committee in the form of one very handsome doctor, Gregory Morgan. Their attraction is instant. So is their animosity . . .

**Pick up *A Good Dose of Pleasure*
wherever books and ebooks are sold.**

Meet Troy Morgan

Gabriella is a triple threat—singing,
acting, and dancing—and has always
lived the life of a princess.
Now, her father is determined to marry her to
someone who can help expand her brand
and the Stone empire, not some ordinary Joe.
Of course, Troy Morgan is anything but ordinary.
But can bad boy Troy take a backseat
to someone with more money, more fame,
and more of just about everything than him?

Troy's story goes on sale Spring 2014!

1

On a warm, overcast day in late September, the forever-grooving-always-moving female magnet Michael Morgan found himself spending a rare day both off from work and alone. After sexing her to within an inch of her life, he'd sent his latest conquest—all long hair (still tangled), long legs (still throbbing), and . . . well . . . perpetual longing—on her melancholy yet merry way. As usual when his mind had a spare moment, his thoughts went to his business—Morgan Sports Management Corporation—and the athletes he wanted to add to this successful company's stable. At the top of the list was former USC standout and recent Olympic gold medalist Shayna Washington, a woman he'd been aware of since her college days who he'd learned had just lost her mediocre sponsor of the past two years. When it came to business, Michael was like a bloodhound, and he smelled the piquant possibility of this client oozing across the proverbial promotional floor. Along with his other numerous talents, Michael had the ability to see in people what others couldn't, that indefinable something, that "it" factor, that star quality that took some from obscure mediocrity to worldwide fame. He sensed that in Shayna Washington, felt there was something there he could work with, and he was excited about the possibility of making things happen.

The ringing phone forced Michael to put these thoughts on pause. "Morgan."

"Hey, baby."

Michael stifled a groan, wishing he'd let the call that had come in as unknown go to voice mail. For the past two months, he'd told Cheryl that it was over. Her parting gifts had been accompanying him on a business trip to Mexico checking out a local baseball star, a luxurious four days that included a five-star hotel suite, candlelight dinners cooked by a personal chef, premium tequila, and a sparkly good-bye gift that, if needed, could be pawned to pay mortgage on LA's tony Westside. Why all of this extravagance? Partly because this was simply Michael's style and partly because he genuinely liked Cheryl and hadn't wanted to end their on-again off-again bedtime romps. But now, several years into their intimate acquaintance, she'd become clingy, and then suspicious, and then demanding . . . and then a pain in the butt.

Michael could never be accused of being a dog;

he let women know up front—as in before they made love—what time it was. Michael Morgan played for fun, not for keeps. Fortunately for him, most women didn't mind. Most were thankful just to be near his . . . clock. He loved hard and fast, but rarely long, and while it hadn't been his desire to do so, he'd left a trail of broken hearts in his wake.

Broken, but not bitter. A little taste of Morgan pleasure was worth a bit of emotional pain.

But every once in a while he ran into a woman like Cheryl, a woman who didn't want to take no for an answer. So when entanglements reached this point, the solution he employed was simple and straightforward: good-bye. But sometimes the fall-out was a bitch.

"Cheryl, you've got to quit calling."

"Michael, how can you just dump me like this?"

Heavy sigh. "I didn't 'just dump you,' Cheryl. I've been telling you for months to back off, that what you're wanting isn't what I'm offering. This has gotten way too complicated. You've got to let it go."

"So what did that mean when we began dating 'officially,' when I escorted you to the NFL honors?"

This is what I get for being soft and giving in. If there was one thing that Michael should have known by now, it was that mixing business with pleasure was like mixing hot sauce with baby formula. Don't do it. *Any minute she's going to start crying, and really work my nerves.* As if on cue, he heard the sniffles, her argument now delivered in part whine, part wistfulness. Michael correctly deduced that she was sad, and very pissed off at his making her that way.

"You've been my only one for years, Michael—"

"I told you from the beginning that that wasn't a good idea—"

"And I told you that I didn't want anyone else. There is no one for me but you. I can't forget you"—Michael heard a finger snap—"just like that." Her voice dropped to a vulnerable-sounding whisper. "Can I please come over just for a little while, bring you some of your favorite Thai food, a few sex toys, give you a nice massage . . . ?"

Michael loved to play with Cheryl and her toys. And when it came to massages, he gave as good as he got. And then there was the sincerity he heard amid her tears. He almost relented. Almost . . . but not quite.

"Cheryl, every time you've asked, I've been honest. Our relationship was never exclusive. I never thought of us as anything more than what it was—two people enjoying the moment and each other. I'll always think well of you, Cheryl. But please don't put us through this. You're a good woman, and there's a good man out there for you who wants what you want, the picket fence and all that. That man is not me. I'm sorry. I want the best for you. And I want you to move on with your life." He heard his other cell phone ringing and walked over to where it sat charging on the bar counter. *Valerie.* "Look, Cheryl, I have to go."

"But, Michael, I'm only five minutes from your house. I can—"

You can keep it moving, baby. I told you from the beginning this was for fun, not forever. Michael tapped the screen of his iPhone as he reached for his Black-Berry. "Hey, gorgeous," he said into the other phone.

"Hey yourself," a sultry voice replied.

"Michael!" *Oh, damn!* Michael looked down at the iPhone screen to see that the call from Cheryl was still connected. "Michael, who is that bit—" Michael pressed and held the End button, silently cursing himself for not being careful.

"Michael, are you there?"

"Yes, Valerie."

"Whose was that voice I heard?"

"A friend of mine. Do you have a problem with that?" Michael had never hidden the fact that when it came to women, he was a multitasker, especially among the women he juggled. But the situation with Cheryl had him very aware of the need to make that point perfectly clear, up front and often. If a woman couldn't understand that when it came to his love she was part of a team, then she'd have to get traded.

"Not at all," the sultry voice pouted. "Whatever she can do, I can do better."

That's how you play it, player! "No doubt," Michael

replied as his iPhone rang again. *Unknown caller.* He ignored it. *Sheesh! Maybe I'm getting too old for this.* Just then, his house phone rang. "Hello?"

"Hey, sexy!"

Paia? Back from Europe already? "Hey, beautiful. Hold on a minute." And then into the BlackBerry, "Look, Valerie, I'll call you back."

"Okay, lover, but don't make me wait too long."

"Who's Valerie?"

The iPhone again. *Unknown caller.* Michael turned off the iPhone. *Cheryl, give it a rest!* "Look, Cheryl—"

"Ha! This is Paia, you adorable asshole. Get it straight!"

Michael inwardly groaned. How could he have forgotten his rule about keeping his women separate and himself least confused? Rarely call them by their given name when talking on the phone. *Baby* was fine. *Darling* would do on any given day. *Honey* or *dear* based on the background. Even *pumpkin* or the generic yet acceptable *hey you* were all perfectly good substitutes. But using names, especially upon first taking a phone call, was a serious playboy no-no. *Yeah, man. You're slipping. You need to tighten up your game.* He'd just promoted this beauty to the Top Three Tier—those ladies who were in enviable possession of his home number. He and Paia were technically still in the courting stage—much too early for ruffled feathers or hurt feelings. At six feet tall in her stocking feet, Paia was a runway and high fashion model, an irresistibly sexy mix of African and Asian features. They'd only been dating two months and he wasn't ready to let her go. He even liked the way her name rolled off his tongue. *Pie-a*. No, he didn't want to release her quite yet. "Paia, baby, you know Mr. Big gets lonely when you're gone."

"Uh-huh. Because of that snafu you're going to owe me an uninterrupted weekend with you and that baseball bat you call a penis. You'd better be ready to give me overtime, too!"

"That can be arranged," Michael drawled. "Where are you?"

"I just landed in LA. But we have to move fast. I'm only here for a week and then it's back to Milan. So whatever plans you have tonight, cancel them."

"Ah, man! I can't do that—new client. But I'll call you later." Michael looked at the Caller ID as an incoming call indicator beeped in his ear. "Sweet thing," he said, proud that he was back to the terms of endearment delivered unconsciously. *That's right, Michael. Keep handling yours.* "This is my brother. I've got to go."

"Call me later, Michael."

"Hold on." Michael toggled between the two calls, firing back up his iPhone in the process. "Hey, bro. What's up?" Just four words in and said phone rang. *Jessica!* Unbidden, an image of the busty first-class flight attendant he'd met several months ago popped into his head. *Was it this weekend I was supposed to go with her to Vegas?* "Darling," he said, switching back to Paia, "we'll talk soon." He clicked over. "Gregory, two secs." He could hear his brother laughing as he fielded the other call. "Hey, baby. I'm on the other line. Let me call you back." He tossed down the cell phone. "All right, baby, I'm back."

"Baby?" Gregory queried, his voice full of humor. "I know you love me, fool, but I prefer *bro* or *Doctor* or *Your Highness!*" Michael snorted. "You need to hone your juggling skills, son. Or slow your player roll. Or both."

2

Michael smiled and nodded as he walked from his open-concept living space to the cozy theater down the hall. "What's up, Doc?"

"Man, how many times do I have to check you on that old-ass corny greeting?"

"As many times as you'd like. Doesn't mean I'm going to stop saying it, though. Plus I know it gets on your nerves and you know how much I love that," Michael confessed.

"If all of those skirts chasing you knew just how corny you truly are."

"A long way from those grade school days, huh?"

"For sure," Gregory agreed. "And girls like Robin . . . what was her last name?"

"Ha! Good old Robin Duncan. Broke this brother's fifth-grade heart. And that was after she took my Skittles and the Game Boy I bought her."

"Using that word *bought* rather loosely, don't you think?"

"Okay, I borrowed it from the store."

"And never took it back. Some might define that as stealing."

"Hey, I pay them back every year by donating, generously I might add, to their turkey giveaway. Not to mention my anonymous donation after that arson fire destroyed part of their storefront last year."

"Payback? That's what you call it? Ha! If Mr. Martinez was still alive I'd tell on you myself. But at least you're letting your conscience be your guide."

"No doubt. Say, how is it that you have time to bug me on a Friday night? You work the early shift?" Michael walked over to an oversized black leather theater seat, sat down, and opened up the chair arm console. A moment after he punched a series of buttons, a track meet video appeared on the screen.

Gregory, an emergency medical doctor, was rarely off on weekends, normally pulling twenty-four- to forty-eight-hour shifts between Friday and Monday and often unavailable for calls. "We're training a new intern. Believe it or not, brother, I've got the night off."

"You don't say. So who's going to enjoy the pleasure of your company?"

"I thought about calling the twins. You up for a double?"

The twins Gregory spoke of were longtime friends who'd grown up in the same Long Beach neighborhood as the Morgans. As childhood cohorts, they'd made pinky promises to marry each other. Unfortunately for Michael, one of them was trying to hold him to that bull.

"No, man, that's a code orange. I'm going to have to pass on that."

"Code orange? Lisa still bugging you to make her an honest woman?"

"We both know what Lisa's doing . . . trying to snag a big bank account. I introduced her to Phalen Snordgrass, told her that he was going to be picked back up this year."

"Talented brother right there. I'm surprised she didn't go for it."

"Man, Lisa picks men more shrewdly than I pick clients. She's looking for someone who has more time left in the NFL than two, three years. I told her she was getting too old to go after the new drafts, that she should stop being so choosy before all of her choices were gone."

"Man, you can handle Lisa's bugging. We haven't hung together for a while. Let's go out."

"No can do, bro."

"Why? What are you doing?" Gregory asked.

"Right now I'm watching the female version of Usain Bolt," Michael replied. "And this country's next athletic superstar." He leaned forward, resting his elbows on his knees—as if he had to change position to view his television screen. His latest electronic purchase was so large that someone manning the space station could see it.

"Is that so? Is she a new client?"

"Just signed her last week. She's coming over for an informal chitchat; we'll just kind of hang out and get a feel for each other."

"She's coming there, to your house?" Michael was sure that this tidbit got Gregory's attention. Michael was long known for not mixing business with pleasure, and bringing a potential client into his Hollywood Hills pleasure palace—revise that, a *female* client to where he lived—definitely sounded more like the latter.

"Yes." Gregory was quiet, and Michael imagined how his brother looked while digesting the story behind that one word. The two men could almost pass for twins themselves with their caramel skin, toned physiques, and megawatt smiles. But Gregory was actually eighteen months younger than Michael's thirty-one years, and two inches shorter than his sibling's six foot two. And while Michael sported a smooth, perfectly shaped bald head, Gregory's closely cropped cut gave him a distinguished look, one completely befitting a man in his profession.

"Shayna's special," Michael continued. "She has that 'it' factor, similar to a Michael Jordan, a Tiger Woods, or, in the world of track and field, a Carl

Lewis. This country hasn't seen the likes of her since Flo-Jo."

Gregory knew that his brother spoke of the illustrious Florence Griffith-Joyner, a world-class track star who in the late eighties was known for her bright smile, long colored nails, and flowing mane. "Since when did you start focusing on track and field?"

"Come on, now. You know I never met a sport that I didn't like."

"You never met a woman you didn't like, either."

"Aw, man. You wound me. I have very discriminating taste. But Shayna Washington is the real deal; on a good day she's the fastest running female in this country."

"Sounds like a winner, my brother. But I still don't understand why she's going to your home instead of meeting you at the office."

"I thought it might help to loosen her up, have a more casual meeting. When she signed, her lawyer did most of the talking. Other times we've met, she's answered my questions, but not much more than that. If I'm going to rep her, I need to get to know her; I need us to develop a camaraderie and trust. Plus, you know how the tabloids have been on me, ever since that last situation."

"All the more reason not to have her at your house!"

"That's just it. I spot them in or near the office

almost every day and that's cool, because security is so on point. But so far my residence is still off their radar."

The downtown LA skyscraper that housed the Morgan Sports Management offices boasted a very efficient and loyal security staff. And chances were that since it was Friday night, he could have suggested this penthouse spread with its 360-degree panoramic view and contemporary furnishings for their meeting. But he liked to play his cards close to his chest. The competition would know soon enough that he'd just landed the next track star sensation. This was what he told his brother.

"I guess I'll have to roll solo then," Gregory said.

"Look, if the meeting wraps up early I might join y'all for a drink. But if you have to take them both on, I'm sure that will be no problem for you."

"Ha! No, that's more Troy's style."

"Maybe," Michael retorted to the comment about their baby brother. "But it's probably been so long since you've had any that you need a double dose."

"Mind your business, brother. The freak days are long behind me, and believe it or not, I've been thinking more lately about meeting that special woman and settling down."

"Will you please tell Mama that so she'll get off *my* back?"

Gregory laughed. "Better you than me. Look, I probably should let you go. I'll take the twins to dinner, maybe even follow them to the latest Hollywood hot spot. I'll send you a text on where we're headed so you can maybe join us later. I've never known a woman who made you afraid."

"Please. You know better than that." A pause and then, "I might meet up for a drink after my meeting."

"That sounds cool. Until then, have a good time with this new honey."

"Shayna is my newest client. Period. End of story." When the screaming silence transmitted his brother's skepticism, Michael continued. "You just told me I needed to hone my juggling skills. With that being so, do you think I'd be adding yet another player to the roster? Don't get me wrong, though. She is one fine specimen of a female."

"Speaking of fine females, remind me to tell you about Troy's latest situation. That boy's a trip." The youngest Morgan was a bigger playboy than Michael and Gregory combined: a fact on which all three brothers agreed.

"You met her?" Michael's eyes never left the big screen. He smiled as Shayna crossed the finish line a full two strides ahead of the second-place winner.

"Not exactly. Stopped at the Ritz for breakfast and saw them cross the lobby. They were on their way out of the hotel."

"How did she look?"

"Very happy," was Gregory's deadpan reply.

Michael laughed. "Sounds like young bro is

doing his thing. And speaking of, I need to get back to doing mine." After again promising Gregory to meet him and the twins, Michael ended the call and got back down to work. Reaching for his beer before leaning back against his plush, custom-made, tan leather couch, he forwarded the Washington DVD to an interview she'd recently done on ESPN. While a bit timid for his liking, she was poised and well-spoken. Further, a certain kind of fire burned in her bright brown eyes tinged with hazel. For a split second, Michael wondered what it would be like to stoke her flame. He discarded the idea just as quickly. He would never again date a client. *Ever.* This lesson had been learned the hard way, when a determined baller with the LA Sparks had refused to accept that their passionate yet short-lived love affair was over. *Just like Cheryl.* He'd finally had to file a restraining order and she'd tried her best to sully his name. *Dang, is Cheryl going to make me have to do that again?* Thanks to his baby brother Troy's top-rate investigative skills, the near-smear campaign barely got off the ground before it was extinguished. Instead, the security firm owner had pulled in a couple favors and the former female phenomenon had been convinced—in an intellectual rather than forceful way—that damaging the Morgan name was not in her best interests. Last he heard, she'd moved to Denver and was dating a Bronco. *Ride on, b-baller, ride on.*

Michael leaned forward once again as images from Shayna attending last year's ESPY awards filled up the screen. She'd looked gorgeous that night: tight red dress on her stacked chocolate body, five-inch heels, and spiky short hair that high-lighted her perfect facial features. Unlike many female track stars with strenuous workouts, Shayna's chest was not flat. She still had her girls and they were perched against the low-cut dress in a way that almost made Michael's mouth water. *Never again,* Michael thought, even as his mind conjured up his mouth and Shayna's breasts in an up-close and personal get-to-know. *This meeting is strictly business.* He placed his legs apart and adjusted a rapidly hardening Mr. Big, repeating the words aloud this time. "Strictly business." And then he worked very hard to believe them.

Yeah, right. Good luck with that.

The Hottest African American Fiction
from
Dafina Books